Lock Down Publications and Ca$h
Presents

AMBITIONZ OF A SLIDER

Thuggin' With A Purpose

Written By

Ira B.

First Edition 2025

Printed in the United States of America

Lock Down Publications
P.O. Box 944
Stockbridge, GA 30281
www.lockdownpublications.com

Like our page on Facebook: Lock Down Publications
www.facebook.com/lockdownpublications.ldp

Stay Connected with Us!

Text **LOCKDOWN** to 22828 to stay up-to-date with new releases, sneak peaks, contests and more…

Like our page on Facebook:
Lock Down Publications

Join Lock Down Publications/The New Era Reading Group

Visit our website:
www.lockdownpublications.com

Follow us on Instagram:
Lock Down Publications

Email Us: We want to hear from you!

Prologue

(Raleigh, North Carolina)

Strapped with a pistol, two kilos of cocaine, and five thousand dollars in cash, Dooley anticipated his mission wholeheartedly. Four hours after Dooley boarded the Greyhound bus to Norfolk, Virginia, it stopped at a local rest stop. Dooley couldn't wait to get off the bus and stretch his legs a little—his butt was numb from sitting down in one spot for so damn long.

"Twenty minutes! Twenty minutes and we're back on the road again," shouted the bus driver as the passengers began filing out of the big bus.

Slinging the backpack over his shoulder, as everybody either headed to the nearest restrooms to freshen up or to the rest stop's inside deli to grab a bite to eat, Dooley snuck around the back of the building. Once there, he wasted no time breaking down a Swisher Sweets cigar and stuffing it with Purple Kush to roll up. Moments later, he was putting flame to his freshly rolled blunt, thinking about his mission at hand.

After dealing with some unfortunate events back at home, Dooley's brother Walt needed to sustain his operation as best he could. Since Cash—who was Walt's most trusted right-hand man and well-respected hustler himself—was locked up doing a county bid for several bogus charges, Walt had no one else he could trust to traffic his work. Cash usually handled it himself, and now that he's locked up, who better than his baby brother to see that things were in order?

At nineteen years old, there wasn't much Dooley didn't know about the game—Walt had taught him, and it was simple. Make it to Norfolk, contact the number that was given to him of the clientele, make the exchange, and get back to Raleigh, NC, with the forty grand promised. The basic instructions Walt had given him, Dooley had no problem following.

"And for any reason," Walt had said as Dooley listened, "if you feel crossed or something strange going on, don't hesitate to use that heat you got. Bust first, get away, and get as far as you can, then call me—ASAP!"

To Dooley, he knew his brother played for keeps on every turn, and whatever he said, he meant. Walt was a gangsta, a stand-up guy amongst others; yet he carried himself respectfully and inspired the same respect in return. Dooley was grateful to have a big brother as solid and thorough as Walt, whom he would, without a doubt, do whatever it took to prove himself just as much. Especially after being paid five grand—the most money he's had at one time. Dooley couldn't wait to show his brother just how worthy he was, to see that the mission was done precisely, and he dared not disappoint Walt for no particular reason.

"Hey!" a voice called out from his right.

When Dooley turned, he saw a girl approaching him. This was the same girl he remembered seeing aboard the bus in passing, but hadn't given her the slightest attention. As she neared him, Dooley stood up from the crate he was sitting on and regarded her attentively.

"What the fuck this bitch want?" Dooley frowned when she stopped before him.

"I wonder what you was doing back here," she said.

Then, to Dooley's surprise, she retrieved a modest-size joint and grinned over at him.

"Can I use your lighter?"

Dooley said, "Look, Ma. I'm just tryna chill and get my head right."

He scanned the area from which she'd come and hoped like hell nobody else showed up.

"Me too," she said, clutching her own JanSport backpack. "I just wanna get my head right."

Damn, this a pretty lil' red bitch! Dooley decided, sizing her up approvingly.

Then, reluctantly, he handed her his lighter. For a moment, there was an odd silence in the air.

"Where you from?" she asked.

Dooley looked at her with sudden scorn. "Raleigh," he said. Then asked, "What's your name, Ma?"

"Takira. But they call me T.K."

"Who is *they*?"

She inhaled weed smoke. "My friends down in Atlanta. I'm from Georgia. Who you be?"

"Dooley."

"Where you headed, Dooley?"

"Hesitantly, he answered, "V.A."

"For real? That's where I'm going too." T.K seemed quite excited by this sudden revelation.

The Kush was kicking in, and Dooley was now zoning, taking another healthy pull from his blunt.

"Whatcha going to Virginia for?"

"To visit my godmother." T.K. then unzipped the small compartment of her backpack and retrieved her MP3 player. "You wanna listen to some music while we chill? I got T.I., Drake, Young Jeezy, Lil Boosie—"

"Lil Boosie!" Dooley was taken aback by the mention of his favorite rapper, and before you knew it, Dooley was bobbing his head to some Boosie BadAzz, smoking responsibly as they talked and vibed to the music.

Watching Dooley with just as much attentiveness, T.K. immediately convinced herself that he was someone she would like to get to know. While he enjoyed himself for the moment, Dooley was oblivious to the last warning call for everyone to board the bus for takeoff. He was too busy lost in his own zone while T.K. enjoyed every minute of it. And just when it registered, Dooley bolted to his feet and dashed around the building where the bus had been waiting. It was too late. The bus was already gone.

"Shit! Shit!" Dooley cussed angrily, refusing to believe the fact that he'd fucked up.

Quietly, T.K. could only just stand there, looking just as pitiful as Dooley was.

"Fuck!" Dooley shouted into the late evening as the sun began to set over the horizon.

Then fear of his brother's disappointment settled in him. He was sure Walt would be highly upset with him—to learn that he'd been diverted of the mission that was given to him. That was what disturbed him the most, for Walt counted on him when he couldn't depend or trust anybody else to do it. This was a lesson Dooley will eventually learn—valuable, but terribly disturbing as well. Then he turned toward T.K. with the darkest glare in his eyes . . .

Chapter 1

"What're we gonna do?" T.K. chimed.

They were now sitting inside the rest stop's food court deli as it was nearing its closing time. An hour had passed, and Dooley and T.K. had yet to find a resolve to their situation, which made Dooley even more angry.

Then he turned to her. "What the fuck you mean, what we gonna do?" he demanded. "The muthafuckin' bus left us! Gone!"

"You ain't gotta cuss at me, Dooley."

"Fuck you, bitch!"

That really got her attention.

"Bitch?" she repeated, regarding Dooley challengingly.

Several patrons took their leave, leaving both Dooley and T.K. alone to their predicament. It was getting late, and the place was about to shut down as the few employees left began situating and preparing themselves to leave too.

"You know what? I ain't gon' even feed into that." T.K. stood up with her belongings. "I gotta go to the bathroom."

"So, bitch—bye! Whatcha telling me for?" Dooley shrugged and turned away from her.

With an audible "hmph," T.K. spun on her heels and left him sitting there, drowning in his silent rage.

"Shit!" Dooley banged the table aggressively, causing the two women behind the nearby counter to look up in his direction. Then he reached in his pocket for the cell phone Walt had given him.

Should I call? Walt's gonna be pissed the fuck off with me if I do. But I still gotta do something, Dooley pondered over the matter.

Again, he'd placed himself in a bind. The last time, he'd gotten shot in the process, and Dooley doubted it would get as bad as that incident had.

Or else Walt would shoot my ass for losing my focus, thought Dooley.

"No," he said to himself. "I can't call my brother."

Nearby, the elder white woman leaned over and spoke to the younger Black woman, whose head nodded in response as they watched Dooley from where they stood behind the counter. Dooley looked out through the glass window into the night as his nerves caused him to shudder with effect.

A moment later, a shadow fell over the table, and Dooley looked up with a startled expression at the woman standing there.

"We're closing down for the night," she said coolly.

For some reason, Dooley couldn't find any words of response to her statement.

Then she said, "Y'all missed the bus, huh?"

Dooley nodded.

With a sigh, the woman spoke up again. "Anybody y'all can call or something?"

He shook his head no. The defeated look in Dooley's eyes was all the evidence she needed to know he'd found himself in a situation.

"Where y'all was headed?" she asked.

"Norfolk, Virginia," Dooley forced out.

"Norfolk?" said the woman. "Shit, you a long damn way from there, boy. Well, not that long. You're in Duck, North Carolina now."

"This shit crazy," Dooley muttered.

"And what are y'all gonna do? You can't stay here, because we about to close up shop."

"What can we do?"

"Where you from, anyway?"

"Raleigh, North Carolina," replied Dooley, not really wanting to talk to no one, but he had no choice—especially concerning the current circumstances.

"Gotdamn, boy!"

Now she was feeling sorry for him after estimating the distance between there and Raleigh, NC.

"Look, I see you need some help, and I'ma see to it that y'all get it. Just give me a minute so I can finish up here, and I'll take y'all to the motel or something. It's the least I can do. Shit. What's your name?"

"Dooley."

Dooley needed another blunt right about now.

"Okay, Dooley, sit tight, and I'll be back!" she said, then turned around and left.

Dooley released a sigh of relief, knowing that he had some kind of help after all. A motel? Shit, it was better than being stranded with nowhere else to go or rest for the night. Who would decline something like that in a situation like this?

Returning from the restroom, T.K. sat back down across the table from Dooley. It was obvious that she was also royally upset and looked a bit exhausted as well.

"I'm sorry, Dooley, for making you miss the bus," she apologized, but Dooley just stared at her menacingly.

He had nothing to say, and so they both just sat there silently for the next thirty minutes.

"All right, y'all, let's go," said Shantel, the young Black woman whom Dooley had spoken to earlier.

Startled, T.K. looked up at the woman.

Dooley stood up with his things and said to Shantel, "Thank you, Ma."

She replied, "No problem."

"Where we going?" T.K. bounded up to her feet.

"To hell if you don't pray," Dooley told her, and headed for the exit door.

***

Fifteen minutes later, T.K. was snoring softly in the back seat of Shantel's Dodge Intrepid, while Dooley sat erect in the front passenger seat. The girl was dead tired after being on the road all those hours without the proper rest, but Dooley was too amped to sleep. All he wanted was to take care of what needed to be done and get back home.

During the ride, Shantel had used her charm on Dooley to convince him to tell her all about himself, and what do you know—Dooley shared with her more than what he intended to. What she learned in the process was beyond what she'd assumed, since she had thought the two were relatives or an item.

"So y'all don't know each other at all?" Shantel questioned, as though she couldn't believe it.

"No."

"Then what you gonna do about her?"

"Fuck her!" Dooley said. "I'm going to Norfolk, and I don't give a damn what she—"

"Listen at you."

Dooley glanced up. "What?"

Shantel frowned. "You can't just leave her like that, Dooley. I don't care what you say. Y'all in this together now and—"

"I came by myself."

"That's true, but you know that y'all all y'all got right now to get through this. I'm not saying it's gonna be easy, but you know she can't be abandoned like that. That's a pretty girl, Dooley, and I doubt for a fact she'd survive without your help right now." Shantel drove on with the music playing in the background.

"Fuck T.K.!" Dooley said for the umpteenth time.

He didn't have time to be caught up with no girl he didn't know nor have any clue as to what her life's like. He had a mission to accomplish.

11

"How old are you, Dooley?"

"Nineteen."

"I have a daughter your age. Passion just graduated and is about to attend college soon. Did you finish school, Dooley?"

Shantel suddenly reached inside the armrest console and retrieved what appeared to be a Black & Mild cigar box. Then she handed it over to Dooley.

"I know you smoke, 'cause I smell it all over you. Look in there and get that blunt out and light it up."

Surprised, Dooley did just that.

"You gon' answer my question?" she spoke up again as the car instantly filled with weed smoke.

"I dropped out in the ninth grade after I got shot."

"What about your G.E.D.?"

"Thought about it. I just ain't got to it yet."

"Well," Shantel reached over and took the blunt in rotation, "you need to get to it, or else you gon' find yourself wishing you had in the long run."

"Yeah," he replied without emotion.

For a moment, there was silence between them. So far, Shantel liked Dooley and thought he was a young, straightforward guy, but it was his lack of respect for women—T.K. to be exact—and the fact that he carried himself as a young thug that she didn't seem to accept. But in all, she figured Dooley was an alright dude; he was just in a bad situation that presented his bad side, partially. *Passion would still like him.* Shantel thought of her eighteen-year-old daughter.

"There's a motel that's close to where I live. I'ma take y'all there because all the other ones are out the way."

"It don't matter," Dooley said.

"It's the only one with 24-hour services anyway," added Shantel, puffing on her blunt elegantly, and then they talked more.

Once they reached the motel, Shantel pulled up into the surprisingly filled parking lot. Then she turned to face Dooley.

"Remember what I said, Dooley. She needs you more than you could possibly need her. Don't leave her out in the cold like that."

"I hear ya, Shantel."

"But do you feel me though?"

Dooley met her gaze and held it briefly. He nodded.

"Yeah, I feel you. I feel you."

"Do the right thing, baby boy, and take care of ya'self." Smiling, Shantel stubbed out the butt of the blunt into the ashtray.

With a deep sigh, Dooley turned and shoved T.K. awake. "Come on," he said, and got out the car.

Awakened with a start, the first thing T.K. said was, "Y'all smoked without me?"

Shantel laughed at her. "Girl, go in there and get ya'self some rest."

Getting out the car, T.K. followed Dooley to the front entrance of the two-story motel building. Night had fallen completely, and Dooley had to admit he was totally exhausted himself.

"All I need is to lay my Black ass down," said T.K. as they entered the building.

Despite the current situation, Dooley had to agree with her—but he wouldn't dare tell her as much. Behind the counter of the main desk sat a middle-aged Spanish female. She was watching the screen of a portable DVD player and seemed glued to the screen in the process. She didn't even acknowledge their presence until Dooley slapped his open palm flat against the top of the counter. The Spanish clerk jumped with a startled flinch and turned a wicked glare in his direction.

"Excuse me, but we need a room for tonight," said Dooley, already digging in his pocket for his cash.

"We're full," the Spanish clerk stated, testily.

"Full?" T.K. said.

"That's exactly what I said. We're full for tonight, sorry," she replied with a smirk. "Bye."

Both Dooley and T.K. exchanged a brief glance, but T.K. wasn't going for it.

"Look, bitch! You gonna give us a room or I'ma come cross that damn counter and whip your lying ass," she threatened, and the clerk regarded her cautiously.

"Man, fuck this shit! Come on, T.K."

"Hell nah! That bitch got rooms for us. She just with that bullshit. But I got something—"

"Let's go!" Dooley took ahold of her and almost literally had to drag T.K. outside.

Once outside, T.K. snatched away from Dooley, which caused him to grow a bit furious with her—but he played himself cool.

This bitch is gonna be a major problem if I don't get rid of her soon, Dooley thought, as he watched T.K. rave on and on.

"I can't believe this shit," T.K. stomped her feet and folded her arms across her chest. "Now what the hell we gonna do? We got nowhere else to go."

"Shut the fuck up. I'ma tryna think!" Dooley snapped.

"And I'm just about tired of you talking to me like that too, Dooley."

"And whatcha gon' do about it?"

T.K. backed away instantly when Dooley moved toward her with that look in his eyes.

"I ain't scared of you," she said nervously. But it was obvious to Dooley that she was, yet he knew she wasn't ready for his type of problems.

Especially at that moment in time, Dooley wanted so bad to retrieve his chrome .380 automatic and give her the business, but he knew she wasn't worth it. There was no need to get violent with T.K. Then Shantel's advice came to mind.

"Where you going?" T.K. sobered up quickly when Dooley spun and began walking away toward the sidewalk along the main highway.

"Somewhere. I can't stay here."

"But where though?"

Then Dooley stopped the moment T.K. took ahold of his arm and stepped in front of him.

"Where, Dooley?" T.K. pleaded with him, as the moonlight shone from the reflection of her glassy hazel-brown eyes. And at that moment, Dooley—again, for the second time that night—was at a loss for words.

There was silence between them.

"What about Shantel? She didn't leave you her number or anything?"

Several vehicles passed along the highway, nearly creating a cool breeze of wind in their wake.

"No," Dooley said, reluctantly.

Then a thought came to mind, and Dooley pulled out his small black cell phone.

"Who you calling?"

"Four-one-one. Information. I just remembered the name on Shantel's name tag."

"Good," sighed T.K., looking back over her shoulder at the entrance of the motel.

From where she stood, she could still partially see the front desk and the Spanish clerk behind it. T.K. contemplated going back in there and beating the woman's ass—just because she could.

"Shit!" Dooley broke her reverie.

"What?"

"I don't know where the fuck we even at. I gotta give them a location in order to get the information—"

"The phone book!"

"Huh?"

"She should be in the phone book. I saw one on the table when we walked in," she pointed back toward the motel.

Thinking fast, Dooley made his way back toward the building with T.K. in tow. And the moment they re-entered the motel's front entrance, the Spanish clerk's eyes widened the size of two moons.

"Yeah, bitch, I'm back," T.K. hissed at her.

The clerk swallowed nervously.

"Collins . . . Collins . . ." muttered Dooley as he flipped through the pages of the telephone book.

Waiting patiently, T.K. kept her eyes on the Spanish clerk. She dared the damn woman to say something slick—better not roll her eyes at her.

"Bingo!" Dooley's heart was pounding brutally in his chest as he memorized the number and punched it into his cell.

Moments later, a groggy voice answered the phone. It was Shantel. Without any greeting, Dooley explained the situation—greatly relieved when she said, "I'm on the way."

There was nothing like someone in your corner when you needed them the most.

Dooley smiled inside.

He had Shantel.

Chapter 2

It was a little past eleven o'clock when Shantel walked through the front door of her house, with Dooley and T.K. trailing behind. The house was remarkably warm and well-furnished, and as soon as they entered the living room, both Dooley and T.K. were greeted by Shantel's brother, Kirk.

Talk about huge—this brotha was standing at six foot-four, weighing every bit of three hundred pounds solid. The definition of an ex-convict who'd just been released four days ago after doing a five year bid in the state penitentiary.

The second they entered, Kirk's hungry eyes immediately locked on T.K. as she stood there in her tight designer jeans that seemed to hug her body perfectly. After following Kirk's gaze, Dooley frowned.

After the introductions, Shantel showed T.K. to her room for the night, and the girl followed. There was little energy left in T.K., and she had to force her legs to cooperate just for a moment longer.

Dooley decided to have a seat on one of the sofas, placing the backpack containing the two kilos on the floor between his legs.

"What's up, yo?" Kirk acknowledged.

"What's up." Dooley sized Kirk up for a brief moment of observation, then sat back on the sofa in an attempt to relax.

"Sis told me about y'all situation. So you from Raleigh, huh?"

It didn't surprise Dooley one bit that Kirk knew about him, but what he didn't want was to know Kirk in return. He was far from friendly and rarely kicked it with those he didn't know, but in his current predicament, Dooley knew he had to just roll with the flow. Tomorrow, he would be on his way.

"Yeah, that's where I'm at."

"I know a few homies round your way," said Kirk. "I just did a few calendars with Sandman and anotha young cat name Dero. That's my lil' podna right there. Lil' nigga got a name for himself round your way."

Dooley nodded in response. "I know Dero."

"I'm sure you do." Kirk watched Dooley closely.

He'd wondered who these strangers were that Shantel had so eagerly accepted and brought into her home. Shantel could be naïve at times; however, Kirk loved his sister regardless of her reckless decisions. Who was he to complain, when he made—and had made—just as many bad choices as she had?

Refusing to lead him on in conversation, Dooley looked around the living room, taking in its scene. The place was really decked out, Dooley thought approvingly.

"I got a coupla playz up in Norfolk too," added Kirk, leaning forward to refill his glass from the bottle of *Crown Royal* sitting on the low table. "Them cats up that way are something to reckon with. Trust me. I dealt with a lot of them when I was down."

"How long did you do?"

"Five years."

No wonder this nigga big as fuck, Dooley thought. All this nigga probably did was pump iron and pretend to be hard, but underneath he was soft as cotton.

Dooley had heard all the chain-gang stories from his brother Walt after he'd done a few years in fed.

"Whatcha went in for?"

Kirk seemed intrigued by the question as he puffed his chest out and flexed his muscles, as though to impress Dooley.

"Got knocked off with some weight and a pistol."

See how easy it is for a nigga to lie? Here Kirk claims to have been caught with a pistol and a lot of drugs and got five years for it. He must take me for a fool or something. I guess he assume I'm not the real true street nigga he pretends to be—and that I'd go for anything. This nigga don't even know the half, Dooley laughed to himself inside. *What a real mark!*

"Yeah. They slammed a nigga on some—" Kirk was cut short when, out of nowhere, stepped Passion, his niece.

Instantly, Dooley was mesmerized by the sight of her. The beauty she beheld was far beyond what he imagined after Shantel spoke so faithfully of her, and for a moment, the two locked eyes, analyzing one another for all it was worth.

Damn, Shantel ain't tell me she was this fine, Dooley swallowed hard.

Standing at five-foot-six, shoulder-length dark hair showering over her bare shoulders as she stood there in her tank top and pajama bottoms, Passion was more than pleasing to the eyes. From her cute bare feet up to those pretty brown eyes, the girl was picture-perfect in her own unique way.

Kirk broke the silence quickly. "What's up?"

"Mama said for you to go get the extra blanket and pillows from out the garage," said Passion, cutting a glance over at Dooley.

"I already did that the first time she asked. They're in the damn room like she said," barked Kirk. "Her room!" he then realized his mistake and corrected it.

"She had said the guestroom, but I'll get 'em." Passion gave Dooley one last look over and retreated back down the hall quietly.

Just as quietly, Kirk watched Dooley over the rim of his glass.

"You hear me, lil' homie?"

"What."

"Don't cross me, yo. She ain't the one—you understand? That's my heart right there," Kirk replied with earnest.

"I'm good, Kirk. But you hear me though?" Dooley retorted in the same tone.

"What it is, yo?"

"Don't cross me. I saw how you was watching T.K.— respect my mind too and don't make that move."

Kirk chuckled. "Understood."

Although Dooley didn't really give a damn whether Kirk found T.K. interesting or not, he just wanted to set him straight. And now that they had an understanding, Dooley was ready to get on with the plan.

Little did he know what was in store for him tonight.

Chapter 3

Just when Dooley thought he was in for the night, he allowed Kirk to talk him into rolling with him to the club. Dooley thought that it wouldn't be no big deal to accompany Kirk when he had time to kill. Hell, he had until tomorrow to board another bus and make his way up to Trenton, and a couple hours in the club wouldn't hurt nothing. No matter what, tomorrow he was going to accomplish his mission regardless.

On the other hand, Dooley had a few dollars to blow while he was at it. Stuffing the backpack behind his passenger seat on the floor, he waited until Kirk finished preparing their third blunt. They got out and headed for the club's entrance.

"Yo, Kirk! Kirk, that's you, homie?"

Kirk turned around and acknowledged the speaker behind him, and once he saw who it was, Kirk broke out in a big grin.

"Cee, what's up, yo!"

"Damn, nigga, when you jumped? Look at'cha all swoll and shit," laughed Cee, one of Kirk's childhood cronies whose name actually was Cory.

"You see it," Kirk bragged and embraced Cory briefly. "What'cha doing out here, nigga? You supposed to be all up in that bitch tonight."

Dooley detected the genuine excitement Kirk showed in the presence of one of his homies. After all, they hadn't seen one another in half a decade.

"Man. I don't mess wit' the scene up in there. I'm parkin'-lot pimpin', yo. One stop shop—million-dollar spot out here. Plus, it's safer too."

"Oh yeah, I appreciate that bread you dropped a nigga when I fell," Kirk said.

"Real niggas do real thangs, bro. What's up, nigga?" Cory turned to Dooley and offered a pound.

"That's Dooley right there. Solid lil' homie." Kirk made the introductions.

"That's what's up! Y'all hold it down now. I gotta get back to the paper. But get at me, bro. You know where I'm at."

"Gotcha!" Kirk promised and resumed his path toward the club's entrance after the minor delay.

Dooley expected that there would be a lot of that tonight once Kirk showed his face in the place, and he was right indeed. The moment they stepped inside the club, they had to stop several times on Kirk's behalf before they reached the bar. And just because, Dooley bought Kirk a hundred-dollar bottle of *Grey Goose* and more cigars, then made their way through the club. The place was packed from wall to wall as they mingled and found themselves a vacant table nearby and sat.

Dooley was glad he chose his *Coogi* outfit to travel in because now he appeared to have dressed just for this same purpose, but that was the norm for him. He never left out the house unless he's dressed fresh to impress. Unlike Kirk, who was dressed in a pair of brown Dickies and shell-toe Adidas, and a fresh, crispy white t-shirt, Dooley earned just as much attention as Kirk's homecoming presence.

"Been a long time coming," said Kirk, pouring himself a drink while Dooley sparked up one of the blunts.

Then Dooley wondered whether he'd made a wise decision by buying Kirk the bottle of Grey Goose.

What if this nigga get wasted, and who will be the designated driver? I guess me since I won't be drinking,

22

Dooley thought. *"But how will I find our way back to Shantel's if this fool gets wasted? He won't even be in his right state of mind to give directions."*

Again, Dooley questioned his decision to come along with Kirk when so much was at risk. Then a thought came to mind: *I'll just knock the bottle over and he'll just have to deal with it.*

Kirk had one more cup.

***

Back in Raleigh, Walt was also pouring himself a glass of Cognac after hanging up his cell phone. Tanisha had just put their son, Bryron, back to sleep after he was heard crying out in his sleep again. Wallow, another one of Walt's street lieutenants—but more a friend and thoroughbred killer himself—sat across from Walt nursing his own glass.

"Man, chill the fuck out. Dooley's good; he can handle his own weight," said Wallow, who was built like an ox.

The brotha was six-foot-six tall and as big as the house they were now occupying.

"I ain't doubting that."

"Then stop stressing and shit, nigga."

Walt sighed. "I'm just worried why he ain't hit me up yet. I told him no matter what, to hit me up at twelve—regardless if he handled that bizness or not. You know this lil' bro's first mission on the road."

"And he knows what to do to get the bizness done." Wallow had much faith in Dooley.

"I hope you right, Wallow."

Then Tanisha came into the living room, dressed in a pair of booty shorts and a wife beater. Walt looked up at her questioningly.

"Another bad dream, that's all. He good now. I left the night-light on," she said, sitting next to her man.

Nodding, Walt took another sip of his drink. Then he turned back to Wallow.

"Hit that fool Zoe up and see what's taking him so long to make that happen," he replied with strong emphasis.

"You need to have a little patience, nigga. Lil' bro gotcha all fucked up right now."

"Just do it, nigga. Damn."

Shaking his head, Wallow made the call for the second time. Yeah, it seemed that Walt was also questioning his own decision by sending his baby brother on that mission—but he would soon find out how effective that decision was.

**

"Damn, that's a bad bitch right there!" Dooley gestured ahead with a nod of his head, and Kirk followed his gaze to a group of women standing near their table.

"Go holla then. Which one you talking 'bout?"

"The one in that blue dress. Ma is bad to death," Dooley complimented, admiring her from where he sat.

"Thicker than the outdoors too!" added Kirk, nudging Dooley in the side, beckoning him to go try his luck.

Far from a stranger to macking up on some honey, Dooley decided to do just that. Getting up from the table, he grinned over at Kirk before making his move. There were five of them standing up alongside the outside railing of the dance floor, observing the scene as they grooved to the beat. All of them had some banging bodies, but it was the one in the blue, knee-high, tight dress that held Dooley's attention the most.

"Excuse me, beautiful?" With a gentle hand, Dooley placed it at the small of her back, but it wasn't until she turned to face him that he regretted even making such a move.

The bitch looked like a Black Mick Jagger, and Dooley—never the one to back down from anything—played it cool.

"What's up?" she asked, regarding Dooley closely.

"Your name, that's what's up." *Man, I gotta get the hell away from this ugly bitch!*

Reluctantly, she said with a mean overbite, "Gucci."

"And I'm Dooley, Gucci. I just wanted to let you know you doing your thing tonight, Ma. I like that."

That brought a smile to her face—well, if that's what you want to call it. To Dooley, it looked more like the snarl of a hyena, but he wouldn't dare say so.

"Thank you, Dooley."

"A'ight, Ma. I'll be looking out for you now. Stay jazzy." And Dooley was out of there after that.

By the time he made it back to the table, Kirk was refilling his cup of Grey Goose.

That's two cups right there, Dooley told himself.

"That was fast. You ain't get the number, playa?" asked Kirk, passing Dooley the half of a blunt.

"The number? Nigga, that bitch looked like Cookie Monster!"

Kirk burst out laughing.

"But that ugly bitch finer than a muthafucka!" Dooley said, looking in Gucci's direction.

She glanced back over her shoulder at him, and Dooley shuddered as a cold chill ran up his spine.

"My turn!" Kirk got up from the table and reached for the hand of a passing broad in a tight bodysuit.

For a moment, they stood there talking, and from what Dooley could grasp, the two knew each other. Then just like that, the broad led Kirk onto the dance floor and they disappeared into the crowd of dancers. Dooley checked his watch and saw that it was 12:41. Then it hit him—he was supposed to call Walt at twelve o'clock as promised.

Quickly, Dooley reached for his cell and was about to get up when something crossed his mind.

Damn, I can't go nowhere yet. Gotta wait till Kirk come back, then we'll duck off in the restroom for me to make the call. Don't wanna be gone when Kirk get back—no telling

25

when the next time I'ma see him if I move now. Walt could wait a little while longer. If Kirk ain't back by 1:00, then I'ma make that move and call Walt. Then what in the hell was I gonna tell him?

In the meantime, Kirk was sliding out the side door of the club. Being the slickster that he was, he used Milkshake, a well-known hood trick, to follow him to the dance floor as part of his plan, and from there he broke away from her and found the nearest exit. Now the snake that he was was on the move.

It was back in Shantel's living room, before he readied himself for the club, that he caught a glimpse that ignited his curiosity. He'd just entered the living room after getting dressed for the club—the same time Dooley was zipping up his black Nike backpack. Plus, he'd wondered why Dooley refused to leave the backpack, always checking it and keeping it close by with every move he made.

Kirk was very observant. He needed to see what was in that backpack. And as he made his way through the parking lot back to his sister's car, Kirk's adrenaline was rushing with anticipation. Once inside the car, Kirk shut the door and reached back behind the passenger seat for the backpack.

"Oh shit!" Kirk breathed. "Oh shit! Gotdamn!"

He didn't expect to find two kilos of coke hiding in the confines of the bag.

"What the fuck this young nigga doing with two bricks?"

Kirk shut the bag and scanned his surroundings after a shadow passed by the driver's door.

"Shit," he whispered, heart pounding.

Think. Think. Think. Kirk racked his brain to figure out what he needed to do to capitalize off this sudden discovery.

This was a major come-up for him, and he'd be damned if he didn't take advantage of the matter. That's when it came to him. Immediately, Kirk tossed the backpack onto the floor on the passenger side. Then he juggled the car keys in the dark before inserting one into the ignition. Took a deep breath, and then he followed his first mind.

You slip. I grip, thought Kirk.

A few minutes before one o'clock and anxious to make something happen, Dooley stood up. Just when he was about to say "fuck it" and find the restroom himself, Kirk came rushing toward him. Dooley looked at him with frowning relief.

"Damn, nigga, where the hell you been?"

Kirk pointed toward the V.I.P. lounge area as if Dooley knew exactly where he was pointing to.

"I just fucked that bitch, lil' homie. My first piece of pussy since a nigga been home."

"What?"

"Yeah. I smashed Ma decent!" Kirk grinned devilishly.

This nigga getting pussy in the club while I'm in this bitch stressing, Dooley brooded to himself.

Then Kirk looked over the table curiously. "Where tha 'Goose at?"

"Some drunk fool knocked it over. Don't worry, I gotcha later, dawg. But I gotta piss like a racehorse right now," Dooley said, hoping Kirk took the bait. And that's when Kirk looked down and pointed to Dooley's front right pocket.

"What's up with that shit?" said Kirk, perspiration covering his face.

Dooley looked down and saw his pocket lighting up from inside. He reached in and retrieved the ringing cellphone. Then he froze when he saw it was Walt calling.

"Where the restroom at, Kirk?"

"I'll show you," Kirk said disappointedly.

How this fool gonna let somebody waste a whole hundred-dollar bottle of Grey Goose without stomping his muthafuckin' head in?

Then his answer came at the thought of those two kilos of coke. *Shit, lil' nigga ain't sweating it 'cause he had it made.*

Dooley knew he should've contacted Walt, and now he was dreading what was to come once he spoke with him—but those thoughts died the moment the club erupted in gunfire.

Then all at once, all hell broke loose. People began screaming, running, falling, and shoving one another as they all rushed for safety. It wasn't long before Dooley was shoved every which way, losing the cellphone in the process, and began moving with the crowd.

Everybody seemed to be making their way toward the exit. In passing, Dooley reached underneath his shirt where his pistol rested and moved with the crowd while also ducking for cover. Just like Black people—they couldn't enjoy themselves long before some fool started shooting up the spot and shutting it all down.

Without further incident, Dooley found himself outside, and Kirk was nowhere in sight. Throughout the ruckus, Dooley looked for Kirk to no avail. Then, remembering where they'd parked, that became his next destination. That was before he saw Cory and made a hasty retreat in his direction.

"Yo, Cee! Yo, Cee!" Dooley called out.

"What dey do, playa?" Cory's eyes were everywhere except on Dooley, but he knew he was there.

"I can't find Kirk. You seen him?"

"Kirk? Kirk been gone. I saw him leave 'bout twenty minutes ago."

"Whatcha mean he been gone?"

"Gone. He pulled out in the whip—You ain't know? Look, playa, the police 'bout to crash the spot, and I gotta hit it. Peace, Dooley."

Just like that, Cory was gone too, leaving Dooley to stare after him confused as ever.

"Hey, Dooley!"

Dooley turned suddenly at the sound of his name moments later. Then he relaxed a little when he saw Kirk trotting his way.

"We gotta go, man."

"Somebody splacked the whip. Somebody stole my sista's shit, yo!" Kirk cried out breathlessly.

"What!" Dooley felt his heart leap.

Bending forward with his hands on his knees, Kirk struggled to catch his breath. People still screamed and were running all over the place, and sirens blared from afar into the night.

Stole the car? Dooley stood there, mouth agape, not really comprehending what was really going on.

"There go my nigga Gangsta! Come on, yo!" shouted Kirk, pulling Dooley along toward the black, shiny Dodge Charger, where Dooley eventually found himself inside.

Ever since the mention of someone stealing their car, Dooley had gone into a dark zone. The only thing he could think about was that Walt was really going to kill him once and for all.

Ten minutes later, Dooley was still lost in thought as to what was going on. He'd lost his cell phone, the car was gone with his brother's drugs in it, and he didn't know what to do.

"This shit is all fucked up!" Kirk banged the dashboard in a raging manner.

Gangsta glanced over at Kirk in the passenger seat.

"Chill, gangsta. We gonna find out what's poppin'."

"I'ma murder me a muthafucka 'bout my sista's shit, yo," Kirk blurted. "Somebody stole my sista's shit!"

Gangsta puffed on his Newport. "We gon' find out who it is. Prolly them young fools over there off Peacan Ave. You know how they do it," said Gangsta, attempting to reassure Kirk that it was more likely the Peacan Boyz, who were well-known for stealing cars around town. And if it was them, he was sure they would give up the car by his word alone—or else they all would have hell to pay in consequence.

Dooley's thoughts were elsewhere. There was a sudden eerie feeling settling over him as he thought more about the situation. Something didn't add up, nor did Dooley believe it was a coincidence that Shantel's car had been stolen. Cory had said he saw Kirk leaving in his sister's car twenty minutes before the shooting. During that time, Kirk was nowhere in sight—for he had supposedly been tricking off with the broad he'd snatched up.

Was Kirk really tricking off with her the whole while?

Then Dooley thought back to the strange vibe Kirk had given him back at the house after he almost caught him with the backpack open. The way Kirk would watch him so attentively, glancing at the backpack every so often. Dooley didn't think nothing of it too seriously then, but now as he thought about it, it made him grow weary.

Something wasn't right.

Could Kirk have peeped the stash back at the house?

"How could we get in touch wit' them young fools before they fuck up the whip, Gee?"

"My homie Lank fucks with Lil' Earl. He supposed to be the head of the clique."

Kirk said, "I don't give a fuck! Hit your homie up and see what's poppin'."

"Gotcha," Gangsta reached for his phone, one-handedly driving through the city. "I'ma get Lank to—"

"Nigga, where my shit at?" Dooley demanded, placing the pistol against Kirk's head from behind.

Kirk froze, stiff and rigid.

"What the—?" Gangsta replied, glancing back at Dooley and seeing murder in his eyes as he held the gun to Kirk's head.

"Dooley, whatcha doing, yo?" Kirk cried out.

"You think it's a game?" Dooley bashed Kirk upside the head with the gun. "Where my shit, Kirk? Don't play with me, nigga."

30

"What the fuck going on, *Gangsta?*" Gangsta wanted to know, turning to Kirk with a serious expression plastered on his face.

"Nobody ain't steal his sista's car—he had did it!" Dooley shouted, and he knew for sure in his heart that he was right.

"I don't know what—"

Boom! The blast that sounded off resulted in Kirk grabbing his left shoulder where the bullet had entered.

Kirk screamed just like the bitch he had assumed and tried Dooley as.

"Oh shit!" Gangsta ducked, swerving the Charger into the next lane before correcting it.

Dooley was beyond fooling around now. He bashed Kirk across the head a second time.

"I'ma ask your bitch ass again. What'd you do with my shit, Kirk?" he sneered.

"Yo, tell that nigga something, *Gangsta!*" Gangsta replied. "Give shorty back his shit, man."

There was no doubt in his mind that Kirk was grimy. He had known him far too long. Kirk had a reputation for pulling grimy moves, and now he done placed himself in a deep situation—a situation he couldn't get out of.

Boom! The second blast seemed louder than the first one. Now Kirk was howling like some wounded animal, both shoulders out of commission now. His cries were so agonizing that Gangsta felt sorry for him. It was a rare thing for Gangsta to do—yet here he was, feeling sorry for his fellow comrade.

"You ready to die, nigga?" Dooley said.

"Alright! I'll tell you! I'll tell you!" Kirk cried, sobbing. "Don't… kill me! I'll tell you."

"Nigga, tell 'em!" Gangsta replied.

"Behind the *RadioShack,"* said Kirk. "I parked it back there."

"Which one? That spot down from the club?" Gangsta asked.

"Yeah."

"You ain't lying to me, homie?"

"No! It's back there behind . . . there." Kirk was definitely hurting now as the strong smell of fresh blood reeked throughout the car. "Back there!"

Now Dooley knew he couldn't let Kirk get away with what he did. He'd crossed the line and had to be dealt with accordingly. Dooley automatically knew that if Walt was in this situation, he'd know what would happen to Kirk. Then his brother's words came rushing back to him at once.

It was then that Dooley decided what he had to do—because if he didn't, not only would Walt be more disappointed, but the chance of Kirk coming back for him would perhaps be a decision he could one day regret.

Then Dooley pulled the trigger, blowing Kirk's brains out without further ado.

"Man, why you had to kill the mothafucker in my car? Now my shit all fucked up!" Gangsta complained as he glimpsed Kirk's slumped dead body over in the passenger seat.

"Take me to get my shit, Gangsta," Dooley demanded, sitting back in his seat—and Gangsta did nothing other than just that.

Dooley still wasn't satisfied. He knew there was more to come, and by any means necessary, he would see that it was taken care of also—because his mission was far from over.

It had just begun.

Chapter 4

It was 3:20 a.m. when Dooley pulled up in front of Shantel's crib led by Gangsta. After retrieving the car and Dooley making sure everything was kosher, he and Gangsta disposed of Kirk's body right there behind the RadioShack. It was a 'move quickly' operation and they'd made it happen without further complications. Gangsta hit the horn and sped off into the middle of the night.

Once in the driveway, Dooley got his backpack and made his exit for the house. It took him a minute to find the right key, but he did—and was in the house, slouching through the entrance hall like a tired zombie. Once he made it into the living room, he froze when, all of a sudden a shadow stood in the dark room. It didn't take him long to figure out who it was.

"Where's Kirk?" Shantel asked.

Dooley frowned in the dark. "Your guess is as good as mine. All I know is that they were shooting at the club, and he stayed back with some homies."

"And you drove my car home?"

Dooley nodded. "Yeah."

A frustrating sigh erupted from Shantel as she held out her hand.

"Gimmie my keys, Dooley, and go get some sleep. "Can't believe Kirk and his bullshit. That boy just won't learn," she muttered, shaking her head and retreating back down the hall to her bedroom.

Now it was Dooley's turn to sigh.

After a while, Dooley headed down the hall to the guest room, where he would immediately pass out in a deep

33

slumber. He was dead tired and mad as hell. Inside the bedroom, he dropped the backpack at the foot of the bed and moved around to the empty side where T.K. wasn't laying.

"Boy, what you doing? You better get outta my bed."

Dooley felt a light shove and froze when he realized what was happening. Instead of the guest room, he entered Passion's bedroom and laid down next to her.

"Oh shit, my bad!" muttered Dooley as he looked back over his shoulder at Passion, who was now sitting up in bed and staring at him sleepily.

"You better go," she warned him forcefully. "Next door."

"My bad," Dooley repeated. Then he stood up and left the room, feeling slightly lightheaded and irritated.

Moments later, he entered the guestroom next door to the sound of T.K's soft snores, where he didn't hesitate to lay down beside her on top of the covers. The girl was all over the bed, and he found the closest available space, turning away from her in the dark so as not to wake her. Then sleep took him over instantly. His last thoughts before darkness settled were how pretty Passion's green eyes had stared back at him in the dark of her bedroom.

(One hour earlier)

"Hello?"

"Who the fuck is this?" replied the angry voice on the other end of the phone. Walt.

Reluctantly, the answer came. "Mo'nique."

"Mo'nique?"

"Yeah."

"Um. Look, Mo'nique, where my brotha Dooley at?"

"Dooley?"

"Yeah. Dooley. You got my brotha's phone, don't you? Where he at?"

It was blatantly obvious Walt was anxious, yet troubled at the same time. You could tell by the tone in his voice. Mo'nique looked across the bar into the vast open space of the club, where the floor was littered with the aftereffects

34

from the club's shooting—law enforcement officials, and potential witnesses. The place was a circus, and she didn't want to have nothing to do with any of it. All she wanted was to finish her shift and go home.

"I don't know no Dooley. But whoever he is must've dropped his phone when they started shootin' in the club."

A brief silence. Then an audible intake of breath.

"Club? Shooting? What club?" Walt demanded.

"This is *Club Blaze* over on Sixty-first and Conway."

Another moment of silence. A longer silence.

"Hello? You still there?" Mo'nique said into the phone.

"Yeah. Whatchu said your name was again?" Walt asked, and she told him once again.

"A'ight. Check this out, Mo'nique. I appreciate your help, and I'ma look out for you. Just hold the phone down till I get there. I'ma hit you back later and let you know where to meet me at, a'ight?"

"That's no problem. But I can't go nowhere right now. I gotta help out at the club before I can leave."

"You work there?"

"Yeah."

"Just hold it down. And I'll get back in touch. Thanks, Ma." Walt sounded a little relieved now, but you could still hear the edge in his voice.

He needed to get that phone and find out where Dooley was.

"One more thing, Ma?"

"What's up?"

"Do you remember seeing a young brown-skin cat with a few golds at the bottom of his mouth? He was dressed in an all-white *Coogi* outfit and *Jordans*. Low haircut—"

Mo'nique interrupted. "I don't think I have, but I don't forget any faces though. Sorry."

"Cool," replied Walt. "A'ight. Stay real, Ma, and I gotcha."

"I will."

That was the end of the call.

Again, Mo'nique looked over the club's inner space and gave a deep sigh. The sound of Walt's concerned voice lingered in her mind as she searched her brain to remember whether she recognized Dooley's description or not.

Then, when she came up empty, Mo'nique took the cell phone and shoved it back in her pocket for safekeeping. Her sole intention was to keep the phone and use it to her heart's content, but when it rang, her intuition made her answer it.

Little did she know what great fruits that simple decision would bring her eventually.

With a pile of work to do, Mo'nique resumed her task, and soon the thought of the phone was all forgotten about.

***

When Dooley woke up the following day, he sat up with a start at the burst of laughter sounding off throughout the house. He didn't even wait until his fogginess cleared up and bolted for the bedroom door at once. Dooley padded down the hall toward the area from which the ruckus was coming.

"Look who's finally up," said T.K., acknowledging Dooley first as she looked up from the kitchen table.

Then she gestured toward him as Passion and another strange-looking girl regarded him with sudden surprise. Then a door opened somewhere to Dooley's left, where he stood in the kitchen's doorway. Shantel had exited the bathroom and was immediately taken aback by his presence.

"Um, I think you need to go back and put some clothes on in my house, Dooley."

Dooley looked down at himself and realized he was clad in just his boxer shorts and tank top. Sometime during the night, he had undressed himself in order to sleep more comfortably. He had a morning hard-on. The girls giggled over at him, and Dooley retreated back to his room.

Then, while he was getting dressed, Shantel shouted in his direction from the kitchen area.

"Dooley, I've already scheduled a 10:30 bus for you and T.K. Passion will drop y'all off for me because I gotta get to work. I'm late as it is. Remember what we talked about and use my advice wisely."

Dooley stepped into his shorts before reaching for his shoes, listening while Shantel talked. In the process, his thoughts traveled back to the night before—the club scene, the shooting, then Kirk's cold-blooded murder, and he and Gangsta disposing of his body behind that building. He didn't feel nothing—no remorse at all—for what he'd done. Though he wasn't no stranger to gunplay, it was the first time he'd actually killed another human being and acted in such a manner in Walt's absence.

His young heart had been hard ever since losing his mother several years before to smoking. Since then, Dooley had become a loose cannon. However, Walt had always been there alongside him when the pressure was on. To look at himself now, Dooley could see how much he'd developed into that young goon he was forced to be.

He didn't choose the life he led—it was choosing him. Now he was in this strange house in the middle of nowhere, with no clue where he even was, and forced to survive it through until he got to where he was going.

"Alright, Dooley. You be good now, and get back home safely," said Shantel, seconds before the front door closed shut behind her. But Dooley's mind and eyes were all over the place as he looked for his backpack.

Before he went into a panic, he remembered leaving it back in Passion's room the night before—and that's exactly where he found it, lying at the foot of her bed on the floor.

Back in the kitchen, he found all three girls sitting right where he had seen them earlier. It was then that Passion introduced him to her best friend, NeNe, who—now that the fogginess in his vision had cleared—Dooley thought was very cute.

"You want some cereal too?" Passion asked, looking up at him with a silent, secretive glance.

Of course, she hadn't forgotten their brief encounter the night before in her bedroom. Dooley gave her a knowing nod.

Shit. I might as well eat something while I'm at it, Dooley thought.

A big bowl of *Froot Loops* was before him in no time.

"You got something on your shirt," NeNe pointed out.

"That looks like blood," T.K. exclaimed.

Sure enough, a patch of blood decorated near the hem of Dooley's untucked shirt. He was a bit surprised at seeing it—and knowing exactly where it came from—but he wouldn't dare tell them.

"And you wearing that out, looking like that?" asked Passion, with a sour look on her face.

"That must've happened last night," he said.

"What happened last night?" NeNe wanted to know, speaking for the rest of them.

That's when he told them about the club shooting, omitting what actually happened after that once he found out about Kirk's sneakiness. They all responded to his story with expected surprise, and Dooley left it at that.

"I got a shirt you can have," said Passion. "You don't need to go out with that blood on your shirt."

"I'm good," he said.

T.K. said, "I got a pack of brand-new T-shirts in my bag if you want one, Dooley," glancing over at Passion briefly.

"I'm good."

"And what? You gonna go out like that?"

"I'ma throw it away and just wear my tank top," Dooley replied, chewing. "No pressure."

"That won't work!" Passion chimed in. Then a thought came to her. "If you want to, we can stop by the mall and find you a better shirt. Y'all got two hours till your bus come."

"Sounds like a plan," NeNe added excitedly.

Then T.K. looked over at Dooley questioningly. They held one another's gaze for a moment, and Dooley shrugged.

"I can do that," he said.

Honestly, it didn't sound like a bad idea. T.K. smiled, and Passion did too. They all were on their way.

Chapter 5

After the first thirty minutes spent in the mall, Dooley thought it was a good idea because he really enjoyed himself. He was feeling himself so much that he gave each one of the girls a hundred dollars to spend however they wanted to. Then thirty minutes turned into an hour, and an hour into an hour and a half. Now it was 9:53 and thirty-seven minutes before Dooley and T.K. were to report to the bus station, which was close by.

Bags clutched in their hands, T.K., Passion, and NeNe were ecstatic about their new purchases. It made Dooley swell up with self-satisfaction as he watched the happiness on their faces, as he now strolled alongside them with his brand-new *Coogi* shirt to match his *Coogi* gear. But all their smiles and good humor came to a halt once they descended the escalator and made the final turn toward the exit doors.

"Damn, what's up, Passion?" replied Reggie, a former schoolmate before he dropped out in eighth grade. Standing near him were four more of his homies, all looking like nothing but trouble; something they brought on a daily basis.

Passion's face went slack of excitement.

"What's going on, Reggie? What's up, Pat, y'all?" she greeted casually.

Reggie was eyeing T.K. at the moment, shooting a quick glance over in Dooley's direction.

"You know how we do it, baby, just cooling it like always."

"What dey do, NeNe?" said Chad, one of Reggie's homies, making a move toward her, but NeNe stepped back

40

cautiously, not wanting to be touched—or better yet, even near him.

"I'm good, Chad," she muttered evenly.

"What's your name, sexy?" Reggie's right-hand man, Cojac, asked T.K., sizing her up like a dog's dinner.

Another group of girls, who were deviously skipping school, circled them and moved on into the mall's entrance. Dooley watched Chad attentively, who seemed to be watching him just as much. There was a sense of tension in the air, and Dooley knew that trouble would become the result if he and the girls didn't leave right away. Instead, Passion made a hasty introduction of T.K. and Dooley to Reggie and his crew, then attempted to leave just as quickly, but Reggie wouldn't be swayed so easily.

"Wait a minute! Where you from, homie?" Reggie stopped before Dooley, causing Passion to quietly panic, for she knew what Reggie and his crew were capable of and didn't want nothing to do with it; especially where T.K. and Dooley were concerned.

"He ain't from round here, Reggie!" NeNe blurted.

Passion added, "We gotta go!"

"What? Dude can't talk for himself. He a faggot or something?" Chad frowned, challenging Dooley with an icy stare.

Don't fall for it Dooley, NeNe thought to herself as she watched Dooley's face expression grow hard.

"Where you from, nigga?" Reggie demanded.

The tension was thick now, and just when Dooley was about to say something, Passion took ahold of his hand, and NeNe did the same with T.K. Then they—Passion to be exact—pushed passed Reggie and headed for the exit. But in passing, Dooley gave Reggie a heated glare in return.

"Just keep walking, Dooley. Them fools just trying to start something . . ." Passion whispered.

"Always wit' the bullshit!" NeNe was saying to T.K. as they exited through the doors into the blazing sunshine.

She definitely didn't want to be around Cojac, who she had dated once a year or so ago. Ever since then, she'd avoided being in his presence for all it was worth.

T.K. looked back over her shoulder and groaned in protest.

"Here they come."

When NeNe looked back and saw Reggie and his crew exiting the mall and heading their way, she sped up her pace.

God, please let us make it to the car before they start with the bullshit, Passion prayed, seeing her car several yards away.

She was glad she'd found a good parking spot closer to the mall's entrance where she didn't have to plow through so many other vehicles to get to her own.

"Yo, Passion, don't try to save that faggot!" shouted Chad from behind. "He act like he got a problem or somethin'."

"He prolly one of them southside niggas . . ." one of the crew members chimed.

"Prolly is," said Reggie. "We ain't having them bitch niggas on this side, yo."

Without a word, Dooley unclasped his hand from Passion's and moved it closer to his waistband where the chrome .380 rested.

Man, I hope I don't have to bust one of them niggas, he told himself.

Then the sound of them approaching from behind got closer as they neared Passion's Honda Civic. Passion pulled out her car keys from her purse, pressed the button to unlock it automatically, and glanced over in Dooley's direction.

"Yo, fuck that punk! Let's whip his faggot ass, Reg! Yeah, that's why he ain't say shit cause he one of them southside cats," replied Chad, amping his comrades up for trouble.

"No, he ain't!" shouted NeNe just when all five of the hellraisers bum-rushed them from behind.

Then the unexpected came. Just when Dooley felt the slightest physical contact he whirled around and upped his pistol, placing it directly at the tip of Reggie's nose. They all stopped instantly. NeNe gave a short shriek when she saw the gun, and T.K. didn't know what to do; but surprisingly, Passion was quiet and placid as ever.

"You want some problems, nigga!" Dooley sneered, relishing the fear in Reggie's eyes.

There was no sound from Reggie nor his crew.

"Oh, you a bitch now, huh! Back the fuck up offa me— all you bitch ass niggas!"

Dooley released the shopping bag that was tightly clutched in his right hand. It fell to the ground, then Dooley spoke up again.

"If you niggas ain't ready to die, I suggest you get the fuck outta my face."

He pushed the barrel of the gun deeper in Reggie's face, who at that moment struggled to swallow past the lump in his throat.

"Let's go, Dooley!" said Passion.

Slowly but surely, Reggie and his crew retreated back the way they'd come, back into the entrance of the mall, as quietly as they came. Releasing a sigh of relief, T.K. looked over at Dooley.

"Boy, put that damn thing up before somebody see it and call the police," NeNe said nervously, scanning their surroundings.

Dooley did as he was advised, and they all returned back to the car. *Thank God* was all Passion could say once they were pulling out of the mall's parking lot, but little did she know.

***

"You what?" Mo'nique said into the phone.

As calmly as he could, Walt spoke up. "I'm nearby. Where do you wanna meet up at?" he asked.

"Nearby where?" said the groggy voice.

Walt sat behind the wheel of his Mercedes-Benz truck, with Wallow on the passenger side looking up at the store's name title overhead.

"I'm at a store called Food Lion over on . . ."

"North Flechard," said Wallow.

Nodding, Walt gave her the location.

"I know where you at. I'm about fifteen minutes away," a sigh was heard over the line. "Gimmie a minute and I'll meet you there, okay?"

"Cool."

"One more thing too?"

"What's up?"

Walt watched the three young niggas hanging out at the corner of the store.

"While you at it, get me a pack of Big Red chewing gum from the store next door."

Again, Walt peered ahead and saw that right where the three young niggas were standing was where a convenience store sat, connected to the building of Food Lion.

"I gotcha. Anything else? A chicken dinner? A soda? What?"

She chuckled and assured him she was alright.

"I'll be there in a minute," she said, and ended the call.

There was a brief silence before Walt turned to Wallow. "You want something outta there too, nigga?"

Wallow shook his head no and continued puffing on his Black & Mild cigar. Then Walt got out of the shiny silver Benz truck, sitting nice on chrome 24" face rims, and made his way to the corner store's entrance. The three young niggas watched him, never saying a word, as Walt entered the store without so much as a greeting.

"Yo, Egg, you know that nigga?" said Roscoe, who jumped down from atop the newspaper stand after Walt went inside the store.

Shaking his head, Egg said, "Never seen dude in my life."

"Me neither," added JoJo, the bigger one out of the three. "But that fool sittin' clean though, I know that."

"Go peep that fool tag, Jo!" Egg suggested.

"Yeah, go see what's up!" said Roscoe, plotting.

Without hesitation, JoJo pushed off the side of the store and headed toward the Benz truck. It was hard to tell who was inside due to its dark tinted windows, yet that still didn't stop him from peeping the license plate for confirmation. Then, as Roscoe and Egg watched from afar, they were soon caught off guard when the passenger side window rolled down. An outstretched arm brandishing a big chrome Glock .40 stopped JoJo in his tracks.

They saw JoJo stand there for a moment, as if he was listening to the warning that was being given unto him, then backpedaled the way he'd come. The boy was obviously shaken.

"What's up, Jo?" asked Egg.

JoJo didn't acknowledge him directly and just took the cigarette out of Roscoe's hand and took a long, hard puff.

"Don't ask me to do no shit like that again," he said nervously—and that was all it took for them to get the picture that they were treading on the wrong grounds.

As always, Wallow put the fear of God in their eyes, and it was clearly obvious that the three young niggas weren't as gangsta as they pretended to be.

***

Dooley sat in the back seat next to T.K., leaning against the door in deep thought, watching as the city passed by him through the window. The girls were still a bit uneasy about what had just gone down in the mall's parking lot, but they kept that part of the conversation to a minimum as they talked along the topic of other things.

Thanks to T.K., she had her MP3 player at the ready when Dooley wanted to zone out as he thought about the current predicament he was in. Then his thoughts went back to Shaliah, who he left back in Raleigh to take this journey. Shaliah was one of the several females he was involved with back home. They were close, lived on the same street, and even played in the same sandbox at daycare growing up. That was before Dooley's mama had died, and his daddy, Mike, had grudgingly accepted the responsibility as the sole parent. Shaliah didn't like Mike one bit, but the girl loved Dooley's grandmother, Mama Lizzy, whom Dooley decided he would live with mostly instead of with Mike or Walt.

Then he wondered what Shaliah would think of T.K. ... Dooley shook his head after realizing just how Shaliah would respond to T.K.'s presence if she ever was to meet her. Shaliah was one stubborn bitch who demanded that Dooley be her boyfriend to no avail. Dooley felt they were too close to have a relationship like that.

And that's when his thoughts went to Jon Jon, his childhood crony—the one male friend he could vouch for other than Cash, who was Jon Jon's older brother. Dooley couldn't wait to tell his friend about the journey. However, Jon Jon had been upset that Dooley decided to take the ride by himself, but he knew it was all Walt's doing, and he had to respect that. So Jon Jon let the matter be and kept it moving.

"Oh my god! The damn police is behind me—fuck!" Passion shouted, peering into the rearview mirror.

"What?" NeNe turned around to look for herself.

"I ain't did nothing," Passion cried out.

Instantly, T.K. glanced behind her, saw the police cruiser behind them, and turned to look at Dooley questioningly.

"Gurl, you speeding or something?" asked NeNe.

Passion bellowed a, "Hell no!"—shuddering in response to her sudden fear when the sound of the police siren blared sharply behind them.

"Oh shit," whispered T.K., heart pounding in her chest.

Sensing something wrong, Dooley unplugged his ears from the earplugs and analyzed the tension in the air. Then he followed everyone else's wide gazes and looked behind him. When he saw the police cruiser close behind, he went into a panic.

"I think he want me to pull over," Passion said.

"Pull over?" Dooley gasped loudly.

"Gurl, you better do something!" NeNe was panicking now.

At that moment, both Passion and Dooley locked eyes for a moment in the rearview mirror. Then T.K. reached over and touched his hand. The expression he saw on hers was of total fear. She knew what position this placed him in and was genuinely scared for him. Though she didn't know about the two kilos in the backpack Dooley was slinging over his shoulders, the gun—she knew he had on him . . .

"I'm pulling over," Passion announced.

She was a nervous wreck.

"I don't know what they stoppin' me for."

A deafening silence hung in the air. Passion veered the car alongside the highway out of traffic, and before anyone knew what was going on, Dooley was out of the still-rolling car and running like his life depended on it. This took them off guard—especially T.K., who was by now too scared to do anything—let alone chase after Dooley, who was clearly on the run now. All she could think was whether she would even see him again.

"I can't believe this shit!" Passion banged the steering wheel.

Neither could any of them.

Including Dooley.

***

The phone rang. Walt didn't hesitate to answer it.

"Talk to me."

"I'm here. Where you at?"

"That's you just pulled up in the black Acura?"

"Yeah. Where you at?" Mo'nique repeated.

Walt saw the shiny black Acura several cars down, parked in a parking space. He also observed two occupants in the car and immediately decided it was two females inside. Though he really could care less who occupied the car, he just hoped they could help him locate his brother.

"I'm in the silver Benz truck. Come get in and lemme holla at you, Mo," he replied finally.

A brief silence.

"Here I come," she said.

Hanging up the phone, Walt waited anxiously to see just who this Mo'nique broad really was.

Damn, bro, I hope you alright, thought Walt, catching a glimpse of her approaching the truck from the storefront.

"Damn, baby look kinda sexy a little bit too," Wallow said, receiving not even a comment from Walt.

After noticing Walt and Wallow inside through the windshield, Mo'nique headed for the back passenger door and climbed in. Then, without reluctance, she handed over the cellphone in between them, which Wallow took quietly.

"Thank you, Mo'nique," Walt spoke up from behind the wheel.

Then, the next thing later, he reached over his shoulder to hand her a brown paper bag.

"Thanks." Mo'nique looked into the bag and gasped after feeling the weight of it, because inside was not only what she had asked for but two packs of gum and a roll of bills—cash money.

"Damn, boy, all this for me?"

"It's in yo' hands, isn't it?"

"Damn," she said softly.

"Now," Walt started. "You remember seeing him in the club last night?" he asked, showing her a recent close-up photo of Dooley cheesing for the camera.

It was the same day he had gotten his golds put in his mouth, along with Walt, who had diamonds and rubies encrusted in his gold teeth. Staring at the photo between her fingers, Mo'nique said:

"Remember I told you I don't forget faces? I was right. I saw him last night—your brother, right?"

"Yeah."

"Hmmm." Mo'nique seemed to be pondering.

"Do you remember if he was with somebody or not?" asked Wallow.

"I don't know."

"Think, Ma," encouraged Walt.

An old couple passed by along the sidewalk in front of the truck and entered the Food Lion. Then a dark sedan pulled up in the slot next to Walt's driver-side door. A young girl exited the car and entered Eckerd's Drug Store a few doors down.

"I don't . . . know," she whispered. Then she said, "Lemme call my girl Lisa over here so she can see. She was in the club last night too."

"Handle that!" blurted Walt, growing impatient.

Mo'nique made the call to her friend Lisa, who was waiting in the black Acura several cars down. Then, moments later, Lisa repeated Mo'nique's footsteps but slid inside the Benz truck behind Walt. This time, Wallow didn't have anything to say—for Lisa was far beyond beautiful and just as sexy as Mo'nique.

Was it that her flawless beauty intimidated him?

Walt acknowledged her with a slight nod, meeting her eyes through the rearview mirror. Then Mo'nique showed her the photo. After a moment, Lisa sucked her teeth and handed back the photo nonchalantly.

"He was rollin' with Kirk last night," said Lisa.

"Kirk?" both Walt and Wallow said in unison.

That's when Mo'nique slapped her thigh. "I knew I remembered! They brought a bottle of Grey Goose."

"Grey Goose? My brotha don't drink no Grey Goose." Walt frowned deeply. "Who is this Kirk nigga?"

"He just came home from prison."

"That's my homegirl Shantel's baby brother," Lisa said, eyes wide when she saw the roll of bills in Mo'nique's hand.

The statement caused Walt to freeze.

"Y'all know where he live at?"

"Of course," Lisa answered Wallow.

With one look at Walt, he already knew what had to be done next. The truck roared to life and Walt sped out of the parking space in reverse. In no time, he was aiming the nose of the truck toward the main highway.

"Which way to go?" Walt wanted to know.

Both women looked at one another and Mo'nique shrugged. Then Lisa shrugged too.

"Make a left right here . . ." she pointed—and it was music to Walt's ears.

Chapter 6

For the past twelve minutes, Dooley had been running as long and hard as he could. Out of breath and all, he still ran until he reached what appeared to be an apartment complex. That's when he slowed down to a walk, trying to catch his breath. Scanning the immediate area, he saw a smaller building nearby—which he assumed was the laundry room—and headed there. He needed to find somewhere to lay low until he figured out his next move.

Then he wondered what happened to the girls.

The second he entered the laundry room, he sensed a presence there but didn't see anyone. Though there were the paraphernalia of bleach and washing detergent, several of the dryers and washing machines were being used, too. Dooley looked over the place and wondered who could it be that was in the middle of doing their laundry.

That's when he heard the flush of the toilet moments before a side corner door opened and a female stepped out.

This wasn't an ordinary female, Dooley thought as she approached the table where her belongings sat.

"What's up, youngin'?" she greeted Dooley.

Dressed in a pair of designer jean shorts stopping a little above mid-thigh, a tight matching wife beater, and a pair of high-top Nike Air Maxes, this beautiful sistah was still eye candy. Caramel skin tone with the measurements of 36D-24-42 shaped upon a five-foot-nine frame, with the air of a true diva and piercing brown eyes. She was nothing less than amazingly beautiful in her own way.

This, Dooley thought, *is the baddest bitch I've seen up this way.*

"Damn, boo, you ain't gotta stare," she said arrogantly. "I know this shit is what's poppin'."

"You ain't all that now," Dooley said.

She laughed. "But my gurl was last night when you was all up in her airwaves and shit."

Her statement caught him off guard, and he asked, "Who your gurl?"

"Gucci."

"Gucci?" The name didn't register right then, but when it did, Dooley gave her a sour look. *I know she ain't talkin' about that Mr. Ed lookin' bitch!*

"Hmph. You know who I'm talkin' about," she added, as though reading his current thoughts.

"I know," he admitted. "She was alright—"

"Boy, please! That heffa damn near ran you up outta there when she turned around. That's my gurl and I love her to death, but that's one ugly bitch. But my gurl got a bangin' body, shuttin' down shit everywhere she go."

Dooley didn't reply, just sat down in the nearest chair while she hopped onto one of the tables, retrieving her half-smoked Black & Mild from its edge and lit it up. She looked over at him curiously.

"What's your name, youngin'?"

"Dooley. What's yours?" he asked casually.

"Andrea."

He just nodded in response.

"You ain't from round here. Where you from?"

Reluctantly, he told her, "North Carolina. Raleigh, North Carolina."

"What the hell you doin' up here?"

Sensing the excitement in her voice, Dooley shook his head.

"I don't even s'posed to be here," he said gruffly.

"Why is that?"

Dooley looked up at her. "You a reporter or somethin'? I mean, you askin' a lotta damn questions."

That made her chuckle. "You the one in a situation, not me. I'm just askin'—"

The buzz from the washing machine sounded off, cutting her statement short. Then she pounced down from the table. Right at that moment, Dooley decided to take a look outside and wished that he was back home in Raleigh.

He couldn't believe his eyes.

Because just fifteen yards away, there was Chad and Cojac, along with one more of their crew members, climbing off the back of a truck's bed. They were heading in his direction along the sidewalk, oblivious to his whereabouts.

"Shit!" he muttered.

Instantly, Dooley drew his pistol.

"What's yo' problem?" Andrea startled Dooley as he spun toward her, eyes wide with worry.

She regarded him with sudden fear. After a moment, Dooley turned back toward the doorway, perspiring nervously.

"What's goin' on, Dooley?" asked Andrea.

"Nothing," he muttered.

She wasn't going for it. Somebody's out there, she surmised quietly. Disregarding the fact that he had a gun, Andrea still approached Dooley cautiously and took a look outside, following his line of vision. What she saw was a young boy struggling to dribble a large beach ball in the street—and the three hellraisers just across the street from the laundromat building. That's exactly where she assumed his sudden alertness was directed.

"Them?" she asked.

"Yeah," Dooley told her what happened at the mall.

"That ain't surprising. I know how to handle this shit," she said.

"Whatchu 'bout to do?"

"Call 'em over here and—"

"What!" Dooley froze, looking at her strangely. "Bitch, are you crazy? I swear on my mama I'll kill all they asses," he threatened, heart pounding brutally in his chest.

Andrea gave him an icy look. "Look, youngin', you gonna have to trust me—"

"Fuck that!"

"Listen, young nigga! I'm the muthafuckin' Queen B around this bitch. Either a muthafucka gonna respect my call or fall, one. This *my* turf!" she snapped. "Now let me handle this bullshit, and you just chill the fuck out."

"I told you . . ." Dooley cocked back his pistol. "Let one of them muthafuckaz jump bad and I'ma body they ass right here. Watch!"

The look Andrea gave him convinced him that she knew he was very serious—and she nodded in understanding.

This young nigga is about his issue, Andrea thought quietly.

She just hoped that it didn't come down to any bloodshed on her turf, and with that, she was determined to see that it didn't. She hollered over at the three young hellraisers. Dooley stepped back from the doorway.

"Check this out for a minute!" she shouted, glancing at Dooley. "Just be cool, youngin'."

From where he stood, just beyond the wall next to the doorway, Dooley could hear their approach nearing as they converged noisily. Moments later, their shadows fell across the doorway.

"What'z happenin', big sis?"

It was Chad's voice Dooley heard.

"What y'all up to?"

Chad again: "Just got back from the mall, fixin' to meet up wit' Reggie 'bout some bidness that just come up."

Listen at him, trying to seem like he was really on some real thug-thrizzle shit, Andrea smirked.

"Oh yeah?"

"You know how we do it, Drea!" Cojac spoke up.

"Yeah, I know. Y'all step in here real quick . . ." Andrea beckoned, gesturing with a flick of the hand.

The sudden presence of his recent trouble approaching and walking through the entrance of the laundromat caused Dooley to stiffen. They didn't see him immediately, but the third one—who was Chad—caught a glimpse of Dooley in the corner with his pistol down, eyes wide with caution, and came to a sudden halt. Then he looked over at Andrea oddly, who stood next to him, and voiced his response to the unexpected situation, which caused the other two hellraisers to literally gasp in fear.

"What the fuck is this shit? What the fuck . . ."

Cojac didn't know what to do.

The other two were too stunned to speak. Dooley then cracked a wicked smirk over at them—unintentionally.

"This that bizness you was talking about meeting up with Lil Reggie for, Chad? So y'all niggas was planning on jumping him after what happened at the mall—?"

"I ain't do shit to him!" barked Cojac.

"Fuck that fool, he shouldn't have been actin' all hard and shit. He pulled out on Reggie."

"Cause you niggas was tryin' my gangsta," Dooley spoke up. "You think I was gon' stand there and let y'all niggas jump me? Fuck that. I'ma blast my way out that shit."

Neither one of them made a reply.

"Look," Andrea started. "This my lil boo, and I ain't havin' y'all sizing his shit. Because I'm tellin' you—you fuckin' wit' the wrong youngin', and I suggest y'all find somebody else to spook. Not this one right here! Do I make myself clear?" She regarded all three of them demandingly.

Reluctantly, Cojac spoke. "Fuck that nigga, big sis. As long as he stay in his lane, then we won't have no pro'lems."

Andrea looked over at the next one. "Lil Earl?"

Lil Earl shrugged but didn't answer. Then she accepted that response and turned to Chad, who was staring holes into Dooley.

"What's up, Cee?"

"You know we don't fuck wit' them Southside—"

"I ain't from no muthafuckin' Southside, fool. I rep Raleigh all day—Riverside, homie!" Dooley replied proudly. "You got that?"

A brief moment of silence. Then Lil Earl: "Fuck that shit."

Without another word, Chad spun on his heels and walked out of the laundromat.

"Cojac. Lil Earl? Respect my mind. Tell Reggie and Scoop I said tighten down and squash this bullshit. As long as y'all don't fuck wit' him, then he won't fuck wit' y'all. Keep it player and hold it down. It ain't nothin' but love on this side," Andrea said, draping an arm across Lil Earl's shoulders.

Nodding in response, Cojac looked over at his comrade. "Come on, Earl. Let's buss one," he said.

Silently, the two young hellraisers took their leave, leaving Andrea and Dooley to look after them with their own personal thoughts of the situation. Dooley released a sigh and walked over to the doorway, looking outside.

"Andrea?" he whispered.

"What's up, youngin'?" she answered.

Dooley looked over his shoulder at her. "If it's all right, I need to use your phone to make a call."

"I gotcha, Dooley. You can count on me," she smiled— and that's all he needed to hear.

***

The look on Walt's face was grim.

"Sorry," Lisa replied. "I thought Kirk woulda at least been home chillin', but I guess not."

"Being that the nigga just came home and poppin' bottles of Grey Goose in the club, the nigga can't have no job. Not already long enough to be splurging like that," Wallow exclaimed.

Then he turned back toward Shantel's house. He then wondered if Dooley was inside even though no one came to the door when Mo'nique knocked and rang the bell to no avail. Walt was thinking the same exact thing. Then vision of his baby brother being tied up and gagged somewhere beyond the walls of that house cause him to boil with silent rage.

"Maybe they in there and couldn't hear you the first time," he said, glancing back at Mo'nique.

Mo'nique said, "What? You want me to go try again?"

"They prolly in that bitch tore down drunk," Lisa remarked.

Then Mo'nique let out a sigh and got out of the truck again.

"If they ain't there, I want you to show me where all that nigga be laying his—" Walt's words came to a halt when all of a sudden Shantel's Dodge Intrepid drove around his truck and into the driveway of the house.

Mo'nique had just ascended the porch steps before turning around at the familiar car's approach then stood there waiting for Shantel to get out.

"There goes Shantel right there," Lisa pointed out.

"Good," muttered Wallow.

Moments later they saw Mo'nique rushing toward the car and opening the driver's door. A second later Mo'nique was kneeling down next to the driver, arms outstretched inside, then she glanced over in their direction with a look of concern in her eyes. At that moment Walt felt something stir within him, some unspeakable dread that left him confused as to what it was.

Lisa broke the silence when she saw Mo'nique helping Shantel out of the car as though she was an elderly lady in need of assistance.

"Something is wrong. I'm fixin' to go see what's up."

"Yeah, go do that."

Walt couldn't shake the feeling, but he knew that whatever it was had something to do with his brother. Then he and Wallow watched as Lisa ran over toward the two women, ass bouncing outta control in her short-shorts and Reebok Classics. An eerie silence hung in between the two homies.

Minutes later, after the women entered the house, Mo'nique bolted through the open front door and headed for the Benz truck, and what Walt detected in her facial expression was worse than the concern he saw earlier. When she stopped outside his window, he wound it down and demanded to know what was going on.

"Umm . . . She's all fucked up right now in there. Shantel just found out that her brother is dead; said they just found his body about an hour ago by the club I work at."

"What!" Wallow bellowed.

"Stay focused." Walt told himself. *"Stay calm,"* but he couldn't deny the fact that the news added on to his unspeakable fear that he now had over his baby brother.

"She didn't mention no other bodies found either?"

Mo'nique shook her head. "But I can make a few phone calls and see what's up. And I really gotta get back there with Shantel."

Wallow interjected. "We coming too. I gotta see this shit myself."

"Word. Yo!" Walt reached for his pistol underneath the driver's seat and checked the clip.

The sudden gesture caused Mo'nique to go stiff.

"That won't be necessary, um, you," she muttered.

Slapping the clip back into his gun, Walt looked over at her.

"It's by any means necessary," he said, and that's when she began questioning herself whether she'd made a wise decision with being involved.

Then fear settled in when she saw Wallow's gun.

***

Passion's heart squeezed with sudden relief after she heard Dooley's voice on the other end of the phone. What made it even better was the fact that he'd remembered to call her. Though her recent incident earlier with the bogus traffic stop by the police had her shaken up a little, the sound of Dooley's voice was all it took to lift her spirits back up.

In the back seat, T.K. was also shaken with relief that Dooley was actually alright. She was so happy to know that, it brought tears brimming at the edge of her eyes. They all had taken a dreadful hit from the situation, and now all was well again.

"I know where you at, Dooley. Matter of fact, I'm about to turn on that street now." Passion spoke into the phone while driving one-handed.

"What did the police say?"

"He stopped me because he said my left back brake light wasn't working. He was just a rookie cop tryna earn some points and shit, showing off 'cause he got a damn badge."

"And you just happy it was that easy to get off." T.K. wanted to say but didn't.

"I mean about me jumpin' out?" Dooley asked.

That seemed to spark her interest.

"Oh! I told him your name was Spud and that I knew you from around and picked you up from the mall to drop you off," she said. "He asked me why you jump out and ran like that, and I told him 'I don't know'!"

"That was real shit," Dooley complimented her on keeping it solid and not mentioning his name, although the rookie cop wouldn't have a clue who he was anyway.

It was the thought that counted.

And you just trying to ear some cool points, T.K. frowned with a bit of jealousy.

"He at the Madison Projects," NeNe replied once she realized where they was headed. "That's where Reggie and 'em from."

Then Passion got a call waiting.

"Hold on for a minute, Dooley, this my mama calling on the other line."

"A'ight.

She took the call.

"What's up, Mama?' she answered with the slightest clue as to what was up because Shantel never called her during school hours unless it was important.

"Kirk's dead, baby. Somebody killed Kirk! Somebody killed my brother!" came Shantel's sorrowful sob.

"What!" Passion gripped the small phone tightly, not realizing that she'd actually mistakenly switched back over to Dooley.

Then the sound of her mother's sobs still lingering in her conscious, and what she had just been told caused her to panic. The car jerked, veered off to the left in the next lane. Another car was heading her way in oncoming traffic. T.K. screamed. NeNe reached for the wheel . . .

What happened next was just a blur before Passion blacked out.

Chapter 7

Seconds before he heard NeNe's yelling, then T.K.'s scream, and the unmistakable sound of the crash, Dooley had just received a glass of soda from Andrea as he held the phone to his ear. Now, that glass was lying on the floor with its contents spilled all over the place as he bolted to his feet. Andrea was startled by his sudden movement, disregarding the fact that the soda was now soaking her new floor rug.

"What's wrong, Dooley?"

He was badly shaken by what he hoped hadn't just transpired.

"I think they just got into a car accident up the street from here. Passion said she was down . . . down the—"

"Dooley!" Andrea attempted to catch herself from tumbling over the low table next to her as Dooley shoved her aside and rushed for the door.

Then he was outside in a flash, running like hell was on fire toward the front entrance of the Madison Projects. What scared him the most was what may have happened to T.K. and Passion as a result of the crash. He didn't know which one worried him the most; he just knew that he had to reach them immediately. He was reacting off instinct, not clearly realizing that he had a federal indictment charge banging against his back as he dashed through the grounds of the Projects.

People watched with instant curiosity as to why he was running like that—like a wild man chasing something unknown to them—but to Dooley, he was chasing his fear of what could be waiting for him just nearby. Once he made it to the top of the apartment complex of Madison Projects, he looked both ways down the main street and sure enough, his fear was heightened at the sight to his right: a crowd of people and other vehicles piled up ten yards away.

Without hesitation, Dooley shot forward and sprinted with unbelievable speed toward the accident. Two cars seemed to have collided with one another—both Passion's Honda Civic and a smaller car. From the angle at which both cars rested, it appeared the smaller car had crashed head-on into the front passenger side of Passion's Honda. Dooley could hear NeNe's cries from yards away before he reached the car. Then the sound of T.K. cursing up a storm invaded his conscious from the back seat as she reached Passion's side door.

"Why the fuck y'all just standing 'round lookin' and shit? Somebody call the ambulance or somethin'!" Dooley shouted over his shoulder at the crowd of spectators before snatching open the driver's side.

Passion was lying limply behind the wheel, drenched in blood and totally unconscious, and just inches away, NeNe was crying out in pain, also bleeding from the face and slumped awkwardly in the front passenger seat. Then, without hesitation, Dooley grabbed hold of Passion and dragged her to the side of the road in the grassy area. He left her there and rushed back to the car, where T.K. was attempting to climb out—he assisted her as best he could.

"Help NeNe! Help NeNe, Dooley," T.K. pulled away, wiping the blood from her mouth.

She obviously seemed a bit alright despite the sudden circumstances, which Dooley took as confirmation and went to NeNe's rescue.

"No!" NeNe screamed when Dooley, from the driver's side of the car, reached over and attempted to retrieve her from inside.

The girl was in pain; something was broken and causing her great agony. T.K. limped over to where Passion lay, looking down at her with sadness in her eyes—but the anger was obvious too.

"I gotchu, NeNe," Dooley whispered, afraid of hurting her any more than she already was. But he knew he had to do something and couldn't leave her there.

Fuck it!

Dooley reached for her again as he ignored her painful cries and pulled her from the car through the driver's side. And to his amazement, Andrea was right there next to him, helping him usher NeNe away. Then came the sounds of an ambulance nearby—and the police!

"We gotchu, Shorty," Andrea assured NeNe as she and Dooley eased her down next to the still-unconscious Passion. The sight of her lying like that scared Dooley immensely.

While Andrea tended to NeNe and another elderly woman knelt down next to Passion, Dooley's eyes became blurry with emotion, as T.K. appeared at his side.

"Dooley," T.K. nudged him, grazing his hand with her own, and Dooley turned to face her. "The police is coming."

"Go back to the crib, youngin'. I got this right here." Andrea regarded him with concern after hearing T.K.'s statement over NeNe's constant sobbing.

Once their eyes met, Dooley knew exactly what she meant.

"I'll see that they're taken care of."

Another graze of T.K.'s hand, and Dooley nodded.

"Whatcha waiting on then?" Andrea said, gesturing toward the approaching ambulance turning onto the street about thirty yards away.

"Shit, ya don't gotta tell me twice!" Dooley decided, and spun on his heels, pushing past the onlookers with T.K. at his side.

***

"...then that's when it happened. I couldn't do shit but scream. I thought I was gon' die!" T.K. was saying minutes later as they walked back toward Andrea's apartment.

Dooley wondered what Shantel had told Passion to make her lose control of the car.

"You think she might die?"

"No!" Dooley replied grudgingly. "I hope she don't," he prayed.

His sudden outburst, answering her question so aggressively, made T.K. frown. With a glance over at him, she knew right then that he cared for Passion—and it bothered her a little that he would respond like that about a girl he just met. Then reality settled in: *We just met too...* So why did she feel offended?

Shaking her head, T.K. refused to admit she'd fallen a little for Dooley—enough to react in jealousy over another girl he had taken a liking to. *A hard lesson about falling . . .*

"We missed the fuckin' bus again," Dooley muttered through clenched teeth. "Fuck!"

The statement made her wince, knowing she wouldn't be with Dooley any longer once this maze was over. She knew he'd definitely force the issue of getting away from there, even if it meant...

A dark black Yukon truck screeched to a stop in front of them, blocking their way on the sidewalk—and before Dooley realized what was happening, the doors opened. Reggie, along with his big brother Twan and the driver, Chuck, exited the truck, brandishing an AK-47 aimed at face level. Dooley heard T.K.'s audible gasp of fear beside him, but he refused to look her way.

"What's up now, bitch boy!" Reggie was the first to speak.

Twan stopped a few yards away from Dooley and T.K.

"You got a problem wit' my lil brah, yo? Word is you upped your gun on Reggie."

"He strapped now," Reggie exclaimed, pointing toward Dooley's waistline where the imprint of his pistol formed beneath his brand-new Coogi shirt—which was now a bloody mess, again!

"Ain't that right," Twan added, seeing the print too. "So you think you a gangsta wit' a gun, huh?"

"Your brotha and his homies tried to run up on me—five of them!" Dooley spoke up bravely. "I did what I had to do."

Stunned, T.K. couldn't take her eyes off the big man with the big assault rifle aimed at her and Dooley. The look in his eyes told her everything—he had no problem using it if the wrong move was made. So she stood frozen, afraid to give him reason.

"Brah, tell 'im to put the gun up and give me one!" Reggie demanded, cracking his knuckles, trying to amp himself up.

A spark lit in Twan's eyes. "You call that, yo? Lil brah want you to shoot him one. You gangsta wit' a gun? Let's see you fight like one, then."

"Fuck your brotha, he sized me up first!" barked Dooley.

"Then do somethin' about it, punk!"

"Hold up, Reggie." Twan held out an arm to stop him. "We gon' see if lil homie can throw down. You call that, yo?"

Dooley looked over at T.K. and frowned at what he saw in her eyes.

"Put the gun up and fight like a man," Chuck chimed in.

His six-foot-three frame and the big gun posed a serious threat in the eyes of anyone not used to situations like this. But not Dooley.

A brief silence passed before Dooley finally spoke.

"Let's do it. But tell your boy to ease up with that shit while I pull out," he said, nodding at Chuck.

Neither one said a word, and Chuck didn't ease up with his aim. After a moment, Dooley doubted the big man would shoot him once he was unarmed—if he was gonna, he would've done it already. So without another word, Dooley slowly reached under his shirt and retrieved the pistol. Then he forced it into T.K.'s hands and started taking off his backpack.

"Hold this!" Dooley shoved the bag into her arms.

"Don't do this, Dooley. What if they kill you?" T.K. muttered under her breath, out of earshot of the others as people looked on from a distance.

"I got no choice," Dooley told her. "I can't back down from this dude, T.K. Don't worry."

The roar of an engine sounded behind them as a black Chevy Impala SS came screeching to a halt in the street next to them. Then, when the passenger door opened, Dooley was surprised to see Gangsta step out of the car.

Immediately, Gangsta rounded the car and stopped next to Dooley, facing Reggie and his brother. Chuck eased his weapon, lowering it from where it had been aimed—now pointed in Gangsta's direction. T.K. looked like she was about to faint when Gangsta glanced at her with cold eyes.

"What's the deal, Twan? You niggas got a problem wit' my little homie right here?" Gangsta asked.

Twan swallowed hard. "This got nothing to do wit' you, Gangsta. This between him and my lil brotha."

"Nah, not no more it ain't. This shit got something to do with me now. Yo, Chuck, your best bet is to put that shit up or I'ma make something happen. This my little homie y'all got guns pointed at."

Gangsta draped an arm across Dooley's shoulders.

"Go get in the car, youngin'. I got this."

All three—Twan, Reggie, and Chuck—seemed at a loss for words. Then Reggie looked up at his big brother.

"You gon' let him do that? I thought—"

"Fuck that lil nigga, brah," Twan muttered.

"That's right! Whatever's going on ends right here, yo," Gangsta said firmly.

"Next time, Gangsta, tell yo' lil homie not to pull his heat unless he bound to use it. That shit ain't cool—"

That's when Gangsta sneered. "What's wrong wit' your boy Chuck doin' just that?" Then he turned to Chuck. "Use it, nigga. Pull the trigger on Gangsta and see what happens. I thought so."

"Come on!" Dooley told T.K., pulling her toward the car as Reggie, his brother, and Chuck turned back to their vehicle.

T.K. followed without hesitation while Gangsta just stood there.

"Yo, Twan!" Gangsta called out.

Twan turned, hand on the truck's door handle. "What's up?"

Gangsta smirked. "You know what's banging on this side," he said, referring to the nation of Gangsta Disciples he led all over the surrounding city. Twan knew better than to go that route—it was suicidal. So, he took his leave without further ado.

Dooley was more grateful than ever.

Chapter 8

The hospital room was quiet, except for the constant beeping of the glowing monitors. Shantel stared down at a sleeping Passion as she lay there all bruised up and bandaged. Just when she needed her loving daughter the most, she realized Passion needed her more. With the pain and agony of Kirk's death still lingering heavy in her heart, she knew she had to be strong for her baby—*especially* after identifying Kirk's body just a half hour earlier. She needed all the strength she could muster.

Andrea, Lisa, and NeNe's mother, Bev, were also present, waiting for an update on NeNe's surgery. Both Walt and Wallow waited anxiously outside the hospital door, hoping to take Dooley home safely. Walt had been unmistakably relieved when Andrea called Shantel—who'd been in the middle of explaining her own involvement with Dooley and his situation—and told him everything. Immediately, they all rushed to the hospital after Andrea's call. She'd later met them in the waiting room. It had been an emotional day for everybody.

"I need to go check on my baby," Bev said the moment the door opened and Walt entered with Wallow in tow.

She eased by them and scurried down the hall in the direction of the ICU. Shantel looked up at Walt.

"They should be here in a minute," she said.

Nodding in response, Walt leaned back against the far wall next to the room door. Wallow held his weight beside him.

"The doctor said she'll be alright. She just got a minor concussion, that's all," said Shantel, stroking her daughter's warm hand.

"She have insurance on the car?" Walt asked.

"No."

"Don't worry about it. I'll make sure everything's—"

Shantel shook her head. "That's okay. I just want my baby to be alright. That's all I want right now."

"I'll buy her another car," Walt said with finality.

She didn't want to argue, so she turned back toward Passion.

Moments later, the door opened and in rushed T.K., followed by Dooley, Gangsta, and Boom—Gangsta's right-hand man—who bumped into the back of Dooley. Frozen stiff, Dooley looked over at Walt and Wallow as dread surged through him. Without a word, Walt reached out and pulled Dooley into a brief embrace.

Everyone watched the two brothers embrace. T.K., standing at Passion's bedside next to Shantel, looked on in silent grief—*but that was before the room exploded with the unexpected.*

"Walt Holmes? Big Wallow! What the fuck?" Gangsta said once he recognized them after tearing his eyes off Andrea, who happened to be his wifey.

Arm still across Dooley's shoulder, Walt grinned at Gangsta. "Bernard, what's up, gangsta?"

"Hold up! Don't call me by my government, nigga. I'm Gangsta, gangsta," Gangsta said, dapping up Walt and Wallow. "Last time I saw y'all two was in the pen three years ago. Now look at'cha, doin' big thangz, huh?"

Wallow shrugged. "We heard you doin' some big things too, Gangsta. I guess you kept yo' word, eh?"

"I stand on my word, homie." Gangsta then looked over at Dooley with a nod. "This your little gangsta right here? A solid youngin', you taught him well."

That seemed to fill Walt with pride as he and Dooley exchanged a brief glance. Then came the introductions: T.K.—since everybody already knew Dooley—and Boom, whom neither Walt nor Wallow were familiar with. After that, Walt pulled his baby brother aside.

"I'll be back," Dooley said, glancing at Shantel, and she nodded silently.

Then he and Walt walked outside.

"T.K.!" Shantel called out.

T.K. turned to look at her over her shoulder moments after Dooley and Walt stepped out.

"Stay put and let them be for a minute."

Reluctantly, she nodded and sat down next to Andrea. T.K. watched the door like a hawk.

"What the fuck is your problem, nigga!" Walt snarled at Dooley. "What the fuck I tell you? Huh, nigga?"

Dooley dropped his head.

"Hold your muthafuckin' head up 'fore I snatch it off your shoulders! Nigga, you get sidetracked by a young bitch? What happened to priorities first? The principle. You know I'm bitter with you, Dooley," Walt glared. "Where my shit at?"

"In the car outside," Dooley stuttered.

"You better get my work, nigga."

Walt placed a large hand on Dooley's shoulder and squeezed—hard.

"You better get my work, nigga."

"I—I gotcha," Dooley said through the pain.

He'd been dreading worse but knew Walt wouldn't punish him out in the open, not at a hospital with people milling around. Still, he knew Walt wasn't even close to done showing how disappointed he was.

Then a commotion sounded from the other side of the door before it opened—and T.K. stormed outside. The moment she saw Dooley, she rushed to his side, tears pouring from her eyes. The door opened again, and Wallow acknowledged Walt with a nod and joined their small circle.

"Dooley, I think we need to talk," T.K. cried, glancing over at Walt nervously.

"This ain't the time, T.K.," Dooley said coolly.

T.K. shook her head. "This *is* the time, and you gon' gotdamn listen to what I got to say," she snapped. "Yes, I'm from Georgia, and no, I wasn't going to V.A. to see my godmother. She's dead! I ran away from home, Dooley, and for good reason. See, my parents are super rich! My mama is an entrepreneur with a billion-dollar corporation, and her husband Frank is some high-class attorney. All they do is fly out to rich-people dinners, conventions, and travel—and show me off to their phony-ass friends like I'm some trophy or something. I *hate* that shit! I hate them for takin' me through that all these years."

"I want a normal life, Dooley, not like that. I'm just seventeen years fuckin' old! Seventeen! I lied to you because I was afraid you'd look at me different, like all my friends back home. Fuck them too! All I want is to be with you, Dooley. Don't leave me hurtin' like this. I need you. Take me with you—I promise I'll be loyal to you. Just don't go without me. Please?"

T.K. was breathing hard, trying to catch her breath as people turned to stare, drawn by her emotional outburst.

Dooley looked over her shoulder at Walt, who was clearly caught off guard by the confession—but the hardness in his expression didn't fade. This wasn't the outcome he'd hoped for. Now Dooley was faced with a crucial decision.

Wallow cleared his throat and looked at his watch.

"Look, Dooley, hurry up and take care of that thing for me so we can get on the road. We gon' try to hit Norfolk up by tonight and get back to the crib," Walt broke the silence.

That's when T.K. whirled around on Walt, glaring up at him with an earnest look he couldn't dodge.

"Take me with y'all, Walt. I don't got nowhere else to go. I'll stay out your way. All I want is to be with Dooley. I don't want nothin' else . . . say you'll take me!"

"T.K...." Walt started, but she cut him off.

"Yes or no, Walt!"

Walt looked over at his baby brother. "Dooley, make that happen. We gotta go." Then he turned back to T.K. "The decision ain't mine, ma. I mean, I feel your pain and all, but you askin' the wrong muthafucka."

With that said, Dooley's heart gave an instant squeeze when T.K. spun around to face him.

"Dooley?"

How could he resist those eyes?

"T.K., we gotta take care of some bizness. I can't involve you in that shit—it ain't gon' work like that."

"Are you takin' me to Raleigh?" she demanded.

"Go get the whip ready, bro," Walt said to Wallow.

A moment later, Wallow was marching down the hall toward the elevators. Dooley was having trouble answering. He started thinking about his mama Lizzy... Shaliah's response... and what life he could have with T.K. if she said she would.

"You'll take me," T.K. said, like she was reading his thoughts.

Then she wrapped her arms around his waist and laid her head against his chest.

Damn! Dooley thought his heart was gonna explode.

"I'll take you, T.K.—but you gotta wait till we double back."

"No!" T.K. cried.

"That's the only way. We can't take you to Norfolk for what we're about to do. I'ma come back for you. I promise." Dooley looked over at Walt.

Walt looked away and tapped his watch.

Now T.K. was crying again.

"Don't lie to me, Dooley. You'll come back for real? When?"

"We'll be back round by in the morning. I'm comin' back, T.K., damn. I gotcha, ma," he promised, hugging her tight. "I won't forget about you."

She sighed, reluctantly. "Okay."

Chapter 9

It was after 1:00 a.m. when they reached Norfolk, Virginia, pulling up in the parking lot of a 24-hour McDonald's. The long ride had been spent blowing on some good weed, lecturing, and bobbing to some gangsta music. Mostly, Dooley was drowning himself in thoughts about his decision to take T.K. back to Raleigh. He wondered whether Walt would really double back and get her. *What if he didn't? Then what may become of T.K.?*

Dooley really didn't want to think about it any longer. From inside the truck, all three of them observed minimal activity going on inside the fast food joint. This was the local hangout spot for a few hustlers in the area, and it appeared quite a few of them were in action. There were three young hustlers total, who sat at a far booth, chopping up dope and rolling up weed right there in the spot. Of course, the place was booming with drug activity as crackheads came and went as they pleased. This was one of the most well-known spots in the area, where you could buy just about whatever you wanted if the price was right.

This was far beyond how they do it back in Raleigh, yet the hustle was still the same—just not in public places. McDonald's, to be exact—or the law would have you buried under the jailhouse there. Both Walt and Wallow were used to the hustlers out in Norfolk, Virginia, after frequenting the spot over the years, since it had been one of their main routes. Cash loved Norfolk with a passion—you couldn't keep him away from the place. Now, he was missing out on the trip.

Together, they all got out of the truck the same moment one of the hustlers exited the restaurant. They entered and walked straight for the counter. They hadn't eaten in hours and decided to have a bite before Walt made his call and delivered the package. In passing, Dooley glanced in the direction of the two young hustlers huddled in one of the booths. They both met his gaze, and one of them acknowledged him with a brief nod, but Dooley kept right on moving to the counter.

"Never seen them niggas before," said Tydron.

Meeky nodded. "Look like some outta-town niggas to me, dawg. And they rollin' good too."

"Sure is. That's why I sent Boogie round back to get Shy and Serg. We 'bout to see what's up wit' these fools."

"I bet they some VA niggas."

"Or Carolina. You know how them grimy muthafuckas be all up on a nigga turf like they some gods or somethin'." Tydron reached underneath the table where his gun rested on his lap.

He was ready for action on every turn—especially when it came down to outsiders treading on his turf. At seventeen, the young nigga had earned his respect in the area, and was determined to prove his gangsta as well.

"If they hurry up and get here before they leave . . ." Meeky said, his back turned toward the entrance, his overweight frame hunched over the table rolling up a Swisher Sweet blunt of sticky.

"Oh, they coming," Tydron reassured him.

"When that shit come, grab that," said Walt. "I gotta go take a piss real quick."

Dooley nodded and watched as he left, just as the food arrived. He and Wallow retrieved their orders, then walked over and sat at a nearby table, where Dooley wasted no time digging into his bag for his chicken nuggets. There were several more patrons present and eating during the late hour, conversing in modest tones. The place was pleasantly warm and not as busy as it would be during the daytime. The few employees on shift were either lounging around until another customer came, stuffing their own faces, or just pretending to be busy at work when they really weren't. It was pretty laid back during the midnight hours.

"He ain't gonna hold it against you, Dooley. That nigga happy as fuck you came back alive. He thought somethin' had happened to you," Wallow said, taking out his double Quarter Pounder with extra cheese and mayo. The big man had three of them.

"Something did happen to me."

"What? Other than you wasn't on point, or we wouldn't be here right now."

Dooley seemed to think about his answer. "I learned a lesson I'll never forget, Wallow. This mission taught me a lot, man."

"We all gotta learn at some point," and that's when he told Wallow about Kirk.

Suddenly, the big man stopped chewing and stared across the table at Dooley with a dark glare in his eyes.

"For future references, Dooley, keep shit like that to yourself. If I wasn't there or Walt wasn't there to see it, then we don't need to know. But you did the right thing—the wrong thing too."

"What?" asked Dooley. "How?"

Wallow was silent for a moment.

"You shoulda slumped Gangsta too. No witness, no case. Fuck that. It's part of the game. Now you better just hope that shit play out smooth. But I know Gangsta—have known him for years—and I'm sure he can hold his tongue."

Kill Gangsta? Dooley thought on that hard.

Then the entrance doors to the restaurant opened, and the same young nigga they passed on the way in entered, along with two others. They bent the right and disappeared behind the wall where the other two thugs were—which was also in the direction of the restroom. Wallow bit into his burger and chewed vigorously, waiting on Walt to come back.

***

Inside the restroom, Walt shook himself off and flushed the commode, hawking up a glob of spit to send down the drain as well. Then he checked the time: 1:40 a.m. Walt exited the stall and stepped over to the sink to wash his hands. After attempting to get soap from the wall dispenser and coming up empty, he checked the one on his left. Nothing. So he moved to the third one on his right and pushed its lever, releasing droplets of liquid soap into his hand.

Good, Walt thought, and ran the faucet water cold. Staring at himself in the mirror, Walt looked into his own eyes, facing what was within them.

He wasn't gonna hold it over Dooley's head—he'd forgive him for not being on point. After all his baby brother had been through since leaving Raleigh, to him seeing him in that hospital room, there was no way he would blame Dooley. In actuality, it was his fault for even sending Dooley on that mission when he could've done it himself. But there was so much going on back in Raleigh that he didn't feel the need to take the trip when he could pay to have it done. However, there were only a few he could trust with two kilos of coke. Cash was locked up in the county jail, so that was a no-go! Wallow was already taking care of some unfinished business to take the trip, and that left Dooley to be the perfect candidate for the mission.

Look how it all turned out. He and Wallow still ended up taking the trip when difficult complications kept Dooley from accomplishing the task himself. *Could he, himself, have waited to deliver the bricks at a later time when he had the chance? Was forty thousand dollars worth the trouble that had ensued? The near attempt on Dooley's life? His only baby brother?*

Walt shook his head and shut off the water. He then snatched down several paper towels to dry his hands before attempting a hook shot at the garbage can—and missed with the used balled-up paper. He left it where it landed.

"I'm hungrier than a muthafucker," Walt thought as he approached the restroom door and opened it.

"You know what it is, homie!" Tydron sneered, placing the barrel of his 9mm against Walt's forehead. "Now back the fuck up and live. Or die."

Of course Walt did as he was told, staring Tydron directly in his eyes. Meeky and Boogie followed suit. Then the door closed shut behind them.

***

Back at the table, Wallow was working on his second burger and fries. Dooley was finishing up his last nugget and anticipating the double cheeseburger he'd set out, along with a single apple pie. They were famished but were quickly solving that problem.

"What the nigga in there doing, shitting?" Dooley complained.

Wallow chuckled, but there was no humor in his eyes. *That nigga got ten more seconds or I'm coming back there.*

He waited.

"Fuck this!"

"What?" Dooley looked up.

Wallow stood up and dropped his burger down onto the table.

"I ain't feelin' this shit, lil' bro," he said, and spun on his heels heading in the direction of the restrooms.

A second later, a gunshot blast rang out over the place.

Wallow froze, looked back at a startled Dooley, pulled out his cannon, and rushed toward the restrooms. The second

Wallow bent the corner, he had his big pistol drawn and was squeezing off shots—but that was before Shy and Serg had already aimed their guns at him, shooting on sight. Like the beast that he was, Wallow took five bullets instantly before killing Serg with a headshot and rushing toward the restroom door, killing Boogie and Tydron the moment they dashed out.

Then the beast fell to his death, just before Shy pointed an already jammed gun at the back of his head to no effect. That's when he saw Dooley coming round the corner with his pistol drawn, blasting Meeky away as he stood in the restroom doorway. Meeky dropped like a sack of bricks.

Then the glimpse of Walt lying dead on the floor through the open restroom door caused Dooley to stop rigid—but Shy was by then already dashing out the side door of the building's exit.

For a moment, Dooley just stood there staring into the restroom at Walt's lifeless body lying on the floor. He observed the scene a moment longer, picked up Wallow's fallen .45, and dashed toward the exit door where Shy had taken flight, losing the .380 in the process. There was no way he could let Shy get away that easy.

Tears blurred his vision as he rounded the building, yards behind Shy, Wallow's gun clutched in his hand, running with all his might. About ten yards ahead, Shy was really stretching it—just before two rapid gunshots rang out behind him. He looked back over his shoulder and saw Dooley gaining on him. Then he bent a quick left onto Bravard Street, at the corner of a paint & body shop building. Shy zig-zagged, bounding from the sidewalk to the street and back to the sidewalk, where two more shots flew past him wildly.

"Shit!" Dooley cursed after realizing he couldn't get a good shot in while running as hard as he was.

A car turned onto the street about a block away, and Shy forced himself to think fast. *Could he flag down the car and hop in before Dooley could get a good shot at him?*

Then the car would have to stop, and he'd have to slow up his pace in order to accomplish the task. Shy doubted that would be a successful risk to take. *Then who's to say the car would stop for him? If only I could make it to my hood...*

The car flew by him in a flash. Then Dooley attempted a burst of two more rounds with no success—but that didn't stop him from running!

Images of Walt and Wallow's dead bodies invaded his mental vision, causing tears to spill from his blurry eyes even more, in which Dooley pumped his legs harder and sped up the pace. Sirens blared close by. Too close. Before they even knew it, a police cruiser was turning onto the street the same moment Dooley lifted his arm, clutching the bigger weapon. With more ease, he let go four more rounds toward Shy's back—who then sprinted across the street to the left just before the police cruiser flew past. The car swerved to keep from hitting Shy, and Dooley ran right past it, taking chase and firing off rounds with the Ruger before crossing the street next.

Up ahead, Shy bent another left onto a side street that led into a nearby neighborhood. Dooley was right behind him. The police cruiser was long gone, heading for the murder scene back at McDonald's, despite the fact that another capital crime was in progress. The cop had literally witnessed Dooley shooting after the victim he was chasing— but it all had happened so fast. *Which incident was the most important? The shooting chase or the five dead bodies lying a block away?* The multiple murders seemed to be the most important.

Yards away stood a group of hustlers on a nearby corner at the entrance of the neighborhood. A few addicts roamed the street and sidewalk as well. Ahead, the hustlers watched the chase approach them from a distance—but when three more rapid shots rang out in the night, they all scattered, ducked, and ran for safety.

Shy chanced another glimpse behind him and ran harder when he saw Dooley close behind. He was tired, cramping up, and desperate to find safety as well. The first opportunity he had, he did the unexpected. Like a pro running back, he hit a strong cut to the right, running through a residence's front lawn, up the porch steps, and burst through its front door.

Dooley made the turn, and up the steps he went into the dimly lit house. Once he was in the living room, he stopped and listened. Chest heaving up and down rapidly, Ruger clutched in his hand, he scanned the surroundings immediately. A shriek rang out down the nearby hallway, and the sound of glass breaking sent Dooley heading in that direction.

It was one of the bedrooms.

Then the bedroom door next to Dooley opened to reveal a stark naked woman, just as the sound of a child's voice shrieked again.

Immediately, Dooley barged into the bedroom to the sight of the terrified face of a little girl staring up at him from underneath her bed in the dim room—but that was until Dooley looked up and saw that his victim had finally escaped. There wasn't nothing else he could do about it.

Shy had fled through the bedroom window.

A pang of disappointment surged through him as he dropped his head in defeat.

He lost his brother's killer...

Then it hit him! The face that belonged to the victim he was chasing was the same face of the young thug he saw after entering the fast food joint earlier—and that's when he went back to the face of the one he had chased, whom he'd also seen clearly just before he ran away. He had the same face as the first one.

Though of course, it didn't take a rocket scientist to know that they were twins.

The two were identical twins! Brothers—and he let him get away.

Dooley will never forget this moment ever in his life.

Never.

And then he cried.

Chapter 10

You could hear her clacking away down the sidewalk from ten yards away in those heels. As if she was on the clock tricking on the block, Anne strutted her stuff proudly. Dressed in a pair of old bleached jeans and a loose T-shirt tied in a knot at her lower back, Anne was really feeling herself at the moment.

Dooley watched her bend the corner away from the main highway and turn into the alleyway where he stood. He'd been waiting patiently for her return, and she'd come back just as promised.

"Here I am, handsome. Mommy got the news for ya," said Anne, holding out her hand, palm up. Without hesitation, Dooley placed a fifty-dollar bill in the trick's hand. It would definitely be worth the services Anne had performed, if anything at all.

"What you got for me?" he asked.

Anne smiled crookedly. "Well, for starters, there's four dead and one still alive. But he was the one they'd just rushed out—"

"What'd he look like?" Dooley knew it wasn't Walt or Wallow, but he just needed confirmation to satisfy his curiosity.

With a pensive expression, she answered, "Some fat kid with those dreadlock things."

Meeky.

"Okay. There was a truck there in the parking lot?"

"Silver?"

"Yeah, a Benz?"

"Nice! Yeah, it's still there."

Fuck! Dooley thought about the two kilos sitting on the floor behind the driver's seat.

What can I do? How would I be able to get the truck back? Better yet, the bricks? The cops was all over the place, and there was no way . . .

"Umm, Anne?"

"Mmm?"

"Where can I use a phone at 'round here? I need to make a very important call."

"Baba's Spot!"

"Huh?"

"Baba's Spot. It's just around the block here. I'll show you where it is," Anne said excitedly, eager to please now that she was fifty dollars richer than the two dollars she started off with.

"Yeah, do that."

"Then let's go, handsome. And maybe Mommy could offer you a nice blow job while we're at it. You'll love it!"

I doubt that, Dooley thought, but he followed on anyway.

Chapter 11

During that same time, T.K. was wide awake, puffing on a solo blunt of Sour Kush, sitting on Shantel's porch. She needed the solitude. She needed to clear her mind—develop some type of understanding of the situation. This was more than what she expected from dealing with Dooley, and now her feelings were involved. She couldn't even think straight without losing herself in thoughts of a boy she didn't even know or had seen in her whole entire life before now. But here she was, stressing over something she was not certain she couldn't control.

T.K. could hear Shantel rummaging about the house and drowning herself in grief over Kirk. Then there was Passion, whom the doctors admitted to remain hospitalized for the night, but Shantel had brought her home anyway. Now she was resting in the confines of her bedroom.

NeNe had suffered two broken ribs and a punctured lung, along with a few cracked teeth and a crushed pride. The car had damaged her side of the accident the most, and her wounds were results that she'd suffered the most. Unlike Shantel, Bev saw that her daughter spent as long in the hospital as it took until she was well treated for her wounds.

But that was the least of T.K.'s worries; for she silently questioned herself whether what Dooley had promised to her was true or not. *After all, he was a stranger, and why would he make a strong commitment as to return for me after all that had happened? Was Dooley's word really gold as much as he made it sound? Did he even have the slightest care for me?*

There was no doubt in her mind that she would do anything for Dooley. Like the incident that happened before Gangsta and Boom pulled up to save the day.

Although she was scared, T.K. had convinced herself she would've pulled the trigger on either Reggie, Twan, or Chuck if Dooley was 'really' in trouble. She couldn't just stand there and allow them to take advantage of him when he wasn't capable of defending himself against the three. She hoped that one day she could really show and prove how down she was for him.

"Just one chance," T.K. thought as she took another pull from the blunt. *"I'ma make him have no other choice but to believe I am down for him. But is he down for me? Only time will tell,"* she decided. *"Only time will tell."*

Then she heard Shantel crying in the night…

***

Baba's Spot was a well-known spot where all the fiends, tricks, hustlers, and stray dogs confined themselves whenever time permitted them to. It was an old two-story house that had seen many years and was still standing strong.

After retiring from the Army two decades ago, Baba decided to have an open house for those who needed a place to hold up for a while. He loved the company. The old man had housed some of the most well-known players in the game. Baba's Spot was mainly one of the busiest crack houses in the area.

Thanks to Angie, Baba's live-in girlfriend and former trick, she kept the house in order. She charged the hustlers to cook and sell drugs out of the house, cooked meals for a set price, kept the telephone on, the house clean—whatever it took, Angie made sure she ran a tight operation. Especially now that Baba was old and often bound to a wheelchair. She saw that his legacy was kept alive and running as successfully as she could manage it.

When Dooley stepped foot inside Baba's Spot, he automatically knew what to expect—or go down—in such an environment. He wanted to get it done fast as he could and get the hell out of there.

Stepping over sleeping homeless winos and inhaling the foul odor the house carried, Anne led him toward the den area where Angie kept her office station.

"There goes my favorite lady," Anne smiled.

"And my number one," Angie replied back with nonchalance.

"Hmph! You say that to all the girls. Anywhoo. I brought you a customer." Anne introduced Dooley as *her handsome one*. "He would like to use the phone. I told him Baba's Spot is the spot to be."

"Local or long distance?"

Angie looked up at Dooley for the first time since he entered the room, and to Dooley's surprise, he found the woman to be young and remarkably gorgeous and well-groomed. He then wondered what kind of woman with her type of beauty and elegance found so compelling in a place like this. *She don't fit.*

"Local," he replied.

"One dollar."

Dooley gave her a five.

"I like him, Anne," Angie said moments later.

"My handsome one, sweetie," Anne beamed and disappeared around the corner in search of some drugs to finally buy.

Dooley found a nearby corner out of earshot and began dialing the number by memory that Walt had given him many times before—but he had never used the number until now. Walt had warned him that this number was only to be used in an emergency, out of the two numbers Walt had him memorize along with names. He always said to reach this number first before he go to the second one, and that's exactly what he was doing.

"Hello?" a Spanish-accented woman answered on the third ring. It was obvious she'd been awakened.

"Can I please speak to Mando?"

"Who's calling?"

"Tell him this is Walt's brother Dooley, and I really need to speak with him. It's urgent!"

Dooley exchanged a brief glance with Angie, who appeared to be watching him intently. Then he turned his back to her.

"Hold on, please," the Spanish accent replied.

Dooley waited.

"Dooley?" came the voice of a Spanish male a moment later.

"Mando?"

"Talk."

"Walt is dead. He got killed. And I got something that belongs to you. But the thing is I can't get it to you—"

"Where are you, Dooley?" Mando cut in.

Dooley said, "I'm in Norfolk at some place called Baba's Spot."

"And who's with you?"

"No one."

A brief silence.

"Sit tight, buddy. I'm sending someone to you. We'll talk once you get here. I'm not far."

"Thank you."

Dooley sighed deeply after hearing those words.

At least I got someone close that Walt trusted who might help me outta this mess.

And with that notion, Dooley allowed himself to relax a little. Help was on the way.

***

An hour later, Dooley was sitting in the vast living room of Mando's modest-sized mansion, drinking a cold glass of pink lemonade. He'd gone over his recent tragic moments twice before Mando was satisfied with what was said.

"Don't worry about the truck. I got someone taking care of that now as we speak," Mando replied, sitting across from Dooley. "But I'd like to offer my condolences to you for what happened to Walt. He was an excellent man, a brave one at that. And—"

Dooley interjected. "It was me he always worried about something happening to. Now it turned out to be him who it happened to."

"You're referring to that incident years ago when you were shot and almost killed? Yeah, I remember. Walt had been quite . . . let's say he'd become a bit reckless during that time."

Dooley did remember that time years ago just as clearly as if it had happened hours ago. Walt had found out that Dooley had been the victim of a drive-by shooting that resulted in him being hit three times; he went on a rampage. He'd drank himself into a drunken state, grabbed his AR-15 assault rifle, and went in search of everybody he'd ever had problems with in the street. It took Dooley's daddy, Mike, to talk some sense into Walt after he'd killed four niggas and challenged a whole entire neighborhood of goons by himself. Then it so happened that Dooley wasn't the primary target but someone else, and Dooley had gotten caught up in the crossfire. That was definitely a day to remember.

"But it didn't take him long to realize that he couldn't be there for you if he kept reacting out of emotions. That day taught him a lot, Dooley. You've made a great impact on your brother's life, man."

"But I failed him."

"How so?"

Dooley looked up at him sadly. "Because if I'd stuck to the game plan, he wouldn't have had to come up here. You may as well say I helped—"

"Don't you dare fix your mouth to say something so ridiculous. You hear me? It's not your fault Walt's dead—"

"Bu—"

"No buts. I don't wanna hear it—matter of fact." Mando stood up suddenly, waited a moment, then sat back down.

A loud sigh escaped from within him. "Look, Dooley. I apologize for blowing up the way I just did. It's obvious that I'm as upset about the matter as you are. Dooley, Walt meant a lot to both of us. Not only did I respect him as an ambitious hustler, but as a man too. A brother in many ways, also. However, never for another second blame yourself for his death. It'll drive you nuts. We got a long day tomorrow, and I need you to be focused."

The tension was thinning out now as Dooley agreed silently. Walt's death had definitely been a painful blow to the heart, and he could tell that Mando was genuinely torn over the situation too. The big, well-dressed Italian had lost not only a business partner but a friend. And as Dooley was shown to his room by the middle-aged Spanish maid, he wondered whether there was a heaven for the real gangsters too.

Because if there was, he thought, *then Walt and Wallow were greeted and welcomed with bottles of Hennessy and some fire-ass weed.*

Fully dressed minus his shoes, Dooley laid upon the large bed, sank into its softness, and stared up at the dark ceiling. Then came the disturbing images of his brother's dead body laying in a bloody mess on that restroom floor—all of it rushing back to him at once.

He wanted to cry out in agony, but bit back his tears, forcing himself to remain strong through the pain. Yet that only lasted a moment before he fell into a fitful sleep.

And that's when Walt came back to him in his dreams. The message was plain and clear.

Chapter 12

It was after ten the next morning when Dooley woke up in a cold sweat. Through the fogginess, he waited till his head cleared before sitting up in bed. When he did, the next thing he saw made him gasp—hanging from one of the dresser knobs was the Nike backpack, and he never expected to see that again. Quickly, Dooley threw his legs over the side of the bed and padded over to the dresser.

"Oh shit," Dooley whispered with instant surprise. *What does this mean?* Dooley asked himself before looking back inside the bag at its contents.

Not only were the two kilos inside, but the forty thousand dollars that was promised to him on delivery was also there. There was no question as to what this meant, as Dooley inhaled the whiff of cold, hard, cash money.

"Damn."

Then the door opened next to him, startling Dooley.

"Good morning, Mr. Dooley. You're finally up," replied the same Spanish woman from the previous night. "Here— Mr. Zantos said for me to give you these. The bathroom is across the hall, and I'll have your breakfast ready when you're done." She then pushed the clothes into Dooley's hands.

Dooley looked down at the bundle of brand-new clothes and observed the brand: Polo. There was also a pair of white leather Polo dock loafers to match the rest of the attire. Mando had seen to it that he was situated properly and handled fairly—as though it was only in his power to do so.

"You like, Mr. Dooley?"

"Tell Mr. Zantos I said thank you."

The woman smiled. "I'm sure you'll have your chance to tell him personally yourself as soon as you're done here. Okay now, shoo! Get on to the shower," she said and took her leave.

Quietness lingered in the maid's wake, leaving Dooley to himself. After gathering his bearings, he headed for the bathroom and showered for the next thirty minutes. Once showered and dressed in his brand-new gear, Dooley went in search of the kitchen, following his nose as it led the way.

When he reached the large, shiny kitchen with marble stove counters and floor, Dooley was greeted by the maid again. Without a word, she took his arm and led him to a table where she placed a healthy plate of food before him.

"Eat," was her only word before she rushed off to the ringing of the phone.

Scrambled eggs, bacon, waffles, pancakes, sausage, and a large serving of grits wafted up from the plate into his nostrils, causing Dooley to wonder if he could eat everything. But that thought simmered down when he picked up his fork and butter knife and stuffed his face without turning back.

"Why did you pay me for the two keys but didn't take 'em?" Dooley asked.

Mando looked up at him over the top of the newspaper and released an audible sigh. Then he refolded the paper back up neatly and set it aside.

"I don't feel right accepting them considering what all you've been through to get it here."

"My brother's life wasn't worth two funky keys of coke."

"I didn't say that."

"But it sounded as if you were going along those lines." Dooley locked eyes with him. "Regardless what you say, that's just how I feel."

Surprisingly, Mando didn't say a word.

"What I get is what I earn, Mando. I'm not on that sympathy-offering bullshit."

"Just take the coke and let it be, Dooley. Don't make the matter more complicated than it already is—please." Mando spoke up, reaching over to relight his cigar from the glass ashtray sitting atop the desk. Then he put it away after several puffs and stood. "Follow me, I wanna show you something."

Dooley hesitated a moment, then rose to his feet. Together, the two exited the study one after the other as Mando led the way down the hall toward the entrance corridor. Then they curved around and began ascending the staircase up to the second floor.

Dooley took in every beautiful wall painting along the stairwell. Without a doubt, he knew each painting was worth a considerable price. So far, the contents of the house had left him marveled—he'd never occupied such a place as brilliant as this one. A house, to be exact.

On the second landing, Mando led him down a dimly lit hallway and stopped before the third door on their left. Mando twisted the knob and pushed open the door.

"This why I feel your pain, kiddo," said Mando, beckoning him to enter.

Although reluctantly, Dooley entered the room. Doctor Walsch looked up from the bedside while checking his patient's vital signs, regarding Dooley with curiosity and silent attentiveness.

What the fuck? Dooley froze once he saw what was laying in the large bed. The man looked thin as a rail, cheeks sunken in, and nearly every bone in his body (or what was left of it) was visible underneath his clammy, pale-looking skin.

What shocked Dooley the most was—as the patient lay beneath the bed covers—just a little below his waist was flat. It was blatantly obvious this man didn't have any legs, and Dooley thought he'd seen some weird people in the hospital the day before after visiting Passion and NeNe. But there was something about this one that stirred something inside him. The question was at the tip of his tongue.

"What happened to him?" Dooley found his voice.

"Cancer, Dooley. That's my brother right there. He's been struggling with it for nearly a year now. The doctors had to amputate his legs just recently. It broke my heart." Mando watched as Doctor Henry Edward Walsch performed his medical duties without the slightest bit of distraction.

The man was good at what he did. Precise.

"Why he ain't in the hospital?"

"Because he refused to be there."

Dooley stared at the sickly man sleeping quietly before him.

"See, this is his home, Dooley. I'm just here to look after my brother whenever I can. Do you understand what it feels like to watch your only brother die slowly, each and every day? A guy who had a big future ahead of him—at twenty-eight years old."

"Twenty-eight?" Dooley looked over at Mando doubtfully.

This guy looked as if he were in his fifties. Mando just stared down at his brother with silent grief. This had become an everyday nightmare for him, and what bothered him the most was that he didn't know when the last day would be. Truthfully, he was scared to death of losing his brother, but there was nothing he could do about it.

Now Dooley was convinced that Mando could actually relate to the pain he was now feeling after the loss of his own brother.

"I'll never be the same if I lose him, Dooley," Mando admitted. "Our sister seems more strong though. You know Lydia—she's a piece of work."

"Lydia?"

"Yes, Lydia."

"Huh?" Dooley had that dumb look. "I didn't know that was your sistah, man."

"Believe me, kiddo, there's a lot of things you don't know," Mando assured him. "Come on. Let's go back downstairs and let the doc work in peace."

Back downstairs, Mando and Dooley made their way into the large, richly furnished living room where they were greeted by Joey. Joey stood up from the couch and nodded in their direction as they approached.

Unlike Mando, this was also an Italian—but smaller and roughly dressed in a pair of old wrinkled jeans, flannel shirt, and some cowboy boots.

The introductions were made. Dooley was ready to leave. He didn't like the feeling of being away from Mama Lizzy for too long, especially now after what had happened lately.

"Dooley, Joey will see that you get home safely. He'll drive you all the way back himself."

"What about my brother's truck?" Dooley asked.

The question was expected, Mando mused. "Of course—that's how you'll be getting back. Unless you—"

"Nah, I'll take it back. I'm ready now."

"I'm quite sure you are, kiddo." Mando squeezed his shoulder.

Joey asked, "Is there anything you need me to do while I'm there, Mando?"

"You know the location, pal. Just make sure everything's in order. And see that Lydia is okay for me."

"Consider it done," Joey replied casually.

Then Mando turned back to Dooley. "Remember what we talked about. And by all means, if you ever need anything, don't hesitate to give me a call. We will speak again soon—we're bonded now," he said and offered Dooley his hand.

Anxiously, Joey slapped Mando over the shoulder and headed for the door.

"Thank you, Mando." Dooley took his offered hand. "But I got one last question, though."

The seriousness in the boy's eyes was ablaze.

"What is it?"

Dooley asked, "What's your brotha name?"

"Michael. Why'd you ask?"

"Because now I'll know who to pray for. It's the least I can do," said Dooley.

Those words meant a lot to Mando.

"You're a good man, kiddo."

"I know," Dooley replied. "I was raised by a good one too." And then he took his leave.

Chapter 13

They had already been on the road for the past two hours and Dooley was growing restless from sitting down for so long. After pondering over whether they should make a quick stop before taking the rest of the ride all the way, Dooley found himself entering the parking lot of a gas station. While Joey handled the gas pump, Dooley entered the gas station.

Minutes later, Dooley exited the store with two big brown paper bags and slid onto the passenger seat of the truck. Before pulling out into traffic, Dooley had broken down a Philly blunt of its contents and was filling it up with the rest of the Sour Kush he'd brought along. Then, to his amazement, he found one of his favorite Rick Ross CDs and had the sound system booming. There was nothing like some good weed and Rick Ross' "Sophisticated" lyrics to ride out to.

"So what are you gonna do now?" Joey asked.

Dooley glanced in his direction. "What'cha mean what I'm gon' do?"

"You know . . . now that Walt's gone."

He knew what Joey meant the first time he asked, but just wanted to stall a moment to find the proper answer.

"Right now I just need to worry about my grandma now. I know I need to be there when she gets the news."

"Are you gonna tell her or wait for her to get the call?"

"It wouldn't be right for me to know and not tell her. I'ma tell her everything—always do." Dooley released a cloud of weed smoke from his lungs. *"I'll never keep anything like that from Mama Lizzy,"* he told himself. *"She don't deserve it."*

Joey nodded. "I've met him on several occasions. Nice guy but very sure of himself. I just hope that you use this situation wisely and learn from it."

"Already have."

"Life is the precious thing one could have on this earth. Many think it's freedom, but you can't have freedom without life, Dooley. So take advantage of it while you got a chance. Live each day like it's your last because you never know when your time's up." Joey stopped talking and just drove on.

That was his message to the young Dooley because for someone to have escaped the rest of his life in prison to flee to this country from Italy—he had the right to say what he'd said. His life was so precious, and he was determined to keep it that way.

For the rest of the ride back to retrieve T.K., Dooley thought about his life. Joey's words of expression had been profound enough to make Dooley come to terms of what he wanted most in life.

How could he keep Walt's legacy alive? What will he do with the two kilos he'd accepted? How can he make an impressive improvement on his past? So many questions. Dooley had enough time to think them all over and find a resolution for them before he returned to Raleigh. Like Joey said, he needed to take advantage of the life he had and live as though it was his last day.

With that notion, his mind was now made up.

Chapter 14

"Girl, stop all that damn crying!" Andrea snapped, standing over T.K. with her hands on her hips. "T.K., you're really pissing me off wit' all this emotional mess."

Shantel stroked T.K.'s back smoothly. "He coming back for you, T.K. Dooley will keep his word."

It was 6:30 p.m., and Dooley hadn't returned as promised. For a moment, even Shantel was uncertain whether he had been true to his word, but there was no way she would hurt T.K. any more than she already was if she voiced her uncertainty. T.K. was really letting it out. The girl was heartbroken.

"He ain't call or nothing, Shantel?" asked Andrea.

She had just stopped by to check on Shantel and her situation—only to find T.K. crying her eyes raw.

"No."

"He will. They prolly just caught up there hangin' out and stuff. Who said they was gon' come right back anyway?"

"He did!" T.K. cried. "He said they'll be back by the morning!"

Both Shantel and Andrea looked over at the clock above the large entertainment center. Shantel shook her head, silent. *Dooley, now why you gotta go and do this to that girl?* Then she spoke up.

"I tell you what then, T.K., you'll stay with me till we find where Dooley—"

"If he don't come, I'm going to Raleigh my muthafuckin' self!" said T.K., angry now. "And I'ma kill his ass for lying!"

They all knew she was talking out of emotions.

In the back room, Passion was dealing with her own personal grief and agony. The girl had been confined to her bedroom ever since returning home from the hospital the previous night. She knew about the two kilos and had put the pieces together. *No wonder he held on to that bag like his life depended on it.*

That very morning, she had woken up and found the backpack lying on the floor in her room. Curiosity got the best of her. She had to look in and see what more she could learn about the boy who'd barged into her life so unexpectedly. Now she knew—however, not enough—which bothered her most.

One day, she promised, *I'll bump into him again.*

Then Andrea spun around at the sound of a car door shutting outside. She went to investigate, leaving Shantel and T.K. to their own worries. Once she pulled the curtains back to look out front, she felt her heart squeeze with relief at the sight of Dooley. All this whole while, everyone had begun to doubt that he would keep his word. Dooley showed up to save the day, and she had to admit, the youngin' did look swagged out in his all-white and cream-colored Polo attire.

He stepped around the Benz truck and spoke to the driver—to Andrea, who appeared to be a white guy from a distance. Then she turned around to look over her shoulder at T.K., who was lying with her head in Shantel's lap. Shantel met her gaze, and Andrea nodded with a smirk. Her smile was still plastered on her face until she turned back to Dooley, which immediately fell into a frown from the sad look in his eyes.

Something in her didn't feel right.

Where was Walt... an' um, Wallow? she thought as she watched Dooley approach the front door.

"Shit!" Andrea scurried over to the door, snatched it open, and took him in her arms.

Whatever the reason he was hurting over, she hoped to reassure him with her embrace that everything would be alright.

"Please come in here and do something about yo' gurls, 'cause they goin' through it right now."

He nodded and stepped inside the house. The instant Dooley turned the corner into the living room, T.K. bolted from the sofa and rushed into his arms. The girl cried for all it was worth as both Shantel and Andrea watched with expected emotion.

"That's all she needed right there," muttered Andrea.

From inside her bedroom, Passion could hear T.K.'s cries of relief that Dooley had actually returned as promised, but she dared not go out there. She didn't want him to see her in such condition. Plus, she was too exhausted and emotionally drained to even move at the moment—though she hoped that Dooley would come to her.

Passion knew how T.K. felt for him, so she didn't want to intrude on her sudden happiness. She would just wait and see—*Will Dooley make the decision to come share with her some part of her own happiness of being with him again?*

Would he come? Or would he leave with T.K. without ever seeing her again? Did he even care enough to. . .?

"Unh uh!" said Passion as she kicked away the covers and got out of bed.

A new boost of energy rushed through her as she pulled her door open and was about to dash into the living room—but Dooley was blocking her way as he stood before the doorway with that quiet, yet sad look in his eyes.

"Dooley!" She jumped into his arms and cried just as T.K. had done moments ago. "I love you!"

Yes, this was all they wanted.

"They killed my brotha and Wallow," Dooley explained—and everybody gasped in unison.

"Who?" T.K. wanted to know.

And so, he gave his account of what happened—leaving out the part where they killed those who had killed his brother.

That's when the truth hit him. The nigga he had been chasing didn't have no weapon on him—but his twin brother definitely had one. So it really wasn't him who'd killed Walt, and Mando had promised to have the alive twin found and brought to him.

Should I tell him to forget about the muthafucka? Dooley pondered and decided to keep things the way they were.

No one gets spared.

"So what're you gonna do now?" Shantel asked.

"Go back home to my grandma Lizzy's crib. 'Cause I know once she find out Walt is dead, she gon' need me close by. I'ma chill with her for a minute. Then I'ma go stay at my brother's crib."

"Oh," muttered Passion.

"And what about T.K.?" Andrea questioned.

Dooley looked over and met the girl's eyes. "She know she got a nigga now. I'ma hold her down."

"We gonna come back up here and visit y'all when everything get situated," T.K. said.

"Y'all better."

"No doubt about it."

Passion felt her heart squeeze.

"I wanna see NeNe before we go."

"Me too," T.K. agreed with him.

"Gangsta would wanna see you too before you head back home," Andrea replied.

"Yea. I know—Oh damn! I almost forgot."

"What?"

"I'll be right back!"

Dooley got up and went outside to the truck where Joey still sat waiting patiently. Joey was one of Mando's most trusted men. He was told to drive Dooley back to Raleigh safely and return to Norfolk after seeing that Lydia was also well.

The Spanish goon nodded at Dooley, whom he'd met a couple of times before, and handed over the small shopping bag through the window.

"It won't be long, Joe."

"Take ya time, man," Joey said.

A minute later, he returned to the living room and handed over the shiny blue shopping bag. Shantel took the bag and looked inside.

"Oh my God, Dooley!"

"That's yours. You and Passion need it more than I do," he said. "That's twenty-five thousand dollars. I'll be able to send more later when I get—"

Shantel shook her head as her eyes watered and pushed the bag back into Dooley's hands. "I can't take your money, Dooley. It wouldn't be right."

"Stop trippin', Shantel. You and Passion deserve all this shit," he said, then dropped the money bag onto Passion's lap.

The girl looked down at all the money with another startled gasp. She had never seen so much money before.

"Gurl, take the damn money," Andrea said.

Shantel looked up at Dooley silently. Then, when he bent down and kissed her cheek, she released her own tears.

Dooley grinned and said, "Thank you. All y'all been real to a nigga. You know what to do."

"Thank y-you, Dooley," Shantel cried.

"Nah," Dooley reassured her. "Thank you, Ma." And then he was gone.

On their way to Raleigh, while puffin' on a blunt in the backseat together, both Dooley and T.K. talked. It was now that they needed to get some serious matters out of the way before reaching their destination. Matters that needed to be discussed sooner than later—but mainly for T.K.'s sake, now that she was about to become a more major importance in his life. The life that they were about to share as a team, a unit—a world that only existed within their solidarity.

"You think she'll like me?" T.K. asked.

Dooley nodded. "As long as you keep it real."

"That ain't hard to do."

"Damn. I can't forget about that dream you said you had."

"Me either," she said with her head on his shoulder. "The same time you was goin' thru all that shit, I was havin' that dream."

He did not make a reply—just smoked on the blunt.

"Dooley, I got somethin' to tell you—"

"What?"

T.K. waited a few seconds before she spoke. "I . . . I had meant for you to miss that bus the other day. I did it on purpose," she admitted.

Then she felt his body stiffen, sensing his reaction.

"What the fuck you mean you did it on purpose?" Dooley shoved her away from him. "Huh?"

"I . . . didn't wanna be alone. I figured that if I get you to miss the bus, then I could be wit'chu. I had been watchin' you ever since you got on the bus—"

Whoop!

Dooley punched her dead in her muthafuckin' mouth. Then came another hook right to her jaw, rockin' her whole world from the impact.

"Bitch! You set me up to miss the fuckin' bus!"

Smack!

Dooley slapped her so hard it sounded like a thunderclap. T.K. shrieked in pain and sudden fear.

"You see what the fuck I had to go thru, bitch?" he shouted. "You the reason my brotha dead, hoe. If you was real wit' a nigga—"

"I'm sorry!" she cried. "I'm s-sorry, Dooley!"

"Nah, bitch!" Dooley pulled the big .45 out and aimed it against T.K.'s head.

She ducked just in time; he squeezed the trigger. The blast was deafening as the bullet shattered the glass window before it was sucked out into the wind. Screaming out of her mind, T.K. reached for Dooley's gun hand and clamped both of her hands around it. Another blast boomed from the gun, sending its second bullet through the front passenger seat.

Joey ducked cautiously as he drove, hoping for dear God that he—

Boom!

The third blast came, penetrating the passenger seat and tearing a hole into the dashboard ahead.

"Stop, Dooley! Don't kill me! Pl-p-please . . . don't kill mmme!!" T.K. wailed as they wrestled with Dooley's gun hand.

"Fuck you, bitch! Phony-ass hoe!" Dooley pounded her in the side of the head with his free hand.

Boom!

This time the bullet traveled through the driver's seat and grazed Joey's head.

"Aaahh! Aaah . . . shit!" Joey cried out, and the truck swerved off the road for a second before he stomped on the brakes and maneuvered it to the side. Fuck it. He wasn't gonna keep on driving like this!

"Get offa me, T.K.! Get the fuck—"

"Pleeeease, Dooley, don't kill me! Don't do me like that, p-please!" T.K. pleaded with him, suddenly and uncontrollably now.

The next time Dooley squeezed the trigger, there was no blast. The clip was empty, and it was all T.K. could do not to sigh in total relief—because Dooley was still in a rage.

The truck had stopped, and Joey wasted no time bolting from it. He raved and cursed like a sailor in Spanish, feeling the burning sensation of the gash along the side of his head.

Just an inch away, he thought. *Just an inch away and I'd be dead.*

Joey dared not go back toward the truck right now. Instead, he pulled out his phone and called Mando.

Tired of fighting and struggling, Dooley released the big gun from his grasp and broke down in a sorrowful sob. This baffled T.K., who just stared down at a crying Dooley. Both of them were crying now—in which T.K. risked the chance of embracing him as they cried together. Together they shared a pain that only two loved ones would understand, far beyond the cries of two young, ignorant children.

"I'm sorry, baby. I just wanna be wit' you, Dooley. That's all I want," T.K. professed from the depths of her soul. "Forgive me, Dooley."

Dooley didn't respond. He just cried...

He just cried.

The young gangsta was hurting.

Walt was dead.

Chapter 15

"Baby, hand me one of them paper towels ova yonda." Mama Lizzy pointed, and T.K. got up to go retrieve one for the old lady.

"Yes, ma'am."

"I always knew one of my boys was gonna fall victim to death out there in them streets."

T.K. gave Mama Lizzy the paper towel and sat across from her at the kitchen table. The old lady was grieving openly now, after Dooley told her about Walt being killed.

Dooley could not stand the pain in his grandmama's eyes, so he left the kitchen for his bedroom. He still had the rest of his grieving to do. Alone.

"First they mama—my daughter—get caught up out there in them streets and got herself killed. Now look at my boy." Mama Lizzy wiped her eyes with the paper towel. "Where do you come in at, baby? Tell me something."

So, T.K. told her the truth. She told her everything. She wouldn't dare lie to this woman who was the grandmother of the person she now fought to love through guilt.

Once she was done, Mama Lizzy frowned and said, "A pretty girl like you with such family like that . . . You know, many people would've been happy to be in your shoes, baby. But I see whatchu mean."

"I couldn't stand being 'used' more than being treated as their own daughter, Mama Lizzy," T.K. said.

"And Georgia, ya say?"

"Yes, ma'am. Thomasville. But I was raised up in Atlanta."

"No brothas or sistas?"

"I'm the only one, thank God," T.K. said with emotion.

Mama Lizzy said, "And now you . . . say you love my baby."

"I do."

"Chile, what is love?"

Now T.K. didn't respond, for the question had caught her completely off guard.

"That's what I thought. You ain't been knowin' my baby but two days and you talkin' about love."

"You right, Mama Lizzy. I don't know what love is. What I had always thought was love was really . . . nothin'. Lies. Just somethin' to say to somebody to somehow make them feel good. But I know one thang—I will stand by Dooley. I will show him better than I can tell him how much he means to me. I owe him my life, Mama Lizzy," she professed, with tears at the edge of her eyes now. "You just don't understand what we been thru together already." Her mouth trembled. "All I know is that I don't wanna be no other place than beside Dooley, and I mean that wit' everything inside of me."

Nodding quietly, Mama Lizzy just looked in the girl's young, flawless, pretty face. She searched for anything to convince her that T.K. wasn't who she claimed to be. She searched for what all she couldn't find. There was nothing that told her that T.K. was just another young girl with puppy love. This young gurl had been through a lot in life, grew up fast, and had evolved into the young, strong, self-made woman she was. Mama Lizzy saw the genuineness in her eyes, the love for her grandson—a young fighter—but she would not be persuaded so easily.

"I hear you, baby. Now let me get on and get y'all some supper outta the way so y'all can eat."

"I'll help you cook, Mama Lizzy." T.K. jumped at the opportunity.

"Baby, no other woman cooks in my kitchen but me. Now go on somewhere, chile!" Mama Lizzy smiled weakly. "That boy prolly want you anyway."

T.K. nodded. "Alright. Thank you, Mama Lizzy," she said and hugged the old lady.

"Whatchu thankin' me for?"

Now it was her turn to smile. "For Dooley," T.K. said.

Mama Lizzy shooed her out of the kitchen.

Dooley heard the tap on the door before it opened, and T.K. stepped inside his room. He was in the middle of a phone conversation and frowned when he saw her. T.K. closed the door shut and entered further into the room. While he talked, she observed his bedroom with interest.

There were Lil Boosie photos everywhere along the walls, as well as some of Jeezy, 2Pac, Bob Marley, Plies, and Rick Ross. To her right sat a shiny black wooden dresser with gold handles, then a twin-size bed next to it. A walk-in closet to her left, which was wide open and displayed multiple shoes and enough clothes to dress an army.

Dooley surely knew his shit when it came to dressing nice.

A large flat-screen TV hung up upon the wall above the dresser, along with a four-foot rack stacked with DVDs, video games, and music CDs for the stereo system. The room was neatly furnished and quite impressive.

Without permission, T.K. climbed upon Dooley's bed and laid down behind him. The TV was on but muted, as the movie *Iron Man 2* was being shown. Cuddling herself onto one of the pillows, she kicked off her shoes and began watching the soundless movie.

Minutes later, Dooley hung up the phone and left the room without looking at her. T.K. sighed deeply and hoped like hell that Dooley wouldn't continue his silent treatment toward her. She didn't know how long she could take that—for she longed to have him talk to her. She needed him to show her some type of attention, for this was the only person who'd really made an impression upon her heart—that which caused her to want nothing other than their attention.

She'd been with a lot of boys, even grown men, but never had no one made her feel the way Dooley does.

There had to be something that she could do to get through to him. Regardless of the fact that she'd told him the truth and had—and still is—getting punished for it. She knew that Dooley cared for her. He had to care, or else she wouldn't be where she was now. He wouldn't have brought her home to his grandmama's.

T.K. shrugged to swallow the lump in her throat as she thought. She would be dead if he didn't care.

And slowly but surely, she drifted off into a quiet sleep.

There were no dreams.

***

Forty minutes later, she woke up to the aroma of soul food and the absence of Dooley. She got up, stepped into her shoes, and exited the room. Seconds later, she found Mama Lizzy still in the kitchen, finishing up the last touches of dinner, who assured her it'd be ready in a minute.

"He out back somewhere, baby," Mama Lizzy said.

For a moment, T.K. just stood there in the kitchen doorway. Then she decided to take a trip outside, and just as she neared the screen door, she heard Dooley's voice—and another girl's!

T.K. paused for a second, thinking, feeling. Wondering. Curiosity made her push the screen door open and step outside onto the porch.

Sitting upon the white porch swing was Dooley and another girl whom T.K. instantly assumed was Shaliah. She was of a yellow-bone complexion, with brown hazel eyes— petite and well-dressed in her skinny jeans and open-toe sandals. The girl wasn't all that pretty, but her unique elegance itself was worth admiring.

Yeah, this was definitely Shaliah.

Both girls met one another's eyes, and immediately they knew—this wasn't gonna be an easy situation to handle. Shaliah wasted no time making it clear, by her attitude and expression, that she disapproved of T.K.'s presence.

"What's up, Dooley?" T.K. found her voice. "Hey," she spoke to Shaliah.

"Hey."

Well, at least the bitch could speak, T.K. thought.

Dooley didn't make a reply but did acknowledge her with a brief nod.

"Mama Lizzy say the food is almost ready."

"A'ight," he said.

Then outta nowhere came another young nigga with a small paper bag in his hand. Jon-Jon. T.K. assumed that was him—Dooley's best friend and comrade. Cash's little brother. Walt's best friend, too. A young goon not to be crossed, Jon-Jon grinned up at his crony as he climbed the porch steps.

"What's up, T.K.?"

"Um. Hey."

"Damn. Bruh ain't tell me you was this fine."

Hmph! Shaliah folded her arms.

"He didn't have no reason to—it speaks for itself, Jon-Jon," she said, and Jon-Jon grinned again after hearing her say his name.

"I know that's right, baby," said Jon-Jon and turned to his crony. "I got them gars, and I hollered at Cuz and copped some bud for the two-five."

"Not now, bruh. Later," Dooley said. "But you can roll 'em up though... behind the truck so Grandma can't see you."

"Man," Jon-Jon started. "What's up wit' them two thangs you was talkin' 'bout? A nigga tryna hustle. These fools gon' be fiendin' now since bruh—"

Dooley interrupted. "Chill, homie. You know we don't talk 'bout that shit here. Are you crazy?"

"My bad."

"Whateva, man."

"Liah, why you lookin' all stuck-up and shit?"

"Erick Daniels, you better watch yo' mouth out there on my porch, boy!" Mama Lizzy shouted from inside the house.

"Stupid!" Dooley muttered.

"My bad, Mama Lizzy! You know I love ya!"

"Unh-huh! You heard what I said," Mama Lizzy added with finality.

All T.K. could do was shake her head. *That damn Jon-Jon is off the chain!*

Then all four of them settled in with some small talk until Mama Lizzy called for them to come in and eat—and to her surprise, she fed two more mouths than she'd intended. Though Elizabeth Janes knew that cooking was her job, and feeding those who wanted to be fed was her passion.

The meal was baked boneless, skinless chicken thighs with gravy, sweet peas and brown rice, homemade butter biscuits, and a whole lot of laughter.

After dinner, and being shooed back out the dining room, T.K., Dooley, Jon-Jon, and Shaliah headed outside. Nightfall had approached, and they found themselves across the street, over in Jon-Jon's backyard. A couple of blunts was being prepared while they all chilled out and vibed like old friends. Though Shaliah still pretended to be uninterested in T.K., she secretly admitted the girl was alright.

T.K. felt the same way. She saw a *her, Passion, and Dooley repeat* coming on all over again in the near future.

"Man, fuck this shit!" Jon-Jon blurted outta the blue. "Let's go cruise around in the whip and burn. Sheeit, ain't nothin' poppin' off back here."

Shaliah shrugged in response. Dooley looked over at T.K., though he didn't know why.

"You know I'm down for whateva, baby," she said.

Yeah, because she really wasn't feelin' this spot right here.

"Let's go then!" And they all made way for the Benz truck.

"Goddamn, bruh!" Jon-Jon said with immediate surprise. "What the fuck happened to the whip, man? Some niggas done shot bruh shit up?" He continued once he recognized the bullet holes and shattered window.

"It ain't nothin', man," Dooley said and slid in behind the wheel of the truck.

Both T.K. and Shaliah got in the back, with T.K. on the side behind Dooley, next to the broken window. And she meant to stay as far away from Shaliah as possible.

"Fuck it! Crank that shit up and let's roll, bruh!" Jon-Jon sparked up the blunt, and they were riding high.

Dooley took them through the city and along the back roads as they smoked and rode out to some good music. It was just what Dooley needed to feel at home again—but little did he know, tragedy lurked just beyond the joy of being home.

"T.K.?" Shaliah called over.

T.K. looked over at the girl. *Now what the hell she want now?* "What's up, girl?"

Shaliah looked up front and saw that Dooley and Jon-Jon were lost in their own vibe and conversation. Then she turned back to T.K.

"I know Dooley already told me about y'all, but I wanna ask you myself."

"Ask?"

"Are y'all fuckin'?"

T.K.'s eyes widened with surprise. "Not yet."

"Not yet, huh." Shaliah seemed lost in thought for a brief moment. "So you don't give a fuck that I love him and that's my man?"

"No, I don't. Why should I—when he told me y'all ain't together. Y'all just friends."

"Just friends…"

T.K. interjected. "So what—you love him? I love that nigga too. That makes two of us, Liah. But I ain't finna sit here and... Look. It is what it is. I don't know about you, but

I am bonded by loyalty to him. And I'd be damned if I let you or anybody else come in between that. Simple as that. Now—" she puffed on the blunt—"you got any more questions?"

Despite the current situation, Shaliah chuckled to herself. *This bitch is really about her issue.*

"Nah, I'm good. I see what it is now. I respect the game."

"And that's all I ask. Respect the game." T.K. passed her the blunt in rotation.

"Turn in there, bruh! Turn in there!"

"Nigga, chill! I got it!"

"C'mon, Dooley!" Jon-Jon said excitedly.

Hitting the blinkers, Dooley turned into the entrance of the Recreation Center on Crenshaw Avenue, a block away from their former middle school. The parking lot was packed with vehicles. People were crawling all over the place, in and out of the big white building.

"They must got some basketball game t'night," said Jon-Jon, releasing a cloud of smoke into the air as Dooley looked for an available parking space.

People watched with curious eyes as the big silver Benz truck crept through the lot, sitting high on chrome wheels. Most knew who the truck belonged to, but rarely ever saw the little brother driving it.

After finding a park, the four of them exited the truck. T.K. went to Dooley's side at once. Shaliah knew she wouldn't be able to take much more of this new bitch that mysteriously appeared in her world.

"It is a game poppin' off in there. Y'all wanna go in and check it out?"

Always the adventurous one, Jon-Jon would surely have made the first suggestion.

"Let's do it!" Dooley said without second thought—and into the center they went.

Chapter 16

After entering the center, which was going wild and crowded with people, the four of them found a nearby cut to post up at. Because it seemed that all the seats were taken, yet none of them felt like being bunched up with strangers, it was best to find their own spot.

Of course, many wondered who the young sexy chick was with Dooley and his boy, and T.K. was aware of the attention she was receiving—though she paid them no mind. It was Dooley only who deserved her time and effort.

"Damn, I'm higher than a muthafucka!" Dooley said to himself as he leaned against the wall.

"You hang out here a lot, Dooley?" T.K. asked, craving for his conversation.

"Not really," he said. "I don't do too much hangin' over here on the west side of town. The only time I used to was when we went to middle school."

"Oh. You play ball too? You like sports?"

"Nah, I don't know shit 'bout it."

"You just a street nigga. Oh, I forgot!" she laughed. "I'm high as hell. That's some good ass weed."

A group of three girls circled the court, glancing in their direction, and kept it moving. T.K. glanced over at Dooley to see if he was looking at them—and he was. *No sweat,* T.K. told herself.

"I'll be back, y'all. I gotta go use the bathroom real quick," said Shaliah.

"Kick rocks then!" Jon-Jon shot back.

Shaliah ignored him and turned on her heels. She walked it out as though she was working the runway.

"She don't like the fact that we close."

"Okay . . . and? And who said we was even close?"

"I said it!" she replied back sharply.

That made him glance at her oddly.

"It's what *you* said. Yeah, we close all right."

"What's that supposed to mean?"

Dooley shrugged.

"One way or anotha, Dooley, I'ma *make* you love me back," she said. "I'ma show you just what I'm really about."

"How you gonna do that?" he asked; he was curious.

"Anyway you want it, Dooley. Like I told you earlier, I'm all the way down fo' you. You name it, and it's done."

Now he begun to question: *Is this bitch really for a nigga despite the flaw shit she did? Can I really trust this bitch's word now? What do she mean by 'all the way down for me'? Should I test this bitch's loyalty—her word?*

"It's whatever, baby," she added, brushing her hand up against his, but Dooley moved his hand away.

"I hear you talkin'."

Jon-Jon shouted, "Bam! That nigga Cliff bamboozled that nigga ass and dunked that bitch!"

The crowd went wild for the home team.

Cliff, a 6'2" Senior rebounder who grew up in the same hood as Jon-Jon and Dooley, was their division's basketball star. Though there were quite a few of them already looking at him for scholarships.

It was then that they realized it was the last points of the game he had achieved.

Cliff, along with his winning teammates, was talking trash to the rival team about beating them by nine points. It was their fifth straight win. Yet all it took was one person to challenge the other and all hell broke loose on the basketball court.

People from the bleachers on both sides, along with those who hung around, made their way to the middle of the basketball court for the brawl.

"Just like niggas to mess up a good night," Shaliah said, walking up to Dooley and the other two.

"Let's go 'fore shit really get down and dirty," Jon-Jon said, and they headed for the exit along with many others.

"Niggas can't take a loss," said Dooley.

"I'm tellin' ya. Dang!" Shaliah commented—and was then shoved aside by another girl.

"Hoe, move outta my damn way 'fore you get stepped on!" said Monica, along with two of her homegirls in tow.

The same three girls who had passed them earlier.

"Bitch…!" Shaliah had to grab a hold onto Jon-Jon's arm to stay balanced. "Watch where you going—"

"Who you callin' a bitch, *bitch*!?" Monica turned around to confront her.

"You the only female dog I see, bitch!"

"Y'all chill, man," Jon-Jon protested against the violence brewing between the two.

"We don't want no problems, Monica," Dooley said. "Let that shit go."

One of Monica's girls eyed T.K. cautiously, obviously ready for her to get wrong.

"Nah, Jon-Jon. I already feel this hoe be on some hating shit anyway."

"Hating on what?" Shaliah laughed. "Hoe, you ain't even on my level."

"Come on, Liah." T.K. took her hand and was about to lead her back towards the truck before the next comment was made.

"Oh, you dyking too? You need the next bitch to hold ya hand and take you home?"

T.K. turned back to face the three girls. "What the fuck you just said, bitch?"

"What's up, sis? What's the problem, yo?" Lil Benny, Monica's sixteen-year-old brother, and his crony Tabby walked up.

Lil Benny was a young hellraiser too, who terrorized the streets on the west side as well.

"These bitches got a problem, and—"

Whop!

T.K. reached back and punched Monica dead in between the eyes, knocking her straight on her ass.

"Watch ya fuckin' mouth!" T.K. spat, and kicked Monica in the stomach, which was enough to provoke the two girls to pounce on her like never before.

Before he even knew what was happening, Jon-Jon was sucker punched in the eye by Lil Benny. Off instinct, Jon-Jon went for the counterattack. Shaliah jumped in to help T.K., who was giving both girls a run for their money.

They had the young Georgia-rich girl fucked up!

One look at Lil Benny's crony, and Dooley hit him with a straight jab so fast it was almost a blur. Dooley whipped his ass just because.

Several other west siders saw what was going on, and all five of them rushed over to help their own. Of course, more grown-ups and authorities were too busy trying to cease the matter inside the Rec Center to know what was happening in the parking lot.

Monica found her footing, reached for her fallen purse, then inside for her pepper spray. Since Jon-Jon was the closest—who was fighting her brother—she waited for the right opportunity to spray his ass.

When that opportunity came, the moment Jon-Jon hit the ground, she let it rip! Jon-Jon's whole entire face was blasted with the pepper spray. He panicked and reached underneath his shirt.

"Shit!"

Bang! Bang! . . . Bang! Jon-Jon hollered as he shot blindly into the midst of those upon him. *Bang...* he hollered some more. *Bang! Bang!*

Jon-Jon struggled to his feet, brandishing the small .25 automatic, not realizing what damage he'd done.

All he knew was that he was burning up and couldn't see.

Bang!

"Jon-Jon!" Dooley rushed over to his comrade and took him by the arm. "I gotchu, bruh!"

"That . . . bitch sprayed me, bruh! It burns. Man. Ahh! Shit!" Jon-Jon cussed, groaning in pain.

"Dooley!" T.K. called out!

"Oh shit!" Shaliah looked in pure shock at T.K. laying on the dark pavement, bleeding from a gunshot wound in the arm. "Oh my god . . . T.K.!"

Dooley damn near died at the sight of T.K., while Jon-Jon hollered in pain and agony. The other bodies were laid out on the ground too—all of whom had been caught in the line of fire. Panicking now, Dooley shouted, "Liah, take him to the truck! I got T.K."

"Dooley . . . it hurts," T.K. cried as Dooley helped her up off the ground.

"Come on, T.K., I gotchu, baby—"

"It h-hurts . . . Dooleeey!"

Sirens sounded off.

"I know, baby. Come on."

Dooley hefted her good arm across his shoulders, and they both ran for the truck. They all piled in, with Dooley back at the wheel.

"We gotta take her to the hospital!" Shaliah shouted over Jon-Jon's steady ranting and groaning.

Dooley knew that taking T.K. to a hospital was out of the question. She was a runaway. They would send her back home, and he wasn't having that. Yet there was only one place he knew for sure to take her:

To Grandma Lizzy!

Chapter 17

"Man, this shit's crazy," Jon-Jon said two hours later as he puffed on a Black & Mild.He was still burning. Dooley didn't reply. Jon-Jon sensed his friend's worry.

"I'm sorry, man. I wasn't thinkin', bruh. That shit had me fucked up."

"You gotta lay low now, man."

"I know."

"Yeah. I know somebody said somethin', and they prolly lookin' for both of us."

"Damn!" Dooley put his head in his hands.

They were sitting out behind Mama Lizzy's house where the truck was parked. For the moment, the night was quiet, but they knew it wouldn't be like that forever. Eventually, the police would show up, and the thought of being arrested disturbed Dooley.

"Man, we gotta get missin' 'til we figure out what we gon' do next. They gon' get both of—"

"Nigga, whatchu talkin' 'bout?"

"They gon' get both of our asses for that shit."

Jon-Jon shook his head. "Nah. I'm the one who pulled the trigger. If they catch me, then I'ma man-up to that shit. Can't let you go down for some bullshit I did."

"It ain't even about that."

"Then what the fuck it's about, Dooley?"

Dooley looked out into the starry sky. The cool breeze would've been comforting under different circumstances, but not tonight.

"If I go in and they fingerprint me, they gon' link me to them murders up there in Norfolk. Walt was already found dead in that place—"

"You left the gun in there?"

Reluctantly, Dooley shook his head yes.

"When we had murked them niggas, my bullets ran out. It was one more nigga left that I had to get, so I dropped that shit, grabbed Wallow's heat, and went after the nigga."

"You left the muthafuckin' murder weapon," Jon-Jon said softly. "Nigga, what was you on?"

"I wasn't thinkin' straight," Dooley said. "The only thang that was on my mind was killin' dude."

"Damn."

"I fucked up."

"Damn," Jon-Jon repeated.

"I just remembered that shit. After all them niggas' heads I bust growin' up, shootin' at niggas behind my brotha bullshit—I never went in. My prints ain't in the system."

"You lucky."

"Lucky?" frowned Dooley. "Ever since bruh had me take that shit to Norfolk, I been havin' *bad* luck outta this world. Everythang been fucked up since then."

An eerie feeling fell over them. The realization of his predicament was weighing heavy on him. Dooley knew he couldn't let the police get him—or else he was fucked.

"What about T.K.?" Jon-Jon asked.

A deep sigh escaped Dooley's system.

"I don't know, bruh. I don't want her in . . . I think I'ma leave her here with Mama 'til I find out how I wanna do this. I can't stay here, Jon-Jon."

"Me either."

"We gotta go, man. I know you got yo' old gurl and all to take care of while Cash ain't here."

"I'll leave her the stash."

"The stash? What stash, man?"

Jon-Jon said, "Niggas I'd been hittin' up, plus some hustle profit I put to the side. I got 'bout fifteen grand saved up."

"Fifteen grand!" Dooley looked shocked. "You had all that money the whole—"

"The night before you left and went to Jersey, I hit this chump up ova on the Southside for thirteen stacks. I was gonna show you, but Walt had told me you had left and went somewhere for him."

There was another moment of silence.

"I got two keys of coke and about twelve grand too."

"You strapped too, huh? Two keys?"

"I'll leave the money with Mama and T.K. Plus, I know where Walt's stash at too. We can get all that and dip."

"Let's do it!" Jon-Jon said.

As on cue, the sound of cars braking to a stop on the other side of the house was heard. Both comrades looked over at each other and knew that the time had come. Jon-Jon pulled out his gun.

"Wait a minute, man," Dooley whispered and crept alongside the house to have a peek out front.

He gasped and rushed back around the house where a frenzied-looking Jon-Jon stood anxiously.

"It's two police cars out in front of yo' house."

"Damn!" Jon-Jon cussed. "My stash!"

"Fuck that! You can get it done another time. We 'bout to hit it now. Lemme go in here and grab my shit right quick," Dooley said with a rush.

"Shit!" mumbled Jon-Jon. "A'ight. Hurry up, bruh. I gotcha back."

"Real quick," Dooley reassured him and ran up the steps of the back porch into the house.

***

"What is it, baby?" Mama Lizzy questioned Dooley's nervousness. She'd just left out from seeing to a now-sleeping T.K. in the guest room.

"I gotta leave again, Mama—maybe for a while this time."

"What you mean 'leave'? For a while?"

Dooley handed her the bag of money while explaining the situation to her as fast as possible.

"What about that chile in there?"

He said, "When I can, I'ma come back for her. I'll be back for both of y'all."

"Boy, I ain't runnin' away from my own home."

Dooley opened the door and walked inside the bedroom where T.K. lay soundlessly.

"T.K.?" Dooley shook her softly.

"Dooley!" Mama Lizzy shot her hand to her hips.

T.K. awoke groggily. "What . . .?"

"I love you, baby. That's what. Get better. I'll get back at you soon. Get some rest," he said. "I love you."

"I . . . love you too, Dooley."

Dooley had tears in his eyes as he bent down to kiss her on the lips and exited the room before either one of them could stop him.

Then there was a knock at the front door, but he didn't stop—just sped up the process and through the back door he went. Once outside, he and Jon-Jon cleared out the truck from all its illegalities and dashed off into the path behind the house. The path led to the next street over on 4th Street. From there, they stole two bicycles and pedaled them both all the way across the town to the Eastside.

Next thing later, Dooley was knocking on the door of a triple-wide trailer—Walt's baby mama's crib.

"What if she ain't home?" asked Jon-Jon, trying to catch his breath. "Damn, I need to stop smoking if I'm gonna be running like this from now on."

In all his eighteen and a half years, that's all he had been doing—ripping and running the streets of Raleigh.

"Her whip right there," Dooley pointed over to the Chrysler 200 parked at the corner of the trailer.

"Oh . . . damn."

A second later, Tanisha called out, and Dooley announced who he was, and the door opened immediately.

"Dooley! Damn… lil brotha," was all she could say as her own tears began forming in her eyes.

"I need yo help, Tee."

"You don't never have to a-ask. You know that."

Then he explained to her his current situation, although he'd spoken with her earlier several hours before. She was the second to know about Walt's death—and that's only because she had his three-year-old son, Bryson. However, the bitch was loyal to Walt on all accounts, and so she deserved to know.

"A'ight, Dooley. Lemme call Kay ova here to watch Bryson, and I gotchu," she said and rushed for her bedroom.

Both Dooley and Jon-Jon slid over into the kitchen and raided the fridge for something to drink.

"We gon' get to bruh condo, grab the stash, and beat it like Mike said."

Jon-Jon nodded. "Where we go after that?"

"Wherever, bruh, as long as it's far away from here. You know—Florida. Miami Beach?"

For that simple reason, Dooley grinned mischievously. "Jackpot," Dooley said. "But the only thing is, them grimy fools we gon' have to deal wit' if we gon' put in some work."

"Whatchu think they made guns for?"

"But guns ain't what save a nigga all the time, man. We gotta use our brains—our intelligence."

"Stay two feet ahead of them niggas."

Nodding quietly, Dooley gulped down more of his strawberry Kool-Aid.

"I know you gon' tell Cash what's up."

"A-SAP," he said. "They can't hold bruh down. He'll be back out in no time. They only got him for a few sell charges and V.O.P."

"County time."

"Ain't shit to him to do."

Tanisha came back out now wearing some hoochie-mama shorts, tank top, and her all-white Air Maxes, but it was what she had in her hand that was something to be questioned.

"I know y'all prolly still strapped, but here go a lil somethin' somethin' to hold down."

"That's real."

Dooley took the chrome 9mm with the two extra fully loaded clips.

"That's Walt's new one right there. I still got the .38 snub-nosed, but that ain't going nowhere."

"Nah. You need that." Jon-Jon couldn't help but stare at Tanisha's body.

At 5'6 and weighing 135 pounds, dark chocolate complexion and with more curves than the state of Ohio, Tanisha was a bad bitch. Oval-shaped face in such a unique way, full pink lips, light brown eyes, and with a Boss Bitch attitude—she was definitely one to be admired... and also hated, due to the many reasons haters struggle to hide the fact that she is to be envied. No wonder Walt chose her as his own.

"Tee, you already know where you stand wit' Grandma Lizzy," said Dooley.

"Of course. That's my Mama, boo," she said, busily splitting a blunt down the middle at the kitchen counter. "Don't worry 'bout your gurl. I'ma make sure she taken care of. You know me, lil brotha—I handle my bizness."

Burning inside, Dooley knew he'd made the right choice leaving T.K. in Mama Lizzy's care. He also knew she was going to be very disappointed at him deciding such a thing, but she would have to understand that he had no other choice. He didn't want to put her back in harm's way again—and that's surely what it would be if he'd taken her too.

Jon-Jon was a very trigger-happy muthafucka, with one of the shortest tempers he knew. Dooley shook his head.

Hell nah! I will not put her in that position right now. But once her stubborn ass get well, there was no doubt she would take care of her own.

"What's up, man?" Jon-Jon looked over at his friend with concern in his eyes.

Dooley shook his head again. "Waitin' on Tee slow ass to light up the damn blunt."

"I'm sayin'! Damn. Slow ass!" Jon-Jon remarked.

"Whateva!" Tanisha put flame to the fat blunt of mid-grade. "As soon as Kay—"

The knock at the door cut her short.

"There it is, yo. Let's get it poppin', man," said Jon-Jon, ready to get to the next phase.

***

The ride took a full twenty minutes to make it to Walt's condo. Dooley, already having the keys to the place, went straight in like it wasn't nothin'. Tanisha followed behind and locked the front door. Without hesitation, Dooley hurried along inside the kitchen area and began taking items out of a certain cabinet.

"Whatchu doin', Dooley?" Jon-Jon asked.

"Look in one of them drawers and find me that flathead screwdriver," Dooley said as he continued extracting all kinds of items from the cabinet.

Knowing that Dooley told him that for a good reason, Jon-Jon did as he was told. He began searching the counter drawers for the screwdriver at once. Tanisha quietly watched with fascination as they worked to reveal the unknown. Once the cabinet was cleared away, Dooley looked over his shoulder at his comrade.

"Damn, bruh."

"Found it—shit! That was a mission."

"Lemme hold the damn thang, man!" Dooley said and began unscrewing each corner of the back wall of the cabinet.

Minutes later, Dooley retrieved the back wooden wall panel of the cabinet and handed it over to Jon-Jon. Now there before him sat an all-black steel wall safe, to which he dialed in the six-digit code—his birthday: month, day, and year. The safe clicked and automatically unlocked.

"Oh… goddamn!" Tanisha gasped.

"This look like some James Bond-type shit," Jon-Jon said.

"Hand me—"

Jon-Jon interrupted. "Walt was doin' his thang, man. Look at all that shit!"

"Man, get the bag," Dooley said. Then he began pulling from the wall safe bricks of coke, heroin, and jewelry, and piled them all upon the countertop.

Tanisha couldn't believe her eyes. *My nigga was really doing it big up in here*, she thought.

Altogether, it was eighteen kilos of coke, three bricks of heroin, and a variety of jewelry that was worth over one hundred grand itself.

Leaving Jon-Jon to handle the safe's contents, Dooley grabbed the screwdriver and hurried out of the kitchen to the master bedroom. He stopped at the door and fell to his knees to unscrew the bottom, where there was another hidden slide panel underneath. A couple minutes later, he reached a finger underneath the door and pulled out the long, three-inch-wide flat metal slide. Then stacks of money began tumbling down onto the floor. Who would've ever known such a compartment stuffed with thousands of dollars existed?

This is how much Walt trusted his little brother—with his life, and his life's savings. Dooley's eyes watered, his vision became blurry with sudden emotions as he thought about his dead brother, but there was no time for emotions. He had a mission to complete.

"What the—" Jon-Jon's eyes bulged widely as he stared down at all the money.

Without a word, Dooley separated half of the pile of stacks and looked up at Tanisha, and Tanisha already knew what was up without any words. Dooley was giving her her share of the money. Little did they know that Walt had actually hit his million-dollar mark in the game—and from both hidden stash spots, including over fifty more thousand dollars already in Bryson's savings account, consisted of that million-dollar mark. Niggas really been sleeping on his hustle.

There was no time for talking with Dooley. He hustled all throughout the apartment, stuffing both duffel bags with the rest of what he felt he needed. Once all was said and done, he hugged Tanisha for a long time. He held her—for strength, Walt, himself, love, and faith that she would do what she had to do to survive and take thorough care of Bryson, his nephew, his brother's only child.

"Love you, sis."

Tanisha couldn't help it, but she sobbed uncontrollably, shaking sorrowfully in his arms. This was a moving moment for Jon-Jon, who looked away as his own tears crept to the edge of his eyes.

"I love you, lil brotha. I'm . . . I'ma represent for ya, Dooley. I got this," she cried. "I promise."

"I know," Dooley whispered. "That's why my bruh chose you."

Then he visited Lydia.

Chapter 18

Thanks to Lydia and her forever graciousness, Dooley and Jon-Jon made it from Raleigh to Spartanburg, South Carolina, with the help of a good friend. From there, the two cronies boarded an Amtrak train all the way to Jacksonville, Florida. Once there, they hopped on a Greyhound for Miami. Though neither of them was really feelin' all the riding for long periods of time, they both knew it was well worth the effort.

"This shit feels depressin' as hell," Jon-Jon complained.

Dooley chuckled. "We almost there, homie."

"Bad luck my ass. We slid from that shit like it wasn't nothin', bruh."

"We did too." Dooley wondered how long it would be before some bullshit happened.

Truly, although he didn't believe in such things, he was beginning to feel like he was cursed.

Jon-Jon said, "Soon as we touch down, I'm findin' me some pussy and some fiyah-ass weed."

"Shhh, man. You loud as fuck! Pipe down, nigga." Dooley shoved him in the ribs.

That's when Jon-Jon looked up and detected several glances from people looking in his direction. He frowned and turned back to Dooley.

"Fuck that. This a free country."

Dooley laughed, shaking his head.

This nigga is a trip!

"So what, we gon' snatch up a house or apartment?" Jon-Jon asked.

"I don't care how we do it, man. The only thang I'm worried about is stayin' alive."

"And get this money."

"Straight up!"

"Maybe I can work on my music while I'm down here. You know this the spot on that music shit."

"If that's what you wanna do, I'm down wit' it."

Then he thought about the two people he killed—Monica and one of Lil Benny's homies. Three more were also hit by stray bullets, including Lil Benny and T.K., but they were now suffering as a result.

"Nah, man. I'll just stick to my grind in the streets. Even if I do do somethin', it'll only be just some shit we can vibe to. No commercial shit."

"Like I said, it's whatever, bruh."

Jon-Jon sighed. "I'm hungrier than a bucket full of starving fat hoes!"

Not caring how loud he was now, Dooley laughed. From the rest of the ride to Miami, both friends plotted and schemed on their next move once they got there.

Dooley was missing T.K. already. Then he remembered his last words to her.

Did I tell that bitch I love her? he questioned himself. *Yeah, I did tell her that shit.*

That's when he quietly searched within himself to see whether what he felt for her was real or not. He couldn't find no reason to feel otherwise.

Yeah, he decided. *I do love T.K.* And with that, he planned to prove just how much he did...

In due time. Starting now.

(Six days later)

Dooley woke up at eight-something that morning to the sound of the stereo blasting loudly throughout the apartment. Then the smell of weed smoke was in the air, and the place was alive with Jon-Jon's usual loud and peppiness. The muthafucka was definitely filled with energy early this morning.

Already having kicked away the cover during his sleep, Dooley slid out of bed and into his Nike slippers. Still dressed in just a pair of boxer shorts and nothing more, he headed down the hallway where the racket was coming from.

"Happy Birthday! Happy Birthday, my nigga!" Jon-Jon shouted over the loud music of Lil Boosie and handed over a freshly lit blunt. Then he started dancing.

To his surprise, there was Mando, all dressed in the finest designer line as usual, grinning from ear to ear.

"Twenty, eh!" Mando stepped up and embraced the young birthday boy. "Got somethin' nice for you, buddy. Go take a look outside. Matter of fact, later. It's party time."

"Huh?" Dooley was stunned as he looked down at the large birthday cake sitting upon the coffee table in the middle of the living room.

Plus, there were two beautiful Spanish model-looking women dressed in bikinis lounging around the living room before they stood and approached him. Both women were all up on him instantly, touching, rubbing, and causing his dick to grow rock-hard!

"I'm Amy!" said the tall sexy one.

"And I'm Cheri," replied Jennifer Lopez's clone.

"And we'd like to say Happy Birthday, Dooley."

Amy then kissed him on the cheek, followed by Cheri's, which was directly on the corner of his mouth.

"Ooooh shit, bruh! Put that shit up, nigga!" Jon-Jon laughed heartily as Dooley's seven-inch dick burst through the front hole of his boxers. "Hell nah!" He covered his eyes.

Mando was tickled himself.

"We know what to do with that matter," Cheri purred, taking his dick in her hand and squeezing it. "Mmmm . . ."

"Yes!" Amy stuck her hand in the bottom of her bikini.

Then Cheri led Dooley back to the bedroom by his dick as Amy followed close behind and shut the door. It wasn't no tellin' when he would come back up for air again.

"Man, now I gotta roll anotha blunt," Jon-Jon whined and just busted out dancing again.

This muthafucka is bugged the hell out!

Now all Mando could do was wait.

Chapter 19

Dooley didn't know where in the hell he was going, but didn't care, because he was now driving his brand new car. It was a 2011 Chevy Impala, the color of midnight blue, rolling on 23" chrome rims, and fogged up with Columbia's best ganja. With Mando riding shotgun and Jon-Jon in the backseat getting wasted, the trio rode through the streets of Miami.

"I love this place," Mando was saying. "The sun never sleeps even when it's dark outside."

"Been tryna get down here for forever now."

"Started from the bottom now we here . . . Started from the bottom now my whole team here!" Jon-Jon rapped along with Drake as he poured himself another cup of Hennessy.

"You'll like it here, buddy. I have a few friends down here whom I will introduce you to. My buddy Al, he owns a coupla diners throughout the city."

"He Latino too?"

"He's black as smut. But he's a good fella, dangerous if ever there should come trouble. As for Rolando, he Mexican, although he acts black as well. He supplies a major stock of coke down here, along with his brother Meechie. Now that's one motherfucker I'm sure would fit in well with your friend back there."

"Jon-Jon?"

"Precisely, yes."

"He must be a loose cannon too, huh?"

Mando nodded. "More like a nuclear time bomb."

Dooley turned onto 118th Ave and cruised close around the same area where his crib was, just a few miles back.

Little by little, he would eventually venture out more in time. For now, he wanted to visit, see, and experience all of Miami, Florida. It was the most beautiful city he'd ever seen, even on TV and magazines. The Sunshine State was remarkable.

"So what are your plans, Dooley?'

"Get rich or die tryin'!" Jon-Jon blurted out and sat forward, bringing his head in between their shoulders.

It was blatantly obvious that he was feeling the liquor.

"We passing by all these honies, and y'all talkin' 'bout nuclear time bombs and shit. Bruh, why the fuck you drivin' in circles?"

"I ain't drivin' in circles. That's just yo' big ass head spinning.

Jon-Jon looked over at him and said, "Oh." Then he sat back as if nothing had happened.

Yeah, that nigga is loose as a goose, Dooley thought.

"You're still gonna answer my question?"

"What question?"

Dooley took another pull from the blunt, and Mando asked the question for the second time.

"I'm just seeing where you stand with this new setup."

"Oh." Dooley blew out a cloud of smoke. "For now, I'm just gonna, you know, chill and get adjusted to the scenery. Then I'ma crank up and get my hustle on. Maybe invest in somethin' with the money I do got now. Walt had always wanted to have a barbershop or car detailing bizness. That was what he was saving for."

"Either or both?" Mando questioned.

"Both if the opportunity arises. I really wanna do the barbershop though."

"And Jon-Jon?"

"All he know is the grind. So I'ma put him in them streets where he wanna be." Dooley said and turned on Citrus Parkway and into the parking lot of Applebee's.

"That's what the fuck I'm talkin' bout! Food food food, goddam! Bout time you do somethin' right, Dooley" Jon-Jon said excitedly. "It better be some honies in here too."

Both Mando and Dooley exchanged grins and shook their heads.

"Here we go." Dooley sighed.

After the trio ate their meals—and Jon-Jon's constant nagging about there being no women in the restaurant to fit his liking—Mando directed them to the next best thing: *Club Fierce*, one of the top strip clubs in the city. It was owned by an associate of Mando's, more like a distant friend to be exact. His name was Sin, one of Cuba's own.

Jon-Jon nearly tore the door open to get in the place. A stack of five hundred ones was his next priority, and then he lost himself in the midst of beautiful naked women. Dooley found him a spot close by so he could keep an eye out on his friend.

"You're not gonna live it up for your birthday, Dooley?" Mando asked.

Dooley shrugged. "Prolly later. I just wanna take it all in for right now," he said.

"Hey, hey Mami! Yea' you. Come here for a minute!" Jon-Jon called out at a very tall, black, fine sista with ass for days—while already receiving a lap dance from another stripper.

The nigga was gone wild!

The place was packed with people from every trade of the game—strippers of a variety of nationalities, but mostly Black. Money was raining down all over the club. Even major celebrities were in the building, such as *Gunplay*, *Omarion*, *Smoke from Field Mob*, and many more who'd come to make their appearances. Club Fierce was definitely where one would want to be to have a good time.

"I'll be leaving back for Jersey tomorrow. Had some business to attend down here which I rescheduled early to be here on your birthday. Now that that's done, I must return to my post," Mando leaned his broad shoulders back.

"How often do you come here?"

"Only when business is ordered. I'd say once or twice every coupla months."

Dooley relit his blunt and glanced around the busy scene. Every male person in the place was intoxicated with the fascinating views surrounding them.

"I'ma have somethin' like this when I get my money right."

"It's a profitable investment."

"Not an actual strip club. I mean, I want somethin' that attracts this much attention on a daily basis."

"Any thoughts of what just that may be?"

"I'll tell you when I know myself."

Mando said, "I know this is a bad time to bring this matter up, but it's better to get it done now."

"What's that?" Dooley inhaled a lung full of weed smoke, relishing the rush.

"You don't happen to know Walt's personal connect, do you? The main one he got his weight from?"

"Heard of him. Why?"

"Correct a few errors, that's all."

Mando's heart was thumping with anticipation now. *It was what he'd wanted from the very beginning—the main reason he'd stuck around this long dealing with Walt.* He wanted Walt's connect, especially after finding out he had the purest cocaine in North Carolina. Though he had his own resources and his own weight, Walt had the real deal. What Walt had was thirty percent purer than what he had. Now Mando's patience was nearly shot. He was losing too much money.

"I only met him twice when—well, that was over the phone though. He would send Cash to go pick the shipment up, or it would be brought to them."

"You got a name? Any idea where he's from?"

For some reason, Dooley was feeling a strange vibe from Mando. Although he tried to brush it aside, the feeling wouldn't budge. Then when he looked up in the big man's eyes, there was no mistaking the ghastly deceit in them.

"I can't just give out his—Shit!" Dooley realized his own mistake. He'd spoken too fast. "I don't know his name, Mando. You'll have to ask Cash that, which I doubt he even know."

He knows, Mando thought. Then his face brightened up.

"No sweat, buddy. I just hope whoever it is doesn't get the wrong idea."

"Whatchu mean?"

"You know. Maybe Walt probably still owed him, or vice versa. We don't need any complications behind that. Because if he does owe Walt anything, I will make sure you get what's owed. And if Walt owes him, I'm obligated to clear that up—now that he won't be able to."

"Man, I need five hundred mo'!" Jon-Jon came up to their table and looked down at them. "I ran out. I'll pay you back when we get back in the whip, bruh."

"You out already, buddy?"

"Nigga, we ain't been in here twenty minutes and you done spent—gave away— five hun—"

"I said I'll getchu back, man." Jon-Jon glanced back over his shoulder at Tall and Sexy.

She waited patiently for him, because she knew she found her a puppet. Dooley saw just as much too, but that didn't stop him from digging in his pocket for his cash.

"Thank you, bruh!" said Jon-Jon, taking his money to go cash it in for five hundred more ones.

Shaking his head pitifully, Dooley said, "Yeah, we really gon' have a pro'lem wit' this strip club thang. I can see it already."

"He just having fun. You both hustlers. You'll get back what you put out," Mando replied.

"That's free money," Dooley said. "Money we could use to benefit from—not trickin' with some stripper hoe."

***

Two hours later and fifteen hundred dollars spent to supply Jon-Jon's stripper habit, the trio was back on the road again. So far, the majority of the day was spent with nonstop excitement. It was almost five-thirty that afternoon and still so much to do and see. Mando made sure that the two comrades enjoyed themselves immensely as he toured them around the city.

"May as well enjoy myself while I'm here," said Mando, eating a plate of curry goat and rice from Jamaica's Way restaurant over in Dade City.

Dooley was fucking up a foot-long shredded steak and cheese El Monterey burrito as they sat in the car waiting on Jon-Jon to return. He was taking a long time to come. As if on cue, he came trudging through the exit of the restaurant with his take-out.

I wonder what he smiling about now.

"You'd never know with him. That guy there is totally unpredictable."

Jon-Jon slid into the back seat of the car.

"That's four phone numbers in one day and some free food."

"Must've been that fat bitch behind the counter wit' hot sauce and bread crumbs 'round her mouth."

Mando bit back laughter in order to consume his food, his face turning red in the process.

"Oh, you got jokes, huh?" Jon-Jon frowned.

Well, at least he was about sobered up a little.

"I call it how I see it, bruh."

Back on the road they went as Mando suggested that they stop by Rolando's place before they settled in for the remainder of the day. After driving for nearly twenty minutes straight, Jon-Jon decided to shoot the question out there.

"Damn. Where the fuck the dude stay, in muthafuckin' China?"

"Just a coupla more minutes, buddy. He doesn't live in the city area," Mando replied.

When those coupla minutes turned to five, he directed Dooley to turn on a dirt road. Dooley turned and drove the short distance to the stop sign up ahead.

"Where to now?" he asked.

That's when Mando pretended to spill his drink into his lap and bent forward. A little too low for a spilled drink. Then came a loud explosion. A boom! That resulted in Jon-Jon's brains splattering all over the back seat of the car, and before Dooley could react to what was happening, Mando came up with a big .40 Glock and shoved it between his eyes.

"I think it's time for you to give me the information to your brother's connect now," Mando hissed like a venomous cobra.

The next thing later, the back door was opened, and Jon-Jon's body was snatched outside, only to be replaced with two masked goons. Once a large double-barrel .12 gauge was now pressed against Dooley's head, Mando drew down his own weapon.

"Now, Dooley," Mando sighed. "One way or another, you will tell me what I need to know. And in the process—" he shot Dooley in his right thigh.

He screamed to the top of his lungs.

"You will feel never-ending pain."

Dooley told him everything. Pressure bust pipes. Then his brains were splattered against the windshield.

Chapter 20

Dooley cried out.

"Brah? Dooley, wake up, man!" Jon-Jon's words exploded next to him as he shook Dooley awake.

"Whad'it?" Dooley said groggily but alert now.

"Man, you alright?"

"I'm good."

Jon-Jon wasn't going for it.

"You was havin' nightmares and shit, hollerin' in ya sleep," he said from the back seat.

"I was hollering?"

"Yes, you were, buddy," replied Mando next to him.

They were still parked at Jamaica's Way restaurant, as Jon-Jon had just slid into the back seat. It was the door shutting closed with a bang that had awakened Dooley from the nightmare he was having—even while taking a catnap.

"Don't be buggin' out on me, Dooley."

"I gotta piss like a muthafucka!" said Dooley. "Y'all give me a minute right quick while I run in there—"

"You'll have to make it fast, buddy. I'd like for us to make a quick stop before we head back to the house," Mando replied.

Just hearing those words made Dooley cringe as he opened the door.

"Be right back," he said.

"Shoulda been did that shit, bro," Jon-Jon said, but Dooley was already exiting the car and heading for the restaurant's entrance.

"Knew I shouldn't've gave that nigga no Chronic!" said Jon-Jon, imitating Smokey from the movie *Friday.*

Mando chuckled and checked his Rolex.

Once in the restroom, Dooley pulled out his cellphone. He had to warn Jon-Jon of his intuition. Moments later, Jon-Jon looked down at his buzzing phone in the back seat and picked it up. He read the text message Dooley was sending him and wondered what the fuck was going on:

Go outside when phone ring. Don't say shit, just go!

While Jon-Jon was reading the message, Mando was in the process of flipping through the CD disc changer. He had no clue what was being transpired. The phone rang.

"Damn, 'bout time this bitch call a nigga!" Jon-Jon said, going along with Dooley's warning. "What's up, baby?" he answered and stepped out of the car.

Inside the restroom, Dooley was pacing back and forth.

Jon-Jon, bruh, I think Mando is about to kill us, dawg.

What're you talking 'bout?

As quick and short as possible, Dooley told him about the conversation he and Mando had in the strip club. Then he went on to tell him about the dream he'd just had, which now had Jon-Jon convinced.

I'm telling you, bruh, Mando is willing to do whatever it takes to get my brotha's connect.

You know who it is too, huh?

"Yeah," he said, thinking about Walt's connect named Fedo.

Jon-Jon glanced over into the car.

We gotta do something, and do it fast, bruh. You heard what he just said. I'm serious, man. I don't trust this dude no more.

I got it . . . Just let me handle it, a'ight?

"Yeah." Dooley sighed. "I'm on my way out now."

"Yeah . . ." Jon-Jon snapped the phone shut and hopped back inside the car. Then he reached for his bag of food and began eating while waiting on Dooley.

"I assume you have a hot date, eh?" Mando said with phony blithe.

"And you know it!" Jon-Jon stated. "If it's lookin' right, I'll have two dates—"

"Oh, you're a player, man."

Dooley exited the restaurant, approached the car, and got in.

"Let's do it!" he said.

"You good now, bro? Don't start that hollering shit . . ." laughed Jon-Jon. Without hesitation, he removed the loaded 9mm from underneath the front passenger seat.

When they were back on the road, Dooley glanced over in Mando's direction.

"Whatchu sayin' now, before I got out the car? Something about making a quick stop somewhere?" he asked curiously.

"Yes. I have to pick something up from Rolando's place . . . I don't wanna wait till it's too late considering his work schedule."

"A'ight then." Dooley and Jon-Jon exchanged a brief glance through the rearview mirror.

There was no turning back now, and Dooley just hoped it all works out for the best.

While Mando directed Dooley, they all maintained small conversations as they rode out, Lil Boosie booming in their ears. Dooley wondered when Jon-Jon would make his move. About ten minutes into the drive, Jon-Jon did just that.

During the ride, Jon-Jon had managed to finish his food in record time and unstrung his shoelaces. He twirled them both together and wrapped each end around both of his hands. Now there was only about five inches of the combined, doubled shoelaces left, which he wasted no time wrapping around Mando's neck. Instantly, Mando reached for his neck with a useless attempt to grab ahold of the shoelaces, which only tightened as Jon-Jon applied more pressure.

"You thought you was gonna off me and my brotha like that!" snarled Jon-Jon, pulling hard to shut off Mando's air circulation.

"No! Jon…" Mando's face was protruding with thick veins as it began to turn red from loss of breath.

Dooley knew he had to get off the road now and was searching for some place to park—away from witnesses!

"Nahhh, mu'fucka! You wanted to be slick… I got ya ass now."

That's when Mando, nearly toward his last breath, reached for his waistband.

"Jon-Jon!" Dooley shouted, reaching over to knock Mando's hand away in a worthless attempt.

Grabbing ahold of his gun, Mando snatched it up and aimed it over his head. Jon-Jon ducked just in time—or else his brains would've been all over the place. Then came two more untrained blasts from the big pistol, as Jon-Jon kept his head ducked while pulling as hard as he could on the shoelaces. Jon-Jon was hollering now, but out of rage.

The blasts of the gun ceased, for Mando had used up all of his strength. His movements came to a stop. There was nothing left in him to fight for.

"Sonnavabitch!" Jon-Jon shouted angrily, minutes later.

When Dooley looked over, he saw that Mando was no longer breathing. Jon-Jon had choked him to death.

"Ah, shit man. We . . . we gotta do somethin' with him, Jon-Jon."

"Fuck 'im!" said Jon-Jon. "Toss his bitch ass out the car right now."

"Not now," Dooley said.

"Whenever. Just as long as we do it!"

Dooley looked over at Mando's dead body again. *Damn,* he thought. *Mando is dead!*

"Fuck 'im!" Jon-Jon repeated, breathing hard. Then he slapped the dead man in the back of the head and laughed. "I should shoot his ass too."

Man, Dooley said to himself, *Jon-Jon is crazier than a muthafucka!*

Bang! came the near-deafening blast.

"What chu doing, fool!" Dooley almost jumped out of his skin.

"He tried to shoot me, bro."

"But he was already dead, Jon-Jon!"

Jon-Jon shrugged as he stared at the hole in the back of Mando's head. "Well . . . I was just making sure he was," he exclaimed.

Yeah, this nigga is crazy as hell, Dooley thought.

***

It was four hours later when Dooley and Jon-Jon walked through the front door of their apartment. Both of them were dead tired, yet not tired enough to fully relax. Their adrenaline was still pumping; they were still on edge from their recent activities.

"You think whoever was waitin' on us to show up gonna come after us now?" Jon-Jon asked, dropping down onto the large sofa with a sigh.

"If they do, we'll just have to go to war."

"They won't come."

"How you know?" Dooley asked.

"Because Mando won't be 'round to tell 'em what to do now."

Jon-Jon found a half-smoked blunt in the ashtray and lit it up. "By the time they find out what's up with him, we'll be good."

"They won't have no reason to suspect us."

"Nah."

Mando . . . Lydia gonna flip out if she find out that he's dead.

Jon-Jon said, "That bitch probably was up on that creep shit too. I wouldn't put nothin' past her ass."

Dooley was shaking his head. "I don't think she would've been down with it."

"Dooley . . ." Jon-Jon looked up at his friend, holding his gaze for a moment. "Don't start that shit. Nobody can be trusted no more. We all we got."

Where did I hear that from before? Dooley thought as he strolled over into the kitchen. *Shantel! Shantel had told me that same shit—and look where it got me.*

From the fridge, he pulled out his favorite Mott's apple juice and drank it from the jug. Then he sat down at the kitchen table and thought: *Today is my damn birthday and already, I almost had to kill somebody. This the worst fuckin' birthday I ever had!*

"What's on your mind, bruh?" Jon-Jon stepped into the bright-lit kitchen.

"What just went down, nigga!"

"Yeah, what about it?" Jon-Jon sat across from him.

"You think that's the end of the—"

"What the fuck you worryin' bout, bruh!" Jon-Jon snapped.

"It ain't the end of nothin'. This shit just started. Even if it didn't come from Mando, it woulda came eventually now that we on other niggas' turf. You think these chumps gonna just allow us to do our own thang without bein' tested? First shot, we need to bomb on them fools, earn our respect, then make somethin' happen."

Dooley nodded because he knew Jon-Jon was right. He knew how he thought—*they'd been friends so long, how could he not?*

"You right, man."

"Straight up though, I think we need to get in touch with that fool Sin and Mando's boys, Rolando and Al. You know, slide in on them like everything's all good."

"Now you talkin' crazy, man."

"Maybe I am. But it's worth a try."

"And if we do slide in on them, what the hell we gonna do? Huh, Jon-Jon?" Dooley questioned, wondering just what his friend had in mind.

Jon-Jon passed the blunt over to him and leaned forward against the edge of the table.

"We don't know nobody down here except for Sin now—plus that mu'fucka Al. We can use Mando's face to get through the door with them. Then once we establish that, we take off from there."

Again, Dooley nodded. "I'm down with that."

"We'll holla at Sin first—tomorrow—since we already got it in good with him."

Dooley thought about Mando's dead body now buried underneath a pile of trash in a local city dumpster.

"You know what else too, man?"

"What?"

"Them two tricks we had today."

"What about 'em? Nigga, fuck them raggedy hoes—"

Dooley cut in. "Wait a minute, dawg. Listen," he said firmly. "We can use them hoes to the best of our advantage. They know people who know people, and with that—"

That's when Jon-Jon interjected. "I already know, bruh. I already know."

From that moment on, the two comrades were on to the next phase. The mission was far from over, but there was a new route to be taken—and by any means necessary. They were bound to pave their own way, even if it killed them tryin'.

It was on and poppin'.

Chapter 21

T.K. answered the door to find Shaliah standing on the other side. Instead of letting her in, she stepped outside onto the porch with her. Since that night of the shooting, both girls had grown very close. Their lives had changed dramatically.

Arm slung in a sling, face tight and serious, T.K. stood before Shaliah and said, "Mama Lizzy said you had called earlier."

"I did, and you sleepin' your life away like you don't have one to live."

"My life is somewhere on the run," T.K. said, referring to Dooley. *I love you, baby.* She remembered his words as if they were being spoken at that moment.

How bad she'd love to hear him say those words of endearment just one more time.

"T.K.!" Shaliah shouted.

"Oh . . . yeah, what's up?"

"Girl, you gone." Shaliah shook her head. "Don't go buggin' out on me and shit. Anyway, Tanisha is on her way to pick us up."

"Where we goin'?"

"I'm tryna find out the same damn thang."

The statement made T.K. frown.

As if on cue, Tanisha's Chrysler 200 pulled up to a stop in front of Mama Lizzy's house. Tanisha tooted the horn once and remained inside the car.

Shaliah turned back to T.K. "You comin', gurl?"

With a pensive look, T.K. glanced back over at Tanisha's car and then at Shaliah. "Lemme go tell Mama Lizzy, and I'll be right back."

147

"Go ahead," said Shaliah, descending the porch steps as she approached the car.

After telling Mama Lizzy what's what, T.K. headed for Dooley's bedroom—her sanctuary, her comfort zone. Immediately she retrieved the .25 automatic pistol she'd found in his closet and tucked it in her purse. Then she went to her stash of the six grand Mama Lizzy had given her out of the twelve Dooley had left them. She took out five hundred dollars and placed it in the purse as well, but little did she know that a hundred more grand was being sent to her through Lydia by Dooley that same day.

"You be careful wit' that arm now, baby."

"I will, Mama," T.K. promised in passing. "I'll bring you somethin' back if you want somethin'."

"Chile, all I want is for you to be careful and come back in one piece," Mama Lizzy said from her rocking chair before the fireplace.

"I will," repeated T.K., and then she was out the door.

"Lord, please watch over that chile if you don't do nothin' else," she prayed for T.K.

Then she went back to her crochet needlework.

***

Sin was a short, stocky-built Cuban who had plenty of money and clout. Although friendly with Dooley and Jon-Jon as they basked in his presence in his large, spacious office, the two friends knew he was a true killer. *Mando had said as much,* but it was how Sin carried himself that was evident enough despite his amenity.

Mr. Club Fierce was a man to surely be admired—but also feared. They figured you had to be someone of importance to occupy Sin's main office. Especially being two young strangers who'd been introduced to him by his close friend the day before. Sin would give the two comrades the benefit

148

of the doubt, for he 'trusted' Mando without so much as a second thought.

It was hard finding those who had the type of loyalty Mando had sustained with him over the years.

"So what can I do for you guys?" Sin asked.

Jon-Jon looked over at Dooley, who had decided to do all the talking.

"We're just here to build our bond, you know, like more stronger," said Dooley.

"I see."

"We family now."

That made Sin's eyes rise. "From my understanding, family is the ones that can't be trusted," he said. "So please, don't use that term with me."

Maya, Sin's most loyal assistant, stepped over to refill his drink behind the desk. Tall, dark, and beautiful as ever, Maya—a former stripper herself—was the crème of the crop of Club Fierce. The first stripper who made the club what it was, and now officially its Vice President.

Sin accepted his drink with a nod.

"Anyway," Jon-Jon decided to speak up, "we're just tryna get in good with you, Sin, since we don't know nobody else down here." Then he looked over at Dooley.

Dooley said, "Another thing too. All we really tryna do is hustle and stack our money up while we down here. But that won't be as easy as it seems because we're on other people's turf. We don't want no problems—just hustle, have fun, and stay below the radar. Therefore, we need your help."

"You need my help with what? I don't deal in drugs, son. I run a respectable business here."

Dooley shrugged. "Who you think you foolin', Sin? If it wasn't for drugs, you wouldn't be where you at now."

Surprisingly, Sin didn't comment, so Dooley continued.

"Now, with your help settin' up shop, we'll pay you forty percent out of every ten grand we make. We got our own drugs, but when it's time to re-up—"

"We'll have our own connect by that time, bruh," Jon-Jon said.

"Right." Dooley thought of Walt's connect. "There's no doubt that you knew my brotha Walt, right?"

"Yes, I knew him."

"Then you should know how I gets down, because everything I know, I learned from him."

Sin nodded and took a sip of his drink.

"But how do we know that you can be trustworthy as we were with your brother?" Maya asked.

"Because we wouldn't be sittin' up in this fuckin' office right now, wouldn't we?" Jon-Jon challenged, and Maya suppressed a smile behind her own glass.

"You're absolutely right, Jon-Jon," Sin said. "Mando wouldn't have brought you here if he didn't trust you guys. And I approve of his judgment of character immensely."

"Then what's more that needs talkin' about?" Jon-Jon blurted out next. "Let's get this shit poppin'!"

That's when Sin held up a patient hand. "There's a lot more that we must talk about, son. Like I said, I run a respectable business here, and I will not jeopardize that without doing what's needed to be done."

"And what's that?" asked Dooley.

Without hesitation, Sin downed his drink and stood up. "Let's go for a ride, and I'll tell you all about it . . ."

***

The car was fogged up with weed smoke as Tanisha, T.K., Shaliah, and Tanisha's best friend Candi rode down Frankly Blvd., bumping some Jay-Z. They'd just picked up Candi and were on their way out to eat and shop. Because Candi was back home for a week from the Air Force, Tanisha decided to do it big for her girl. Both Shaliah and T.K. hit it off good with Candi, although Shaliah had already known her before.

It was another form of medicine for T.K.'s healing process, Candi had said—and with that, all four girls were on their way to having a good time.

"Where y'all wanna go first, to the mall or out to eat?" asked Tanisha.

"I need some food, gurl—some soul food, Italian, somethin'!" replied Candi in the back seat next to Shaliah. "That's all I wanna do the whole time I'm home. Eat!"

"Damn. They don't feed y'all in the Air Force?" T.K. asked.

"Yeah—dicks. And a bitch can't even get full off them." Candi laughed at her own joke.

"Bitch, you crazy as hell."

"Ain't nothin' wrong with eatin' a little dick every now and then."

"Hmph!" Shaliah puffed on the blunt.

"Hmph what, Liah? Don't act like yo fast ass ain't sucked no dick before, so don't go there."

"Better not let Cash hear you talkin' that shit," Tanisha said. "You know he'll get on that ass!"

"And I'll suck that dick too, get that fool mind right."

Everybody burst out laughing—except for Candi, who was now actually thinking about Cash. *How could one ever forget their first love?* Although Candi and Cash couldn't make it as a couple, the two were just as close as could be. They were the same in so many ways that it was difficult for them to maintain a decent relationship. However, you couldn't separate the two for nothin' in the world when it came down to the love and respect they had for each other.

"Speaking of Cash, what's goin' on with my boo anyway?"

Tanisha said, "He should have about a month or two left to do in the county."

"I'll go see him tomorrow."

"He prolly done gone slap crazy by now with what happened with Jon-Jon. You know how that fool is about his little brotha."

"No different than how Walt was about Dooley. Them four fools right there was made for each other," Candi professed.

At that instant, T.K. felt a pang of loss that her Dooley was not there with her. However, she knew without a shadow of a doubt that *wherever he's at, he'll do what needs to be done, and that she will see him again. Dooley will come back for her,* T.K. thought. *He wouldn't be gone forever from me; he loves me too much not to come back and get me.*

While they talked among each other, T.K. drowned herself in thoughts of the boy she'd grown to love.

Quietly, Shaliah glanced over in T.K.'s direction, knowing exactly what her new friend was feeling—and that same pang of loss ached inside her own heart for Dooley. She knew no matter how hard she tried to convince herself otherwise, she had to respect the game and let her have Dooley. Though it wasn't an easy task, she'd rather see him happy with T.K. than not see him at all. That's when T.K. turned and glanced over her shoulder at Shaliah, and just that brief eye contact of true understanding explained it all. As painful as it was, Shaliah let go.

***

The moment Dooley stepped through the door, the machete came down hard on the dead man's left leg. The limb was immediately detached from the body and tossed aside like a stripped chicken bone. Then the cutter did the same with the other leg. Shocked and caught in sudden fear, Jon-Jon and Dooley stared in horror at what was being done before their eyes.

"You see here, Dooley, Jon-Jon." Sin gestured toward the bloody mess in front of them. "This is what could happen to you if you ever cross me."

"What . . . did he d-do?" Jon-Jon stuttered, and it was then that Dooley recognized the now-dead man as Caesar—one of the several people Mando had spoken with briefly the day before.

The bartender at *Club Underground*. Then his head was severed savagely.

"Do you really wanna know, Jon-Jon?"

Jon-Jon looked over at Sin, answering him with his eyes.

"Well. Let's just say I've learnt of his and Mando's dealings behind my back," he said. "Connivance."

"Mando!" both Dooley and Jon-Jon said in unison.

At that moment, a side door opened and in came another body. Unlike the dismembered one before them, this one was a woman—and she was still alive!

"Oh shit!" Jon-Jon swallowed the lump in his throat as he and the woman's eyes met.

Bound and gagged, the big, three-hundred-pound goon shoved her through.

"Remember her well, don't you, Jon-Jon?" Sin spoke up again.

Again, Jon-Jon swallowed nervously as the big, massive goon threw the stripper face-down onto the plastic-covered floor of the basement. She was the Spanish beauty he remembered from the day before also—the same one who he'd had in his lap alongside the tall and sexy Black sistah.

"That's Pepper," said Sin. "She's a relative of Mando and had been playing a part in his and Caesar's scandal. Because of them, I've lost thousands and thousands of dollars in my club. It took a while for me to catch on. However, it has finally come to an end."

"What did they do?" Dooley asked.

"Made a fortune selling their own personal stock of liquor and champagne—among other things—in my club. Mando would come twice a month to pick up his pay and restock while pretending to pay a social visit to his long-distant buddy: me."

Now . . ." Sin stopped talking when Pepper, still gagged, screamed behind her gag as the large goon bent down and snapped her forearm in half like a pencil.

Both Dooley and Jon-Jon winced and flinched at the sickening sound of her bone breaking. All the while, the goon—who was drenched in blood and gore—was still hacking away on Caesar's mutilated body. There was no reason for him to do nothing other than his job as was demanded of him. Dooley was surprised to see that it was Joey.

"Remember that conversation we had earlier about trust, son?" Sin looked at Jon-Jon, then over at Dooley.

They both nodded.

"Good. Um, excuse me, Joey?"

Joey looked up from Caesar's body pieces and said, "Yeah, Boss?"

Sin reached out to him. "Give him the knife," he said, gesturing over at Dooley.

Without hesitation, Joey stood up and approached Dooley with the big, vicious-looking machete. Dooley took a cautious step back and pulled out his pistol at the same time. Joey stopped and looked at Sin questioningly.

"Give it to him," Sin said firmly, smiling for some odd reason.

Joey presented the machete handle-first, which Jon-Jon snatched from his hand instantly.

"What the fuck you got goin' on?" Jon-Jon demanded over the loud, agonizing cries of Pepper.

Then he flinched when he heard the snap of her second arm breaking. Jon-Jon felt very nauseated all of a sudden.

Nodding silently, Sin spoke up. "Now this where you will prove your trust—right here." He glanced over at Dooley. "Your choice, Dooley. You can kill everybody in this room right now, but I guarantee you, son, you won't make it outta here alive. It's a threat, but not intended. I just felt I should warn you, since it appears to me that you have murder on your mind. But allow me to assure you that I'm the one—me, Sin—you can trust, if only you'd just believe."

"What do you want, Sin?" Dooley asked.

"Your trust." Sin nodded over to Pepper.

Both Dooley and Jon-Jon exchanged glances.

And I thought Jon-Jon was crazy, Dooley thought. *But this Cuban is the craziest muthafucka!* It was then he came to the realization that Mando—who he thought was a true head honcho—was just a peon to Sin.

Sin was the real deal. Then a thought came to mind, and he turned to Sin. "I got a question. What's gonna happen to Mando now?"

Jon-Jon was lost in his own wicked thoughts at that moment. After a brief second of pondering his next answer, Sin offered Dooley another one of his evil grins.

"There's not much to do to him when you and your friend there already took care of him."

"What?"

"Don't get surprised. I had my boys follow you guys the moment you left my club yesterday. And I must admit—I was impressed with the results."

Now both of them was looking stuck on stupid.

"So you was gonna kill us yesterday too, huh?" said Jon-Jon.

"If it came down to it, yes. But I owe Walt much loyalty. He was a good man—my buddy, to be exact. However, my plan was to keep you both alive and warn you, like I'm doing now."

That seemed to satisfy Jon-Jon's curiosity. *At least the mu'fucka was straight up with a nigga*, he decided.

"So, are we clear on that?" Sin asked next.

"Yeah. I guess," sighed Dooley.

"Okay." He again gestured toward Pepper.

Without a second thought, Jon-Jon walked over and slammed the blade of the machete onto Pepper's arm, and just like melted butter, her arm was completely sliced through and separated from her body.

"Gotdamn! Oh shit!" Jon-Jon hollered.

Pepper's scream tore through the basement—high, raw, and blood-curdling—until it broke off into a choking gasp and silence as she collapsed unconscious. Blood was everywhere.

"Now you," Sin looked over at Dooley.

Reluctantly, Dooley stepped over alongside the now-bloody woman as they all looked on in silent anticipation. With the pistol still clutched in his hand, he aimed the barrel down at Pepper's still head. Then he looked over at Sin.

"This is where loyalty stands, Dooley," he said.

Dooley squeezed the trigger. *Boom!* Killing Pepper just like he had killed Kirk—with no remorse.

Chapter 22

The second Iris saw Shaliah and her crew enter the Applebee's restaurant, she called her cousin Dina. Soon as Dina got the word, she called her girl Londra, who then called Kerry—Lil Benny's big sister. From then on, other calls were made in response to what was about to transpire.

Iris, the instigator of the trouble that was soon to come, remained at her post behind the counter and watched them attentively. The bitch lived for drama!

The place was busy as usual for a Friday, diners moving to and fro throughout the restaurant in delight. And of course, despite T.K. with her arm in a sling, she and her girls were an interesting sight. They talked, ate, and laughed to their heart's content—the center of attention. None of them was aware of the threat lurking near. They were too caught up in their gaudiness.

Candi burped loud. "Damn, that was some good ass lemonade!" she exclaimed.

"Eww, you dead wrong for that, bitch," said Tanisha. "That was so unladylike."

"I learned how to do that in the Air Force."

That made T.K. laugh.

The sight of Shaliah approaching from the restroom caused them all to look up, but it was Candi who caught the serious look on her face and questioned it.

"Gurl, what's up with you? You fell in the toilet or something?"

But no one laughed this time.

Shaliah came to a stop at their table but didn't sit down.

"It's 'bout to be some bullshit poppin' off outside."

"Liah, whatchu talking 'bout?" T.K. frowned.

"Monica, is what I'm talking 'bout. Her and about ten more bitches standing out in the parking lot lookin' crazy and shit."

Candi looked over at Tanisha. "Who the hell is Monica... oooh, that young bitch y'all got into it with." She turned back to Shaliah.

"Her." Shaliah nodded.

T.K. grabbed her purse that was sitting in her lap.

"And you say it's 'bout ten of them out there, Liah?"

"At least, yeah."

That's when Tanisha reached for her cell phone. She stood up to go see for herself while dialing someone's number. Sensing the sudden tension spreading throughout the place, people looked up in growing curiosity, abandoning their food for the moment. Behind the counter, Iris anticipated the show that was about to go on. Both T.K. and Candi were now up on their feet, no longer interested in their food.

When Tanisha made her way to the other side of the restaurant that overlooked the parking lot, she scanned the group while speaking to someone on the phone. After a moment of observing, her eyes bulged, and she sucked her teeth in that stubborn way she always did.

"Gurl, and guess who I'm lookin' at out there too...Pam Jones and ol' crusty-ass Shannon Boo...You do that and get back with me. Aight, bye!"

"Who was that, Nisha?" asked Candi, coming up next to her.

"That was Chilly. Remember that bitch Pam Jones, Cee?"

Reluctantly, Candi answered. "The one I whupped up back in the day at Club Ready?"

"That same bitch is out there too."

"Let's go see what they got on their chest then," Candi suggested. "You know I gotcha back no matter what."

Both Shaliah and T.K. glanced at one another, and T.K. shrugged.

Shaliah replied bravely, "It's gonna happen anyway, so I don't really care."

Then Candi looked at T.K. with concern.

"I'm down for whatever, Candi."

"You sure?" Candi said—and that's when T.K. opened her purse for the pistol and headed for the exit door without a backward glance.

Seeing the gun in her hand, Shaliah panicked. Tanisha and Candi went after her.

***

At the same time, Dooley and Jon-Jon were back on the road in their own car now, heading to Rolando's place. The two had been silent for quite some time, sharing a blunt while lost in their own thoughts. What had just gone down in the basement of one of Sin's hideaway buildings was beyond what they expected. Even now that they'd gained his trust, the situation still disturbed them—a little, if not a lot.

Of course, Jon-Jon was okay with it now that they'd won the favor of one of Miami's most feared men, but Dooley felt uncertain about taking orders from anyone other than Cash or Walt. He felt his position demanded just as much clout now that the torch had been passed to him. It was his job now to make sure the original code of the game was upheld, now that neither Cash nor Walt was around to enforce it themselves.

This the part Walt been preparing me for all along, Dooley thought.

It was Dooley's time to step up and demand his respect—however it had to come.

Filling in my brother's shoes gon' be a task, Dooley decided. *But I'ma do just that, whether I planned for it or not. Ball in my court now.*

"What we gonna do about this Mexican, Rolando?" Jon-Jon finally broke the silence.

Dooley exhaled smoke. "The same shit we went to Sin for—minus all that other shit if he on that too."

"But it's the only way we can get down wit' muthafuckas like that."

"Nah, man," Dooley said.

"Whatchu mean 'nah'?"

"Just what I said. The way we carry ourselves and handle our bizness gon' show if we trustworthy or not. We ain't gotta prove shit to nobody . . . We a force of our own. And we don't trust the next muthafucka either. They should be proving to us they can be trusted. We got just as much power as Sin or Rolando. All we gotta do is use that shit, bruh."

Jon-Jon nodded. "I see whatchu saying."

"If Rolando on some bullshit, then we get to steppin'."

"Or else we light his ass up too wit' hot lead."

"You just trigger happy."

"I just don't give a fuck! Shit, I damn near upped that steel on Sin and 'em too, but I waited to see how it'd play out," Jon-Jon said, taking the blunt in rotation. "I still can't believe they was on Mando's trail like that, and we ain't even know."

"Now we know." Dooley hit the left blinker and turned onto Prospect Road. "Mando really didn't know who he was fuckin' with. He was small news compared to Sin."

"Well, we 'bout to see what's up wit' this Mexican now."

"Straight up though, it's his brother I'm worried about. Fuck all that super-friendly shit he might be on just to peep our swag—"

"He'll get done in just like the rest of 'em."

"If it ever comes down to it, yeah. He gonna have to."

A minute later, they pulled up in the parking lot of *Rolando's Place*, a large Mexican restaurant over in South Beach. The building was one of those colorful two-story joints that wafted with the smell of rich Mexican food. Even Taco Bell wasn't interesting no more when Rolando's Place was involved.

"This a big-ass muthafucka!" Jon-Jon said, marveling.

"Which means we're about to walk in on some major money. You ready, man?"

Jon-Jon looked at him with an earnest expression. "Nigga, I been ready ever since we got off the bus."

Then he checked the clip of his pistol, slapped it back in, and got out the car. Dooley shook his head and did the same.

***

It was nine girls in all, standing out in the parking lot, waiting anxiously for Shaliah and T.K. to come out. There was no jewelry or high heels on any of them—they came ready to get it down. Just when Kerry, Lil Benny's and Monica's older sister, was about to say *fuck it* and go inside, T.K.'s exit from the building was what she least expected.

Gasps were heard throughout the group as they watched T.K., pistol clutched in her good hand, make her way toward Tanisha's car. She glared at them all, hoping they wouldn't give her a reason to use it. None of them said nothing to T.K. Iris didn't know what to do, watching from inside the diner. Several cars away from the half-shocked, half-scared group of girls sat Tanisha's Chrysler 200, and T.K. headed straight there.

"What's all this shit you got goin' on, Pam?" Candi couldn't help but question her former enemy.

"This got nothing to do with you, Candace," said Pam— a six-foot, plump-looking **Foxy Brown** lookalike.

"It got everything to do with me."

"Me too," Tanisha said, glaring at Shannon Boo. Then she looked at Kerry and said, "Y'all done had enough trouble as it is. I'm sorry 'bout what happened to your brotha, but keep fuckin' around, and you just might get burned too."

Kerry glanced over at T.K., who'd stopped halfway to Tanisha's car and turned around.

"Is there a pro'lem? 'Cause if there is, we can get it done now," said Candi, facing the crowd head-on.

It wasn't the fact that T.K. was packing heat that made her speak the way she did—she'd always had heart and didn't back down from nobody. And being trained in martial arts, she knew damn well none of them stood a chance in a fight against her.

"My brother is dead, Tanisha," Kerry spoke up.

"So... what do my sistahs got to do wit' that? Seems to me y'all came way over here to start some trouble—nine of y'all bitches! Well, it ain't goin' down like that today—or any day."

"The beef was between Shaliah and Monica, and they already handled that like women," Candi added. "Whatever happened after that ain't had nothin' to do with them."

"It's Monica's fault it went down the way it did—comin' at Liah with all that hating shit. Plus, she the one who sprayed Jon-Jon with that mace."

"That's enough, T.K. We don't owe these hoes no explanation. They know what happened." Shaliah walked away toward the car.

"One last thang." Tanisha turned to face Kerry, her former classmate.

Kerry interjected. "Y'all dead-ass right," she said. "What's done can't be undone—my brother still gon' be dead regardless. However, I came here to get—"

"Your ass beat if you test my gangsta!"

"Cee!" Tanisha held up a hand at Candi. "Anyway, if Monica or you feel like y'all got something else on your chest, then meet us at Madison Park. If not, then move on and keep it movin'."

Just like that, Tanisha turned and made her way to the car.

"I'll whup all you bitches . . ." Candi smirked at the group.

"Come on, Cee!" Tanisha called out.

"Bitch!" said Candi, glaring at Pam before walking off.

After watching them all pile into the Chrysler, Monica turned to her big sister.

"You gonna meet them at Madison Park?"

There was a brief silence that swept over the group as everybody waited for Kerry's answer. Laughter floated from the car as Tanisha and her girls sped out of the parking lot onto Broadway. Still not sure what she really wanted out of this situation, Kerry looked at her little sister with worry in her deep, dark brown eyes.

"No, little sistah," she said. "They ain't the ones who killed Benny."

"Then why'd we come here?" Shannon Boo asked.

"I don't even know my damn self." Kerry sighed and walked away.

And that was the end of that matter.

***

"How may I help you today?" said the sweet-faced Mexican woman clerk behind the counter.

"We're here to see Rolando," Dooley said.

The woman frowned. "I'm sorry, sir, but Mr. Rolando isn't—"

"It's alright, Patricia. I'll take it from here," replied a medium-height, well-dressed Mexican who exited through the door behind her.

"Oh, Mr. Rolando!" she sounded surprised.

Dooley glanced at Jon-Jon briefly, then back at Rolando.

"I assume you're Dooley and Jon-Jon, am I right?" Rolando extended his manicured hand across the counter.

"You already know," Dooley replied, taking his hand firmly.

After taking Jon-Jon's hand—after a bit of hesitation—Rolando led them both back behind the counter and through the door. Instantly, multiple pairs of eyes looked up as they entered the large, noisy kitchen and stared at the newcomers. Some even nodded in passing while maintaining their positions. Jon-Jon followed behind Dooley with Rolando taking the lead.

"This is where it all happens—the essence of this restaurant," Rolando explained, stopping every so often to shake hands with one of his fellow employees.

"How long you had this one here?" asked Dooley.

"I'd say about ten years now. And there's seven more just like it spread out across the city."

They passed the vegetable section and rounded the corner to where the large stock shelves sat next to the massive refrigerators.

"This was my very first baby here. Then it grew and birthed another one a year later, and it was history from there to now."

"Everything's Mexican food?"

"Absolutely."

"I just may try some before we leave."

"Good," Rolando smiled. "Don't forget the special."

A moment later, they stepped into a closet-sized elevator that took them up to the second landing. Then Rolando led them into his plush office as both comrades looked around in awe at the unique setup. There was no doubt whatsoever that Rolando was a man of class and abundant wealth. The Mexican boss had gold all over the place! From the picture frames to his coffee mug—it was all made out of gold. There was even a large shiny black stone desk with gold trimming.

"You got two gold pistols that Nicolas Cage had in *Face/Off* too?" Jon-Jon asked with a straight face.

Rolando laughed. "One of my favorite movies, I must admit. But no—I don't have them. It's a good idea though."

Dooley took his seat before the desk while Jon-Jon remained standing, marveling over everything he saw.

Look at this nigga. He ain't even on point! Dooley thought with a frown, but when Jon-Jon threw him a quick glance and smirked, it was at that moment he realized he actually was.

Then he turned to Rolando, ready to get down to business. "How did you know we were coming?" he asked.

Lighting his cigar, Rolando said, "Your partner Sin phoned me and acknowledged your presence before you arrived."

That caused Jon-Jon to settle down now.

"I know all about Mando's disloyalty. Who do you think told him of Mando's deception?"

There was a silence that came over the room.

"Young man, we are a system here. Sin and I happen to be quite fond of one another's position. However, we've established a solid bond that will not be broken. As for Mando—he confided in me, and I trusted him just as he trusted me. But when disloyalty is involved, I must bring it to the attention of my own."

"What he did to Sin he could've did to you," said Jon-Jon.

"And you're absolutely right."

Dooley said, "Once a snake, always a snake."

"I agree."

"So you know why we're here too, then?" asked Dooley.

"I give everyone the benefit of the doubt, Dooley. Yes, I know why you are here. I presume it's the same reason your brother Walt came to me as well."

"What?" Dooley was alert now.

"The truth is what, Dooley," Rolando's eyes stared directly into Dooley's for a moment. "I am who Mando has so desperately wanted to know about. But you kept your tongue. And there, young man—there ain't no further need to question where your trust lies."

"Man, what in the fuck is you talking about!" Dooley demanded, feeling strange all of a sudden.

"Why, Dooley . . . I am Fedo—Walt's most faithful connect. And I've been waiting for a chance to meet you."

"Fedo?" Dooley's eyes widened. "You the Fedo . . . hell nah!"

Rolando smiled brilliantly. "The one and only, Dooley. Mucho gusto."

Then Dooley said, "Tanto gusto, too, amigo."

Jon-Jon looked at both of them as if they had gone slap crazy. "Y'all fools buggin'!"

Chapter 23

A couple months flew by like it wasn't nothing. Now that Dooley and Jon-Jon had the key to the streets of Miami, they jumped into the midst headfirst and hadn't looked back since. The two cronies' names were ringing like Christmas bells, and money was coming in from every direction. This was what Jon-Jon had been so eager to do ever since he stepped into the game. With weight to work with and Dooley at his side—along with Sin and Rolando's vouching for him on every turn—he couldn't be stopped.

Including Cheri and Amy, the two Spanish models who were playing their part under Dooley and Jon-Jon's influence, a newfound operation was definitely in order. It had been a long time coming. From coke to crack to heroin, the two cronies had it all. Within the month, Dooley had copped the '71 Chevy Caprice with the 24-in. chrome rims to complement its candy apple red paint job. The sound system was ridiculous—beating so hard like two gorillas was in the trunk wrestling.

The Dodge Magnum that Jon-Jon chose was by far the most beautiful thing he ever had—second only to his mother. Sitting on 26-in. rims and double-coated in its charcoal black and chrome exterior and paint job, you couldn't tell him his shit wasn't the cleanest. As far as the Chevy Impala Mando had given Dooley for his birthday, he had special plans for that.

Thanks to Sin's graciousness, Jon-Jon was allowed to hustle out of Club Fierce. It was actually his main post, other than using Amy's crib over in Dade City. Why Sin chose only him to grind out of his club, he didn't know, but Jon-

Jon was definitely taking advantage of the new setup. He was really cashin' out!

Playing the role of a hustler as well, Dooley still maintained himself as the young "boss" that he appeared to be. Especially now that he'd sent for T.K., he was sure to keep up his appearance. Accompanying her would be Lydia and Tanisha. Yeah, Dooley felt it was good to keep Lydia in the picture after what went down with Mando—and still, his body had not been found none whatsoever. After he and Jon-Jon dumped his body in that city dumpster, Sin's cleanup goons went to retrieve it and dispose of it at another location.

What bothered him and Jon-Jon the most was the fact that they couldn't attend Walt's funeral. So the two of them popped champagne in honor of Walt's death. It was a celebration of his legacy—which still lived while his soul didn't. *Though God may have made a haven for a gangsta, Walt was there amongst the rest of them. There was a palace for them all, be it dead or alive.*

"One more week and my nigga'll be home," Jon-Jon spoke through the diamonds encrusting his gold teeth—all sixteen of them!

"And then get some of his paper too."

"Why you think they call 'em Cash, bruh!"

Dooley sat anxiously behind the wheel of his car in the airport's parking lot.

"Trust me, I know."

"He gonna trip out when he see this shit," Jon-Jon said, refilling his cup of Hennessy. "All he know is that I'm alive and doing my thing." Then he looked over at the silent Dooley. "You can't wait to see T.K., huh?"

"Man, you know how long I been waitin' on this moment?"

Jon-Jon cocked his head to the side. "You really love that bitch, bruh. Just 'cause we ain't never really talked about her and shit—I can see how much you care for T.K."

"I love that gurl, Jon-Jon. It's crazy . . . I don't like all that silly emotional shit, but that bitch got me fucked up in the head," he professed, taking another hit of the blunt. "Remember when I told you how it all started?"

"Yeah, she was on some creep shit."

Nodding in agreement, Dooley released the weed smoke. "But somehow T.K. became *the one*, dawg. I mean, it was like this shit was meant to be, huh."

"Had to be, bruh."

"Yeah, it was. Even Mama Lizzy said the same shit when I texted her one day."

Jon-Jon burst out laughing. "You texted Mama Liz? Hell nah!"

"Oh yeah . . . T.K.—"

"You know what else too, Jon-Jon?"

"Please don't talk my damn head off with that mushy-love shit, bruh. For real, dawg—"

"You don't even know what I was fixin' to say," frowned Dooley.

"After everythang is everythang with T.K., I'ma send for Passion and her mama—NeNe too! I owe them, dawg. Everybody that stood by a nigga when I was down and going through it, I'ma bless 'em—"

Boom! came the thunderous slap against the hood of the car as both Dooley and Jon-Jon nearly jumped out of their skin. When they turned to see what it was, they were surprised to see a grinning Tanisha bent down, looking at them from the driver's side window. Immediately, Dooley reached for the door handle.

Tanisha jumped into Dooley's arms with total glee, hugging and kissing his face tenderly.

"My baby! I miss you! I miss you! I miss you soooo much!"

"I miss you too, Nisha." Dooley tried to remain calm.

"Damn, can a nigga get some love too?" Jon-Jon said, opening up his arms.

"Much love, lil brotha!" Tanisha hugged him too.

The ultimate moment was when T.K. and Dooley stood before each other. Dooley's heart gave a warm, gentle squeeze as he observed her from head to toe. She'd cut her hair short in a Halle Berry style that brought out her beautiful features. She'd also toned her body up to that perfect shape—and *damn*, she was wearing them jeans! Dooley couldn't believe his eyes. Emotions rushed through him all at once, leaving him speechless for a moment.

Then the tears came pouring from her pretty eyes as she stood there.

Damn, my gurl is so beautiful, Dooley thought.

Tanisha, Cheri, and Jon-Jon watched in silence. Then Dooley reached over and pulled her into his arms, kissing her forehead.

"I love you, T.K. I miss the fuck outta you!" he whispered.

"I love you too," T.K. cried happily, squeezing her man with all her might. "I love you so damn much."

And that's when a tear escaped his own eye, knowing at that moment he didn't ever want to be without her again.

He wanted this *forever*. Now he was happy again.

Chapter 24

Dooley licked his lips in anticipation as he stared down at T.K.'s beautiful, naked body. Then he leaned down between her legs, trailing his tongue across her jawline on up to her earlobe. When he bit down gently, she released a groan. Grinding his body onto hers, Dooley reached underneath to squeeze her ass, breathing heavy as his hands began to explore. Then he kissed his way down her body to her perfect titties and sucked a nipple into his mouth. T.K. arched her back and sighed pleasurably, digging her nails into his flesh, but it wasn't until his hand found her pussy—penetrating her with his finger—that she cried out.

T.K.'s body shivered in ecstasy, and just as smoothly, he trailed sweet kisses down her stomach and stuck his face between her wetness, then gave her a vicious tonguing. As she wiggled and bucked against his face, T.K. tensed and screamed as she climaxed for the very first time.

Feeling her quiver under his caressing and wicked tongue, Dooley drank up her sweet juices and sucked on her clit thoroughly.

"Mmm . . . Dooley . . . That feels sooo good, baby. I love you . . . I love you . . ." cried T.K. as her body shook.

In one swift motion, Dooley entered her womb, loving the way she felt and staring up at her. There was love and passion glazed in her sparkling eyes, her bottom lip caught between her teeth.

"Mmm, baby, you're so tight…" groaned Dooley.

As best as she could, T.K. met him with each stroke.

"All for you, baby . . . I love you, Dooley. Don't ever leave me no more."

"I won't." He pushed deeper inside her.

I can't leave her, Dooley let out a deep cry of pleasure.

Speeding up his rhythm, Dooley let out a series of moans and grunts as waves of pleasure erupted from him into her at the same time. They both came together, and T.K. drifted off into a peaceful sleep minutes later. The girl was drained—but also filled with satisfaction and love.

Then Dooley left her, but little did he know what he'd just actually did to her mind.

At Dooley's entrance, Jon-Jon looked up at him with a grin. Without even a word, he handed Dooley the glass of milk he'd just poured himself and filled another glass. With one turn, Dooley gulped down the milk and reached out for a refill.

"You got hands, nigga. I ain't your fucking maid." Jon-Jon pushed the jug of milk across the counter.

"We gotta handle that business in a minute."

"That's why I slid thru to scoop you up."

Dooley downed the second glass in the same fashion as the first one.

"I already got two bricks ready for dude."

"I still think we should tax that nigga for them two."

"Eighteen apiece is a good deal."

"Next time, he coughin' up twenty for each. That way we'll be doubling our money from what we get from Fedo."

Placing the glass into the sink, Dooley turned back toward his crony. "Give me a minute so I can get ready," he said. Then he made one more reply. "Where Lydia and Nisha?"

Jon-Jon snorted a laugh. "You already know! Both of 'em down at the beach wit' Cheri and Amy."

All Dooley did was shake his head and retreat back to his bedroom. T.K. was still sleep, snoring softly. He left a message on her Samsung, then readied himself for the mission.

Thirty minutes later, both Dooley and Jon-Jon were heading toward Opa Locka to meet with their clientele,

Wizdom. They'd been supplying him for a little over a month now. Jon-Jon had introduced him to Dooley after connecting with him in Club Fierce. However, Wizdom was a local underground rapper who hustled major coke on the side. Especially after hustling his mixtape CDs out the trunk of his car and cutting hair for a living, he decided to invest his profits into the dope game.

Down in Miami, everybody hustled—whether it was washing cars, being hitmen, or selling lies for profit. It was the norm. If a muthafucka wasn't hustling in Miami, then they had no life whatsoever worth being of essence in the sunny city.

Now Dooley and Jon-Jon were having their turn.

After reaching their destination, Jon-Jon checked both of his 9mm pistols and tucked them back in his waistline. Dooley did the same and reached back to retrieve the Polo shopping bag.

"Let's get this paper, bruh."

"And don't let the paper get us," Dooley finished their new saying.

Together, they exited the Dodge Magnum and scanned their surroundings briefly before approaching the big white house. The whole entire area was crawling with children playing in the road and front lawns, niggas hanging out on their street corners while the hood chicks maintained their positions. This was the ghetto for sure, as the whole neighborhood seemed to reek of weed, pissy Pampers, crack, and fried pork chops.

The hood reminded Jon-Jon of back home.

Once at the door, Dooley knocked. Jon-Jon surveyed his surroundings thoroughly while waiting. The door opened to reveal the old Black woman named Flo, who stepped aside to allow them to enter.

"What's up, Ms. Flo?" Jon-Jon greeted.

"Nuthin' much, baby. Just coolin' it… tryna stay off these old knees," she said.

Dooley embraced the old lady as always and dropped a hundred dollars in her robe pocket.

"Still looking good as always—"

Then she snapped, slapping him across the arm. "I ain't gon' keep tellin' you, baby, to stop givin' me yo' money. Wiz pay me enuff money as it is. Now take this back—"

"I don't do that 'cause I—"

"Don't back talk me, boy! Huh, take this back now." Flo pushed the money back into his hands. "Just havin' yo' company for a little while is all I need."

"Yes, ma'am."

"We gotchu, Ms. Flo," grinned Jon-Jon.

"Now go on and take care y'all bizness and sit wit' me for a little while. I got some banana bread and pound cake ready fo' when you come back," she said with the sweetest voice.

"Yes, ma'am," Dooley repeated.

Then the both of them walked throughout the house, down the hallway and out the back door. Wizdom waited on them next door, standing out on the back porch. It was their usual course—to be a step ahead of the game just in case the law ran down on them. That way, when they burst down Flo's door with the attempt to apprehend them on a drug bust, they'd already be next door getting rid of the drugs or hiding it safely as they possibly could. So together the two made their way over.

"I thought Flo was gon' hold up the money, fool. I heard her fussin' all the way ova here."

"You know how she is, man."

Wizdom dapped them both off in turn.

"But I love her old ass as if she was my own mama. Let'z see to this bizness tho," he said, and led them inside.

Once inside, the trio walked through the short hallway and made a left into the kitchen, and to both Dooley and Jon-Jon's surprise, a half-naked female sat at the table rolling up a Swisher blunt. She glanced up at them briefly and returned back to her task. Jon-Jon's eyes wandered every inch of her.

Setting the shopping bag onto the countertop next to him, Dooley said, "Two thatngz…"

Nodding, Wizdom opened the refrigerator and knelt down to retrieve the cash for the product. Then, all of a sudden, voices were heard somewhere in the living room across the hall, which Jon-Jon was now alert to. He looked at Dooley; Dooley looked at him and gave him a silent nod.

It didn't take long for Jon-Jon to click into beast mode, but he held steady and firm with his back against the wall. This way, he could watch both directions while Dooley directed his attention on the main target.

"Thirty-siz stackz on deck, fool!" Wizdom stood and set the bundle of money onto the table next to the chick.

Dooley moved over to the side of the table and began counting the money himself.

"Yo, Lyric, get right and see about that there."

"I gotchu, Wiz," said Lyric, finishing preparing the blunt and handing it over to Wizdom.

Then she stood up in her two-piece bikini and stepped over to the counter where the two bricks were. Her 44-inch ass jiggled so out of control that Dooley fucked up his count and had to restart. Jon-Jon willed himself to stay focused and alert, though he took a peek at just what she was working with in the ass department.

"Nice," whispered Jon-Jon, readjusting his dick in his Coogi shorts.

Wizdom looked at him with a smirk.

With a knife, Lyric split open one of the bricks and made herself a line right there on the counter, and with just as much preciseness, she snorted the healthy line of coke in one take. Eyes shut, head tilted back as the high instantly took effect, Lyric grinned.

"It's the real deal, baby. And when I say the real deal, I mean the real-deal!" she replied with emphasis.

"And that's every shot, dawg," said Jon-Jon.

"I don't doubt that, fool," said Wizdom. "But you know how the game go."

"See, that's the pro'lem, homie. It ain't no game. It's the real deal," added Jon-Jon, sneaking another glance at Lyric. "And I mean the real deal."

Lyric laughed. "I can't feel my face."

***

After reading Dooley's message twice for reassurance, T.K. padded down the hall into the kitchen, where she fixed herself a drink. She downed two cups without a problem and returned back to the bedroom after realizing she was still naked.

T.K. changed into the brand-new outfit she'd brought along with her and strung up her brand-new Air Jordans. That's when she saw the fresh-rolled blunt laying atop the dresser. Then she switched on the stereo system, and Meek Mill's *Church* track boomed from the speakers. Lighting up her spliff, T.K. toured the apartment for the very first time since arriving there.

Damn, my baby got this bitch decked out! T.K. marveled in silence.

Everything was black, leather, shiny, and elegant with each landing her eyes fell upon.

"I know that's right!" T.K. snapped her fingers when Nicki Minaj's smooth flow poured from the speakers throughout the apartment.

Then she decided to step outside into the wonderful sunshine. Before she even realized what was happening, a young boy flew past the door the moment she opened it. He was being chased by another young boy his age or a bit younger, as they both laughed in total glee.

They were on the second landing, the top tier, which T.K. could partially overlook the parking lot area from above. With the sound of children's laughter and music playing behind her, T.K. found herself in a peaceful state. She was content with her life now—satisfied in a way she'd never even imagined.

"Hey!" a voice called out to T.K.'s right.

Leaning against the railing, T.K. looked over to see another girl around her age closing the door next to Dooley's apartment.

"What's up?"

"What's yo' name?"

"T.K."

"I'm Missy," the girl said, stepping over to stand next to T.K. "Where you from, T.K.?"

"ATL, Georgia."

"Oh." Missy seemed thoughtful for a moment. "You Dooley's wifey . . . the one that got shot."

The statement caused T.K. to flinch and turn to look at Missy oddly.

"He told you that?" she asked.

"Gurl, that boy been representin' you since day one. By now all the gurls know Dooley is locked in wit' you."

"Well, that's my husband."

"A true one too," said Missy. "It's hard findin' niggaz like that these days. You got yo'self a winner, gurl."

Trust me, I know, T.K. wanted to say, but her lungs were too filled with weed smoke.

"But you'll have to be careful round here. These skanks are very disrespectful—"

"I got ninety-nine problems, and a bitch ain't one."

"I sure hope so."

"Look . . . Missy. I came down here to be with my man as happily and as easy as I could, you feel me? And if the next bitch can't respect that, then I'm shuttin' shit down. Simple as that. Fuck how many, how bad, or how big—bitches better beware when it comes to that one muthafucka right there."

T.K. looked straight in her eyes.

Now Missy was aware of T.K.'s gangsta side, which appeared to be exactly what she expected. The fire in her eyes and the love in her heart for Dooley was blatantly obvious. Missy knew that eventually, T.K. would really have to be tested no matter what. She just hoped that T.K. would be ready for what lies in waiting for her.

"While we at it, put me up on game. I need to know everythang and everybody who poses any problems round here," T.K. spoke up again.

"Shit, that's just about everybody," Missy said.

"Then tell me about everybody."

***

"It's all there," said Dooley as he began placing the money into the same shopping bag.

"Of course it is fool." Wizdom replied as weed smoke wafted from his mouth. "I do you the same way you do me."

"And that's the right thang."

Then Wizdom said, "And that why I fucks wit' you."

Lyric was now sitting at the table, stuck, eyes wide as moons as she worked on catching her drain.

"When you gon' slide thru and let me cut you up, Doo? Lemme get some of my money back."

"So you can give it back to me later?" Dooley decided to just dump the money inside instead. *"Fuck that neat shit!"* he thought. "It's 'bout that time anyway. But I gotta run right now, man."

"You know where I'm at."

"I'll hit you up on that soon." Dooley dapped him off and both he and Jon-Jon retreated to the back door.

The warm sunshine was comforting as they descended the steps of the porch and made their way next door. It was best that they retreated their steps for no other purpose than that of which they'd come.

"You wanna chill wit' Ms. Flo or what?" Jon-Jon asked.

"For a few minutes then we gone."

"You seen that bitch, Lyric bruh? I swear I'd nail that bitch to the cross if she get caught solo. That's a bad bitch right there." Jon-Jon climbed the steps first.

"She straight."

"She thick like Buffie."

"Nah, Buffie thicker than Lyric."

Jon-Jon was about to argue the matter but thought better of it now that he opened Flo's back door. At once there was an eerie feeling came over Dooley as they entered the house.

"I smell that pound cake too," muttered Jon-Jon.

With each step forward Dooley eyes surveyed all over the place. The quietness was what seemed so disturbing to him. Coming upon the living room Flo was not there sitting in her favorite chair waiting on their return like she always did. So they made way for the kitchen, and when they got there they found a dead Flo sitting at her kitchen table with her eyes wide open.

"Oh shit! Oh Shit!" Jon-Jon panicked.

"Hell nah!" Dooley rushed to the old lady side and touched her arm.

Her skin was cool to the touch in the warm kitchen. Dooley stared at the old lady as she sat back in the chair upright, but head tilted slightly to the side.

"Dawg, we gotta get the fuck up outta here!" said Jon-Jon, refusing to look at the dead old lady.

Instantly Dooley thought about his Mama Lizzy as a sudden pang was felt in his heart.

"We can't leave her like this man."

"What the fuck we suppose' to do, drag her out the whip and go joyriding or somethin'!"

"I'm fenna call Wiz and let him know. Then I'm hit up—"

"The police? You gonna call the fuckin' police!"

"Chill, Jon-Jon."

"Fuck chillin', I say let's leave her old, wrinkled ass and dip!" but Dooley was already calling Wizdom's number and explained what was going on.

"A'ight little fool, 'preciate that." Wizdom sounded sad all of a sudden. "I'm 'bout to send Lyric over there to take care of everythang"

Dooley hung up with Wizdom, kissed Flo's cheek and made his exit, but before he stepped back out into the bright sunshine; he could've sworn he heard Jon-Jon sniffle behind him. Then when he looked back over his shoulder at him, he could've sworn he saw his best friend's eyes glazed with tears that he fought to keep at bay. The monster in Jon-Jon still remained with emotions after all. Dooley couldn't blame him for Flo was actually one of the good women left. Now that same good was taken away from this world. However, he just hoped it was from old age instead of anything else.

"That's fucked up," Jon-Jon murmured once they got into the car.

Dooley said, "But she'll never be forgotten."

Then they were off toward their next destination.

Chapter 25

Days had gone by without any further incidents. Dooley and T.K. were getting along well, living a life that had been promised to many who've never experienced it. Sin, Rolando, and Al were all taken by T.K.'s no-bullshit demeanor and loyalty to Dooley, but it was Rolando's brother Meechie who adored T.K.'s appearance. Jon-Jon, having been the one who shot her, did everything he possibly could to prove how truly sorry he was for hurting her.

Lydia and Tanisha shopped out of control, basked in the sunshine, and Dooley was happy to be a part of their own blithe. There wasn't nothing in the world he wouldn't do for them, but their time was coming to an end down in the Sunshine State. Neither one of them was ready to leave just yet. However, Tanisha had to retrieve Bryson from Mama Lizzy's care before he drove the lady crazy. The boy was an animal! So their last day was spent as a family gathering. That morning, Dooley sent the girls out to the salon to get themselves did up nice and pretty, took them out to eat and a movie, then showed out later that night in Club Ace. They popped bottles, smoked lovely, ate fried and barbecue hot wings and shrimp in the club. They did it big for their last visit together.

The next morning, both Lydia and Tanisha were on the plane heading back to Carolina.

"I swear, Nisha, next time I go back I'm staying," said Lydia as they rode first class. "That was more than a damn tease, honey. That was a change of life."

"Who you tellin'!"

"Dooley's done quite well for himself."

Tanisha nodded. "And I'm proud of him too. He's really grown up a lot."

"I see so much of Walt in him."

"Of course! That's who made him who he is today. After they Mama went to prison and died, Walt was the big brotha and the daddy. Plus, Mama Lizzy molded both of them well too," professed Tanisha. "Then my Mama . . ."

Lydia cut in. "I envy T.K.," she said.

That made Tanisha laugh. "You wild! But I like that though. T.K., that's my lil sistah right there. I love how much she care about Dooley; her loyalty is like no other."

The flight attendant strolled down the aisle with a cart loaded with snacks and drinks. The blonde-haired woman was tall, sleek, and pretty as hell! From several seats down, the flight attendant and Lydia's eyes met. She smiled, and Lydia felt herself tingle inside.

"Looks like somebody's feelin' somebody," Tanisha remarked with a smirk.

"Hmph!" Lydia watched the flight attendant. *Just as long as she don't cross that line. And if she do . . .* Lydia shook her head. *I will have my cake and eat it too.*

Tanisha laughed.

"Is there anything you want during your flight, ladies?"

"Plenty," Lydia said, licking her lips.

"Well," said the flight attendant, whose name was Cynthia, "I think I could manage whatever you desire, ma'am."

"Lydia," said Lydia. "Call me Lydia. However, I won't mind having a couple of 'nuts' before the plane lands."

Smiling, Cynthia said, "Yes, I definitely can manage that."

Lydia couldn't be happier. Tanisha could only shake her head.

"Y'all is a trip."

***

The Chevy Impala was tricked out just to T.K.'s liking as she drove through Carol City with Dooley on her side. Sitting on 20-inch rims and the color of cotton candy blue, T.K. was in love with her new car. You couldn't keep her from behind the wheel.

"You sure 'bout this shit, T.K.? 'Cause I'm not coming out here for no bullshit!"

"I'm tellin' you, baby, my cousin is straight," T.K. exclaimed, firmly. "Nadja won't say nothin'. I know she won't. She don't even like my mama's phony ass either."

"And how long she been living down here?"

"For about five years now. She graduated from the University of Miami, and now—"

Dooley interjected, "She got a man?" he asked. "'Cause I'm not feeling this shit as it is, and I ain't got time to deal wit' no country-ass nigga."

"I don't know," she said. "All I know is that she be modeling and stuff, doing music videos. Nadja's good people. She's my uncle Chuck's daughter."

"Well, we'll see," he replied.

The day before, after wrestling with the decision, T.K. told Dooley about her cousin Nadja. She feared he wouldn't want to have anything to do with her, but after pleading with him, he agreed to meet T.K.'s cousin. His only concern was Nadja running her mouth and telling T.K.'s whereabouts to her parents. Losing T.K. was his only fear at that moment— especially now that his heart was involved.

I've lost too much as it is, Dooley thought.

He'd hold court in the streets about T.K., and no doubt about it.

"Lemme ask you something, baby."

"Ask," he said.

T.K. passed him the blunt. "Do you trust Cheri as much as you seem to?"

"Why you asking me that? You know something I don't know?" he was curious.

"It's just that she deals with so many niggas . . . I don't know. I don't think she'll hold firm under pressure when one of them fools get on some dumb shit."

"To her or me?"

"Either or. But I doubt they'd come for you knowing that you stay on point. They'll try to use her to get to you."

"What made you come to that conclusion?" Dooley asked before taking a hit of the blunt.

T.K. looked at him with a stubborn expression. "C'mon, Dooley, I ain't that lame. A nigga pullin' some creep shit is what to expect in the streets. Especially when there's some major money involved—a nigga'll try his luck regardless whether you got your shit right or not. It's the norm, baby."

Dooley nodded and exhaled the weed smoke. "It is what it is. If a nigga—"

"I'ma see just where Cheri stand at with you for real."

"How you gon' do that?"

She glanced at him. "Put that pressure on her ass. We'll see, one way or another, if she's true or not. 'Cause I'd be damned if I allow a weak bitch to be the reason my man is fucked up."

"What about Amy then?"

"Oh." T.K. smirked. "I put her ass to the test yesterday. And if Cheri is anything like her, then we got some loyal bitches," she said sternly.

"Do whatchu do, baby," Dooley replied. "Do that."

"Believe me, I am," she promised with finality—and that was the end of that conversation.

***

Seventeen minutes later, they pulled up in front of Nadja's townhouse dirt driveway. She had met them a couple of blocks away after T.K., not knowing the rest of the way.

From there, she led them to her home, which she shared with her female friend Diamond. Though Diamond wasn't there, it wasn't long before Nadja brought her friend into the conversation—even in her absence.

Immediately, Dooley was strongly taken by Nadja's ghetto demeanor. The way she dressed to the way she carried herself—she was definitely someone he could grow used to. All T.K. could do was smile and look at Dooley with eyes that said, *"Told you my cousin was straight."*

"Well, at least I got fam down here wit' me. Though I'd never expect it to be you, though, Takira," said Nadja, referring to T.K. on a more formal basis.

"Just as long as you don't—"

"Chile, please!" Nadja rolled her eyes. "I know the game... I *am* the game!"

In all, Nadja was happy to see her cousin.

"So, what're you doing for yourself while you down here?"

Both T.K. and Dooley looked at each other.

Nadja caught on and said, "Housewife shit? Naw, lil cuz, you in Miami now."

T.K. interjected. "I just got down here a week ago. I just wanna get adjusted first, then see. Maybe I'll..." she shrugged. "I'll find something."

"What about you, Dooley, what do you do?"

"I hustle," he said simply.

Eyes raised in response, Nadja drank her Smirnoff wine cooler.

"You hustle, huh? What kinda hustle your lil ass doing?"

"Is it necessary?" Dooley said coolly.

"Yeah, it is—when my cousin is involved! Regardless if you her man or not, I need to know where the fuck you stand. 'Cause I ain't finna have her riskin' her freedom and life over no petty—"

"Petty!"

"That's what I damn-well said, lil nigga."

As calm as he could, Dooley put his glass down on the coffee table in front of him.

"Straight up, Nadja, if I want to, I can buy five of these houses you living in right now. Questioning my hustle is none of your goddamn business. But to reassure you, my hustle's so good that T.K. won't never have to work a day in her life—a young boss nigga! You got that, big cousin?"

Stuck on stupid, Nadja downed her drink then stood up to retrieve another one. She didn't even look Dooley's way at all. T.K. looked over at her man quietly with nothing but love and respect in her eyes.

This bitch think you fuckin' wit' a peon, T.K. he said. *She don't even know!*

"She don't . . . Now she know."

Then there was a knock at the door, and T.K. stood up to go answer it.

"I got it, cuz!"

"You don't answer nobody else damn door, T.K."

"This the problem, baby. It isn't just a nobody—it's my cousin's door," she shot back over her shoulder.

Dooley reached for his pistol tucked—but came up empty handed, for he'd left it in the car.

I need to tighten my game up for real, he told himself. *I'm slippin', and I can't afford to do that. Shit!* he muttered.

Then his cellphone rang, but the male's voice at the door held most of his attention. He answered his phone anyway.

"What's up?"

"Dooley, my man! How's it going, buddy?" replied Rolando's merry voice.

T.K. and the middle-aged guy stepped into Dooley's view, and he stood up. Nadja came into the living room next from the kitchen.

"Chillin', man. What's the deal? You hollered at Jon-Jon yet?" Dooley asked, eyeing the stranger.

"That's why I'm calling, buddy. I was supposed to meet with him at noon—it's going on two o'clock now. Any word from him yourself?"

"Nah." Dooley was instantly worried now. "You tried both of his phones?"

"The house phone also."

"How about Cheri's crib?"

There was a brief pause. "I should've known. I'm about to do just that right now."

"Do that and let me know what's up. That's where he prolly at anyway." Dooley watched as Nadja served the stranger a few bags of weed and sent him on his way.

Muthafucka! Dooley thought to himself. *This bitch is a hustler too.*

As if reading his mind, Nadja looked over at him with a devilish grin.

"Alright, buddy. I'll hit you back soon," Rolando said. "Oh—one more thing!"

"Yeah, what?"

"Me and Olivia thinking about going out for dinner tonight. What'd you say you and your girlfriend tag along with us—if it's not out of your way or anything? You know Olivia's anxious to meet T.K."

"I'll see what T.K. talkin' 'bout and call you back later."

Dooley really didn't want to go. But if T.K. wanted to, then he was game.

"Okay, sorry to have bothered you."

Dooley hung up with the Mexican boss and sighed. He didn't understand Rolando's friendliness yet—especially with him being a man of his position. Or was it that he wasn't used to genuine kindness and amity from people when all he'd ever dealt with was drug users and phonies? Rolando's consistency with being this kindhearted, respectful, innocent-type person *irked* him—when he knew good and well the man was a cold-hearted killer. Rolando was one surely to be feared.

Fedo, to be exact!

"What's wrong, baby?" T.K. asked, coming up to him and looking in his face with concern.

Without hesitation, Dooley leaned forward and kissed her on the top of her nose. T.K. blushed.

"Nothing's wrong, baby. I just love you, that's all."

"I love you too," T.K. hugged him.

Looking past T.K.'s shoulder at Nadja as he held the girl he loved, Dooley met her eyes and held them. There were no other words that needed to be discussed when loving T.K. was involved. Because it was then, as Nadja saw in his eyes, someone whose love was of a *sure thing.*

Secretly, Nadja became envious.

She needed to be loved too.

Chapter 26

That evening, Dooley decided to take up Rolando's dinner invitation. How could you decline such an invitation from one of the most well-respected, ambitious drug lords in the game? Especially when the person who holds his heart would be present as well. Dooley made his decision faithfully.

Without failure, T.K. was immediately taken a liking to by Olivia and had played her position as elegant as she could. Though she hated wearing heels and attending such gatherings, she knew it would please Rolando and his beautiful wife.

Jon-Jon was laid up with some bitch in the hotel, getting his nose treated. Since meeting Lyric on the low and being in possession of some of the best coke in the city—and having an addiction herself—he fell in line. It wouldn't be long before he was strung out on the powder, or Dooley found out about his new cocaine habit. Once that was out of the closet, there wasn't no telling what the outcome would be.

After dinner, Dooley and T.K. cruised around the city, smoking weed and enjoying one another's company. They talked, laughed, and even became a bit intense at one point before T.K. sucked his dick and got him off—then they headed back home to finish what was started. But it wasn't until Dooley's cell rang that he got the surprise of the moment. He and T.K. were cuddled up in bed when the call came, and to Dooley, it was the best news yet.

"I'm here, lil brotha. Y'all niggas come scoop me up!" said Cash, sounding very excited.

"I'm on my way!"

Together, Dooley and T.K. hurried up and got themselves dressed to go retrieve Cash from the airport.

"Shit!" cussed T.K. "Jon-Jon ain't answering his damn phone again! I'ma kick his ass when I get him—watch!"

Dooley didn't say a word but just drove toward their destination.

However, Cash had been home a little over a month now. He had to handle some unfinished business. He wrapped up some loose ends and situations himself before actually making the trip to Miami. Cash was anxious to reunite with his baby brother and Dooley again, for he understood what all they had been through, and he desired nothing more than doing just that.

When he saw Dooley—after sending T.K. to retrieve him—Cash embraced his young comrade and laughed out loud.

"Damn nigga, you just about big as me now," said Cash.

"Been eatin' good, man."

"Where Jon-Jon?"

Dooley said, "Earning himself an ass whuppin' when I catch up wit' his ass."

At that time, T.K. was calling his phone for the fifth time.

"I left 'im a message. Prolly somewhere up to no good."

Cash settled into the back seat of T.K.'s car. Then he laughed again just for the hell of it.

"'Bout fuckin' time yo no-good ass answered the phone."

"Wait a minute, boy, somebody wanna say something to you," she said and handed Cash the phone.

Cash grinned and said, "Heads up, lil brotha. It's on and poppin' now—what'z happenin'!"

"Cash!" They all heard Jon-Jon's loud excited voice yell through the phone.

"In the flesh, dawg!"

There was a pause, then Jon-Jon said, "Let's get this paper, big bruh!"

"Fo sho', dawg. Fo' sho'!"

Jon-Jon laughed. Cash laughed. And everything was alright again.

***

It didn't take long for Cash to reclaim his position in the game where he belonged. After two weeks of getting reacquainted with Dooley and Jon-Jon—and even Fedo and Sin and Al—Cash couldn't be stopped. He wished Walt and Wallow were there with him, as they usually were together getting money. But since they weren't, he was determined to live as if they were still there with him. It was him and his two young comrades now—who would take the places of the lost ones.

As for T.K., Cash respected her so much as far as Dooley and her relationship goes. But he wasn't too fond of sharing the game with T.K. at all, no matter how much she impressed him with her loyalty and love for his brother and Dooley. That was before Nadja came into the picture and tore down all those walls of uncertainty he'd built around him when females in the game was involved.

She'd come to change all that. And now Cash was introduced to a new part of the game—where bitches did exist. Now you couldn't keep the two apart from one another.

Dooley saw it coming before Cash even realized it had been staring him in the eyes all along. Cash had been bitten by a true diva, which literally changed his whole outlook.

Now Jon-Jon was extra cautious with his cocaine habit, now that Cash was back on the scene. He'd be damned if either he or Dooley was to find out. There were certain things—or habits—one can't break so willingly.

The same thing with T.K., who refused to break her concentration as she sat on the edge of the tub. She was waiting patiently for the results of her pregnancy test, and when it came, she rechecked the instructions to make sure she was reading it right.

"Oooh shit!" T.K. whispered softly.

She had been two weeks late from her period and knew it had meant only one thing. The results from the test confirmed it. Heart banging in her chest, T.K. ducked her head as if to pray, then stood up.

"I'm pregnant. I'm pregnant with Dooley's baby," and that's all it took before the tears came falling.

T.K. struggled to control herself, knowing how much Dooley hated when she cried. He said it did something to him.

Then she exited the bathroom and went straight for the telephone and called her confidante.

"Hey, baby gurl, what's up?" came Tanisha's voice.

"Tee . . . I'm . . ."

"Gurl, what!"

"I'm pregnant. I just found out—" but T.K. didn't get the chance to finish before Tanisha started shrieking happily into the phone.

"Does Dooley know?"

"No, not yet," said T.K. "You... think he'll be—"

"Don't start that bullshit. I already know what you fixin' to say. Bitch, you got the real one. So there's no reason for you to question that," Tanisha said firmly.

T.K. sighed. "You right, I'm trippin'."

Then Tanisha giggled. "I'm about to be an auntie!"

T.K. couldn't help but laugh and reach for her stomach. A wave of love and affection drowned her at once.

"I should go see a doctor, huh? To make sure it's . . . official."

Tanisha agreed.

The knock on the door interrupted their moment, and T.K. felt something in her heart squeeze.

"Somebody's at the door, Tee. I'll call you back later."

"You fuckin' better, bitch. You know what's up!"

After quickly hanging up with Tanisha, she went to go answer the door—but it was who she saw on the other side that made her frown as her happiness was just washed away.

When she opened the door, Cheri was standing face to face with her.

"Hi, T.K. is . . . Dooley here? I tried his phone but he's not picking up." Cheri replied.

"That's 'cause you called the wrong one, bitch!" *T.K. wanted to say*, but instead she said, "He went across the way over in Brown Sub for a minute. Come in."

Cheri was allowed inside, and she immediately saw the two suitcases next to the door. Both had just been emptied of multiple bricks of coke and were soon to be stored until further notice.

"Where you going?" asked Cheri, bringing the large McDonald's takeout bag into the living room with her. "You going somewhere?"

T.K. seemed to be taken aback by her question, and instantly a thought came to mind.

"Yeah, I'm about to go somewhere," she lied.

The lie made Cheri's eyes widen with curiosity, and before she could shoot out another question, T.K. excused herself to her bedroom.

I'm 'bout to check this bitch, muttered T.K. as she retrieved the chrome pistol from her Gucci purse atop the dresser. *May as well see about this bitch now while I got the chance,* she decided.

By the time T.K. made it back into the living room, stacks of cash were piled atop the table in front of Cheri. It was the re-up money T.K. had had in the bag, and Cheri was managing to stack it as perfectly as she could in neat rows along the table.

"I assume Dooley's going as well," she said, without looking up to see the menacing look T.K. was giving her.

Reluctantly, the next thing out of T.K.'s mouth was, "No the fuck he isn't. And for your information, I'm leaving him."

"What!"

"I'm leaving his unfaithful ass and takin' all his shit wit' me—so put all that money back in the bag, bitch. 'Cause I'm takin' that too—"

"No!" Cheri protested. "I can't let you do that, T.K."

Good, T.K. decided, and pulled out the pistol, smacking her across the face with it. "You wanna die over that nigga too, bitch?" T.K. hit her again—this time across the back of the head.

"T.K., no!" Cheri cowered over to the other side of the chocolate-colored leather sofa. "Please… just leave…Don't do this!"

"Nah, bitch, you know too much." T.K. snarled, heart beating fast as her adrenaline rushed through her.

The Spanish bitch cried. "I don't know anything! I swear to you—I don't know—"

"Where the rest of the stash at that Jon-Jon keeps at yo' crib? Huh, bitch?"

T.K. grabbed her by the hair and placed the pistol against her cheek.

"Where it at, bitch? I'll kill yo' ass right here—plus I know you fuckin' my man too!"

"No, T.K.! I'm not!"

"Don't lie to me, Cheri."

"I'm only . . . just Jon-Jon! Why are you doing this?"

Cheri froze when she heard T.K. pull the hammer back on the gun.

"Fuck that! You gonna tell me everything right now! Bitch, I'll blow yo' fuckin' face off if you don't tell me where that stash at. You got three seconds. One!"

T.K. saw the fear in her eyes, but she didn't see nor hear Cash when he came into the apartment with Nadja. They both stood quietly and watched, trying to understand what was going on. They'd heard it all, and without second thought, Cash had pulled out his own pistol—though Nadja was too occupied with the scene to be aware of Cash's discreet behavior.

"Please don't kill me, T.K.! Please . . ." Cheri sobbed uncontrollably.

"Two!" T.K. stepped back and aimed the pistol at her.

Cheri sensed T.K.'s seriousness and knew she had no other choice. She wasn't really built for this shit, and she didn't want to die—so she surrendered out of fear.

"Alright! I'll tell you everything," she sobbed harder now. "Just don't kill me. Don't kill me—I'll tell you everything you wanna know," and she did just that.

"I knew it!" T.K. shouted angrily. Then she tucked the pistol behind her. "You phony bitch. You snake-ass hoe! You'll flip my niggas 'cause you can't stand pressure."

"I . . . I . . ." Cheri bawled.

That's when T.K. beat her ass nearly senseless, cussin' her disloyal behavior at the same time. All the anger and disappointment T.K. felt toward Cheri was unleashed, as she dragged her all over the place—beating her into a bloody mess.

All Nadja and Cash could do was smile, now aware of Cheri's hidden weakness. Cheri was a snitch—a rat—and there was a cold place for them in this part of the game, a place Cash knew exactly how to get to. *If Dooley could be here now . . . better yet, hear the things that was said.*

The half of his whole—his only love—the realest bitch in his corner right now, had just saved his life in more ways than one.

***

Missy and T.K. had become extremely close after learning the fact that—without having any clue at the beginning—they were just the same. Especially after Missy confessed that she wasn't actually from Miami, but from New Jersey, who just four years ago came to Florida with her twin sister. They'd escaped the life of being the victims of an abusive father who only drank wine and beer, and gambled his life into a major crisis.

Sissy, Missy's twenty-one-year-old twin sister, was now attending college while her other half chose the street life. Leaving their alcoholic, gambling father behind in Jersey, the two sisters made a life of their own—much better than the one prior.

Single, pretty, and with a two-year-old son of her own, Missy had had more than her share of the streets. Her baby daddy, a hustler in a class of his own, also had a solid reputation. Flex—whom Dooley was already aware of—was a renegade. Missy even regretted ever having met him, but he was her son's father.

Now, as she, Nadja, and T.K. left from the hospital after having the doctor see to T.K.'s fractured hand, she wondered if her friend was in danger or not. Because she knew Cheri personally—and who her brother Etho was. He was a lunatic about his baby sister. And if given the chance, Cheri would surely turn to him.

She'd told T.K. as much, which T.K. brushed off with nonchalance.

"I really don't give a fuck, 'cause he'll get some too," T.K. had said coolly.

"I'm just sayin', gurl."

"And I'm just sayin', Missy."

Nadja broke in. "You think Etho the only bad mu'fucka out there? He'll only just be recreation for them fools that's in our corner," she exclaimed.

"I'm not worried about him," said T.K.

Little did she know, Cash, Dooley, and Jon-Jon were burying Cheri's lifeless body far back off in the woods over in Miami Lakes. Etho would never know what actually happened to his baby sister.

"Anyway," Missy stated. "How about we stop by and get something to eat somewhere?"

"We can do that."

T.K. pondered on whether she should tell them about her pregnancy.

"I gotta taste for some curry goat and yellow rice," said Nadja. Then she added, "Jamaica's Way is what's up! My boy Ziggy'll hook us up. Y'all down for that?"

"Hell yeah!" both T.K. and Missy said in unison.

That's where the trouble lies—and neither one of them knew it.

Chapter 27

While Cash and Dooley were inside the store, Jon-Jon sat behind the wheel of his whip, getting high. He snorted the line of coke he'd made on his cigarette box from his pack of Newports. As always, the effects became active immediately as he whipped up the rest of the lingering coke with his finger and ran it over his gums. Then he lit up a Newport and stepped outside the car.

Killing Cheri and burying her was a disturbing ordeal, for he'd never thought for a moment she would turn out the way she did. *It is what it is,* he thought. Soon as the thought left his mind, he felt a pang in his heart—just a small buildup of emotion he'd held for her—but she had sold him out through a test of loyalty by T.K., which he was grateful for in the end. At any given time, she could've been the reason he lost everything—including his life—if ever the opportunity rose for a potential goon.

"Fuck it!" he muttered. "Can't trust them Spanish hoes anyway."

"Excuse me?" a female replied from across the hood of her car next to his.

He had been so caught up in his thoughts that he didn't realize she had exited the store.

"Didn't you just say something to me?"

"Oh, nah, ma. I'm . . . Nah. My bad," he said.

The female eyed him for a moment. "Aren't you Lyric's man?" she asked with a straight face.

"Lyric?" Jon-Jon looked confused and snorted back his drain.

"Like you don't know who Lyric is. She definitely knows who you are." She shook her head.

"I don't know whatchu talkin' 'bout."

"Chile please, I saw y'all all up in the club together. That's my gurl whether you know it or not."

"The only thang I wanna know is your name, ma," Jon-Jon said, moving around the shiny Dodge Intrepid to face her closer.

Damn, this a fine-ass Black bitch right here! he complimented her with his roaming eyes, licking his lips to punctuate his interest.

"I'm J-Baby," she said with that straight face and sparkling eyes.

"They call me Jon-Jon," he said smoothly, taking her hand.

"Doo, bruh. Check'im out!" Cash nudged Dooley inside the store and pointed outside.

Dooley looked up from over the top of the Debbie Cakes and pies section and grinned.

"Nigga stay puttin' his game down."

"I taught 'im well, huh?"

"Nigga, you was scared to holla at that bitch when she was just in here."

Cash laughed. "You got me fucked up. I pull everything I get at, lil nigga."

"Right," Dooley grabbed two Star Crunch pies, a bag of Hot Cheetos, and a Mr. Goodbar.

As they both made their way over to the beverage cooler, a big Chevy donk sitting high on 26" rims pulled up in the store's parking lot. The big, shiny white car roared to a stop behind Jon-Jon's Dodge Magnum, and two niggas jumped out.

Jon-Jon sensed trouble before it even appeared but reacted too late, as the two grimey-looking niggas closed in on him.

"What's up wit' all this shit, fool? You tryna get fucked up messin' 'round wit' my bitch—"

"Don't start no shit, Bean. It ain't nothing serious," J-Baby replied, stepping away from Jon-Jon toward the short, stocky, gold-toothed brotha with four-inch dreadlocks.

"Nah, fuck that! You young fools—"

"Listen, homie. You know the game. Who you need to be checkin' is yo bitch, not me. I don't know you, bruh. And you don't know me—"

Jon-Jon ceased when Bean's friend upped his big .45 and brought it to his face. Jon-Jon swallowed and stared in the nigga's eyes.

"You talkin' gangsta, fool," said the second one.

"Yeah dawg, he think he gangsta," added Bean, stepping up to Jon-Jon and slapping the cowboy shit out of him.

"Bean, stop! He ain't do nothin'!"

Whop! Bean gave her the same treatment—but hers was a backhand.

"Get yo ass in the fuckin' car, bitch," growled Bean, and turned back toward Jon-Jon. "I treat you young niggas like hoes too."

"Bitches!" said the second one, still aiming the gun in Jon-Jon's face.

"But you a gangsta behind the gun tho," said Jon-Jon, glancing in the store's entrance direction as Cash and Dooley exited.

"Nigga!" Bean drew back and was about to slap him again—before his face was splattered with blood and brain fragments.

Frozen, shocked still, he watched his homie's dead body crash to the ground beside him, and that's when Jon-Jon went for his gun and emptied more than half the clip from his 9mm into Bean. Majority of the shots were to the face, as J-Baby screamed in horror from inside her car with every wicked blast from Jon-Jon's gun.

"C'mon, bruh! Let's go!" shouted Cash as they all headed for the car and peeled off. But it was the look that Jon-Jon had given J-Baby that warned her to keep her mouth shut.

For the murderous glare in his eyes was far beyond any she'd seen, and she knew to do nothing other than go against his warning threat. *After all, Bean and his homie brought it upon themselves.*

***

During this time, T.K., Nadja, and Missy were sitting down at their table inside the Jamaican restaurant. The place wasn't as busy as it usually was during the afternoon hours. However, most customers would order take-out and begin eating. It wasn't long before they were all laughing and having a good time.

There was good food, music, and vibes circulating throughout the place—just as well as weed smoke, among other things. Jamaica's Way was legendary. No wonder it was the second-top urban Caribbean restaurant in the city. It was where one wanted to be.

"I'm pregnant," said T.K.

Nadja choked back her food, and Missy nearly broke her neck snapping it back to look at her friend in surprise.

And then T.K. told them everything.

"I'm about to be an aunt." Missy grinned broadly.

"That's the same thing Tanisha said."

Nadja looked bothered for a second.

"You told her and didn't bother to come to me first, T.K.? Damn, you just gon' put me on the back burner like that?" Nadja was literally hurt that her baby cousin didn't come straight to her when she found out.

T.K. saw the hurt in her eyes and shrugged. "What's the difference? I'm still pregnant with Dooley's baby."

"It's all good, we still happy for you, gurl."

"Which means you need to be more careful now."

"I'm always careful." T.K. took a bite of her jerk chicken and spooned up some fried rice.

"You know what I mean. I'm talkin' 'bout cuttin' the fool like you did earlier today."

All T.K. did was nod and chew her food. Then, all of a sudden, the entrance door swung open and in rushed two masked goons with a shotgun.

"Ohmigod!" Missy whispered in sudden dread.

"Open that shit up and gimme the money now!" barked the taller one out of the two.

"And don't nobody move or I'ma bust a hole in yo ass on sight!" threatened the other jackboy with his own shotgun.

He glared over at the three occupied tables in the dining room area. Missy could've sworn the second one was looking her dead in the eyes when he said that. The young female clerk did as she was told and filled a bag with money from the cash register. Too bad Ziggy wasn't working today—if he was, one or both of them jackboys would be dead. Because he'd be damned if he allowed someone to rob his daddy's restaurant.

Once the bag was stuffed with cash from the registers, the taller one headed for the exit. T.K. reached under the table for her pistol.

"Hold up, fool!" the other one called out and moved quickly over to where they were sitting. "Everybody empty yo pockets and take off all yo jewelry right now!"

Without hesitation, the two girls at the table near T.K.'s did as they were told, while the older woman and her two young boys did the same.

"Fuck them, fool. Let's go!"

"Nah! I got this!" shouted back the second one. "You bitches hurry up 'fore I let loose on y'all ass," he said, looking directly at Nadja, sneering behind his mask.

T.K. was looking at Missy and Nadja like they were crazy as she removed her rings and tennis bracelet.

"Hurry up, fool!" shouted the first goon, standing anxiously at the exit door while keeping guard.

Sneaking a glance up at the masked goon, T.K. squeezed her thighs tight so that the gun wouldn't fall between her legs onto the floor, and that's when Missy kicked her foot under the table from the other side. Both friends gave one another a brief glance that spoke many words.

"Don't play, bitch. Take that chain off . . ." growled the goon as he pointed the shotgun at Nadja.

"Alright. Damn!" Nadja said and reached behind her neck to unclamp her necklace.

"The rest of y'all pile that shit up!"

The second the goon took to look over at the two females at the next table over was all the time Nadja needed, and like a striking cobra, Nadja pounced from the table while the big gun was still aimed at her and took ahold of its long barrel.

Boom! The explosion was thunderous, but T.K. didn't flinch as she bolted from the table with her own gun and blew the goon's brains out while he struggled under Nadja's assault. The shit happened so fast that T.K. didn't even remember getting up from her seat. All she knew was to act and take advantage.

Then all hell broke loose at the next table over. The first goon was already tearing out the restaurant at that crucial moment.

"Ohmygod!" Missy gasped in horror as she watched the female a few feet from her table lying on the floor, screaming in agonizing pain.

She'd been in the line of fire of the shotgun blast. Now she lay shaking with a large hole in her right side, as chunks of her arm were blown away. The two little boys and their momma cried almost helplessly as they watched the woman's life slowly bleed away into her death.

So much blood.

The whole entire restaurant was now up in total chaos. Then T.K. pulled the dead goon's mask off.

"Go, cuz. Y'all leave," said Nadja as the sound of police sirens blared from a distance.

"What!" T.K. looked at her stupidly.

"Just go and get Mis—get her out of here." Nadja nodded at the still-shocked Missy.

"What about you?" T.K. looked into the dead goon's bloody face.

"I'll call you when I clear up this mess. My handprints on this gun... and this the only way I can help you. Now get the fuck outta here! Go!" Nadja's voice was sharp and demanding now.

For a few seconds, T.K. just looked at her cousin in what appeared to be confusion.

"Bitch, leave!" Nadja shouted, and so T.K. left, snatching Missy along with her.

"Now," Nadja turned to those who remained inside the restaurant, "what I'm about to say is what y'all need to say when the police get here . . ."

***

Two dead bodies in a matter of minutes.

The second Cash heard about what happened at the restaurant—as Missy told him—he felt a stab of dread for Nadja's sake. But he knew his girl well. Nadja was thorough when it came to dealing with such circumstances. The bitch was on top of her game. But while Cash and his crew were in the process of meeting up with T.K. and Missy, Sin was receiving an unexpected phone call.

"Stuart, what can I do for you?" said Sin once he was aware of who the caller was.

"Your boys, man. I'm on the scene of a double homicide by your new team."

"I'm listening." Sin sat back in his swivel chair behind the large desk.

Stuart continued. "It's over in Liberty City at a Shell Station. There's a video of the whole incident that my guys have taken into evidence. And I'm more than sure these are your boys. Though one of them—"

"There's nothing else to talk about concerning this matter other than destroying that tape," Sin said with a dangerous calmness that was quite disturbing.

"It's gonna be difficult—"

"Do it, or you're truly going to have a hard time walking for the rest of your life."

There was then a short moment of silence.

"Do I make myself clear to you, Stewy-boy?"

"It's done," sighed Stuart.

"Yes," Sin said. "We don't want you ending up like Richie, do we, Stewy?"

"No."

Then the phone went dead as Sin allowed his threat to linger in the crooked cop's mind. After six years of being on his payroll, Sin still wasn't quite fond of having to deal with the cops. Even when they were working for him as well, he could never become too relaxed about the fact. One could only be trusted to a certain extent.

Not even myself, muttered Sin, and he picked up the phone again.

***

"You what?"

"You heard what the fuck I said, Dooley."

Dooley shot up to his feet and spun abruptly to face her. "Why? I mean why the fuck you ain't call me when—"

"Does it matter, nigga—"

"Don't do it, Dooley. That's yo' gurl now," Missy cut in when Dooley reached back and was about to slap T.K. for getting smart-tongued with him.

"I wish you would, muthafucka!" T.K. rose slowly from her seat and faced off with her man.

Without a word, Dooley just stared into her eyes.

"You got me fucked up, nigga," T.K. sneered and headed for the front door, then walked out.

Flinching at the sound of the door slamming shut behind her, Missy turned to Dooley.

"You should be happy to have a real bitch pregnant, Dooley. I'm disappointed in you." Then she went after her friend, but the sound of T.K.'s car was already spinning out of the parking lot.

"What's going on?" Jon-Jon looked over at Cash, who sat puffing heavily on the blunt with a glass of straight gin in his hand. It wasn't hard to see that he was worried about Nadja's situation.

"What's up, bruh?" Jon-Jon then turned to Dooley. But when Dooley looked up into his crony's face, he frowned like a madman.

"What?" said Jon-Jon.

Dooley chin-checked Jon-Jon with a hard left. Then he was on him like a panther, but Jon-Jon refused to back down or cower away. He counter-attacked Dooley, connecting a sharp jab to his cheek. Cash just sat there watching his two loved ones tear up the living room as they fought. He'd grown up watching the two best friends fight, and this was no different than the others—or so he thought.

Little did he know.

Jon-Jon slammed Dooley on top of the low coffee table, crashing it to pieces under Dooley's weight.

"Chill, bruh!" shouted a bloody-mouthed Jon-Jon before Dooley reached out and connected with his jaw.

"Fuck you! Fuck you!" roared Dooley, now wrestling Jon-Jon across the floor.

When Missy came back inside the apartment, she glared over at the sitting Cash and rushed to Dooley and Jon-Jon.

"Y'all stop that shit!" she punched Dooley's arm. "Y'all better than that—"

"Lemme go! Lemme go, nigga!" Dooley struggled against Jon-Jon's bear hug as they rolled over the floor.

"Cash, you just gon' sit there?" Missy turned to Cash and eyed him nastily.

"Let 'em handle it like gangstaz," said Cash.

"Gangstaz? They brothaz!"

Missy knelt down to hold Dooley so Jon-Jon could get up and away from him.

"Stop, Dooley. Stop! Stop this bullshit!"

Jon-Jon jumped up and wiped his bloody mouth.

Dooley's mouth was bleeding too as he pulled himself up to his feet.

"You fuckin' wit' that coke, nigga? You snortin' that shit up yo' nose?"

Now Cash was alert and sat down his glass.

"What?" He looked up at his little brother.

The look Jon-Jon gave Cash was all the confirmation he needed of the truth claimed against him.

"Fuck this shit, bruh!"

"Jon-Jon!" Missy yelled at the retreating Jon-Jon as he stormed out the door next.

"Fuck him!" Dooley shouted. "Fuck you, nigga! Fuck yo' coke-head ass!" he barked at the open door.

Cash felt like the ceiling had crashed down on top of him. He couldn't believe what had just been revealed to him. A newfound fear awakened inside him as he looked over at the open door; his brother had just exited in a rage.

"I can't believe this shit!" Missy stomped her feet.

Neither could Dooley, and same with Cash. None of them could believe any of it.

Chapter 28

"Muthafuckin' ungrateful muthafucka!" T.K. snapped as she drove, tears in her eyes, speeding through Carol City.

The city flew by in flashes as she searched for peace of mind while venting to herself. The pistol lay on the passenger seat next to her. T.K. rode to her ghetto tunes, hoping to find comfort in them. It was hard, though, when the music booming in her ears was Ace Hood and his gangsta concept.

For some reason, she found herself pulling into Club Fierce's large parking lot. Tucking her pistol close, she exited the car and made her way to the club's entrance.

"What's up wit' my gurl?" said Big Lee, the club's 5'4", 265-pound bouncer at the door.

"Needin' my space, that's all."

"Then you came to the wrong place for that, T.K."

"I'm here now, Big," she said, and she was allowed entrance.

Inside, T.K. went straight to the bar and ordered a glass of Long Island Iced Tea. Then a cigar to roll her blunt up. From there, she mingled through the crowded strip club and found herself a seat at a vacant table.

As Maya descended the stairs from her office next to the VIP section, she saw T.K. immediately. Dressed in her pinstripe business suit, she ignored everything except the seriousness on T.K.'s face.

"What the hell is wrong now?" she muttered softly.

When T.K. looked up, she found Maya sliding into the padded leather seat next to her. She finished what was left of preparing her blunt without a word.

"Do I have to ask or just act like I'm not concerned with that crazy look in your eyes?" Maya said. "Hmmm?"

"I'm good, gurl."

"So we lyin' to each other now?"

"I'm just not in the mood for conversation," said T.K.

Maya wasn't going for it. "Don't make me push you, T.K."

"And I'll push you back!"

"Hmph."

Lighting her blunt, T.K. avoided eye contact and focused on her task at hand.

"So that's how it is now?"

"Look, Maya."

Maya interjected. "No, *you* look, T.K.! All I'm tryna do is help you not make whatever you goin' through worse. I'm not gonna kiss yo' fuckin' ass either."

Then T.K. turned a furious gaze on Maya. "Listen, bitch! If I wanted somebody to talk to, then we wouldn't be going through all this shit. You'd already know what's up. But I just want my space . . . I *need* my space. So please get the fuck outta my damn face."

For a moment, Maya just looked dumbstruck, then she rose from her seat.

"I'ma let you have that, T.K."

"Bye," said T.K., blowing out smoke.

Shaking her head, Maya left her sitting there without a backward glance—and T.K. got what she wanted . . . *Yeah, only for a moment.*

***

Jon-Jon walked along the grounds of the apartment complex, puffin' on his solo blunt. As he neared the park nearby, where a soft, brown-skinned sistah was also headed with her young son, he was lost in thought. He knew it wasn't gonna be long before his cocaine addiction was in the know. Now he wondered how far his consequent consequences would go now that they knew.

Entering the park, Jon-Jon walked over to the big sliding board and sat down at the edge of its shiny end. There were several other kids present and one other grown-up, another female—who he knew as Kim.

His jaw was still aching from Dooley's wicked blow. He and Kim met each other's gaze, and he nodded involuntarily at her.

"What's wrong witcha, playa?" Kim came walkin' toward him in that bowlegged way she do.

"Just blowin' off some steam."

"Why? What happened?"

Jon-Jon exhaled a cloud of weed smoke. "Me and bruh got into it and shit."

"I see," she said, gesturing toward his busted lip. "I never would've expected you to go through it wit' yo' boy. I thought y'all was tight."

"We is," he exclaimed. "Just some bullshit went down, and shit got outta hand."

To his right, he watched the young boy come runnin' toward him and Kim with laughter in his voice. He fell after trippin' over a stump in the rooted ground, and Jon-Jon bolted from the sliding board.

Kim watched as Jon-Jon, blunt still in his mouth, helped the little boy up—who now sported a busted bottom lip too. There were tears in his eyes as he looked up at Jon-Jon's vague expression.

"You a'ight, little homie?"

"Uh . . . yea'," said the young, teary-eyed boy.

"Slow," Jon-Jon turned at the next voice.

Approaching was the boy's mama, steppin' in her designer jean shorts and Air Force Ones.

"That boy is so clumsy . . ."

"Nah, I saw when he tripped," said Jon-Jon, standin' upright to face her.

"Hey Gucci, gurl," greeted Kim.

"What's up, Kay? That damn Skeetah been buggin' 'bout the park all day, and now—"

Jon-Jon interrupted, "He good. Little homie just doin' his thang, that's all."

From that moment, the three of them started talkin', and Jon-Jon shared his blunt with Kim. Skeetah was back to runnin' all over the place. The rest of the kids didn't slow down a bit.

"Y'all heard 'bout that shootin' over in Liberty City a couple hours ago?"

"Which one?" Kim asked.

"Damn, how many was it?" Gucci retorted.

Quietly, Jon-Jon just looked at both women as they spoke.

"My cousin Jazi said they found Baby Boi's brotha dead in that Jamaican restaurant."

"Which one—Vick?"

Gucci nodded. "And they say it was one more, but he got away."

Lil sis handled that shit, Jon-Jon thought as he listened.

He was finally aware of just how dangerous T.K. was. But this was just her first stage—she was now steppin' into her darker side. Then memories of his first kill came rushin' back to him all at once.

"Well, you know who that could be."

"Who?" Jon-Jon asked.

Kim said, "Loomy, that's who. That's that nigga Vick's partner in crime—his right-hand man."

"If so," Jon-Jon said, "he not only gotta worry 'bout the police lookin' for him. Them crazy-ass rude boys gon—"

"Swang . . . swang!" said little Skeetah as he tugged on Jon-Jon's shirt and pointed at the swings.

They all was occupied 'cept one, and it was clear what he wanted.

"Oh shit, gurl, there go Malik!" said Kim.

"Malik?" repeated Jon-Jon.

"Malik?" Gucci spun around so fast and saw Malik—her baby daddy—exiting his black Buick Cutlass and headin' their way.

"Gucci's baby daddy," Kim replied.

Skeetah was still clingin' to Jon-Jon's shirt when Malik approached, fire in his eyes. The big, black nigga was movin' fast in steady, heated steps.

"Here we go again," muttered Jon-Jon. *I know I ain't fixin' to have to kill*— Jon-Jon stopped his train of thought when he realized he ain't have his pistol on him. He'd left it in the car!

"Gee, what the fuck you got goin' on here? Got my son all up on another fool—"

"Please, Malik, it ain't even that serious," said Gucci. "You know how Skeetah is."

She watched her son charge his daddy and hug his long legs in a happy squeeze.

"It's that serious, hoe. You fuckin' round wit' other niggaz 'round my son. What kinda shit you got goin' on?"

Kim glanced at Jon-Jon with an uneasy expression. He was now starin' straight at Malik.

"C'mon, damn. Let's not do this in front of Skeet."

"Nah, take him in the house."

"You too," said Gucci, seein' the look in his eyes. And to her surprise, Jon-Jon turned and walked away.

"Boo-bye!" waved Skeetah at Jon-Jon.

"That's what you better do, bitch nigga. Don't lemme catch you 'round my son again," Malik said firmly.

Jon-Jon stopped and turned around. "Whatchu jus' called me, nigga?"

"You—"

"Come on, playa." Kim cut Malik's reply off and went for Jon-Jon. "Let's go, baby. We don't got time for this shit. Gucci, gurl, I'll see you later, a'ight?" she shouted over her shoulder and took Jon-Jon's hand.

"Fuck that fool!"

"Chill out, Malik. Damn!"

As they walked away back toward his apartment, Jon-Jon could hear Malik and Gucci fussin' behind him.

"Just keep going, playa. We don't got time for no more bullshit," Kim grumbled as she treaded alongside him.

He didn't say a word.

***

After Dooley received the call from Maya tellin' him where T.K. was at, he dropped everything and jumped into his whip. Then he was speeding toward Club Fierce in Carol City. During this time, Cash was on his way to retrieve Nadja, while Jon-Jon, Kim, and Missy remained back at the crib. By the time Dooley reached the club, he'd convinced himself he was doing the right thing.

"I was wonderin' when you was gon' show up, dawg," Big Lee said the moment he saw Dooley.

He'd just seen her car parked and was sure T.K. was there. Dooley entered the club.

"'Preciate it, Big!"

"Puppy love," muttered Big Lee, but he had no clue what kind of love he was referring to when it came to T.K. and Dooley.

Maya nodded in the direction Dooley should go to find T.K. as she sat on a tall barstool at the bar. Dooley headed straight there without halting his strides. Still sittin' at the same table, two empty glasses and the butt of the blunt she'd smoked in front of her, T.K. was nursing her third fresh drink. Eyes were on Dooley as he peeled through the crowd and slid in beside his girl.

"I don't think our baby should be drinkin' at a young age," said Dooley, takin' the glass from her hand and kissin' her on the cheek.

T.K. didn't acknowledge his presence. She just sat there, watchin' the scene before her.

"I'm sorry, baby," he apologized. "That's my bad for actin' like that and shit. A nigga just had went through some shit—didn't mean to take it out on you, T.K."

T.K. glanced quickly out the corner of her eye at him. Then she looked away and reached for her glass again, but Dooley was too quick.

"Let's go home, T.K."

"Getcha damn hands off me, Dooley!" she snatched away from him with a glare.

Dooley's eyes widened. "So I can't touch my—"

"No, you can't, nah!" she cut him off and turned away from him.

Then a shadow came over them as a well-dressed playa in the game stopped at their table, along with one of his allies. Dooley looked up at the two and frowned.

"Don't you see the lady don't wanna be bothered, lil foof?" said the smooth-talkin' brotha who'd made a move on T.K. earlier—and got curved.

"Who the fuck are you, her fuckin' daddy? Nigga, you better back up and live," Dooley said, now in his gangsta mode.

Mr. Smooth looked over at his boy.

"Check this out, fool." Mr. Smooth's homie stepped up as he neared Dooley.

"Nah, *you* check this out, nigga!" Dooley came up with his pistol and placed it at the tip of the dude's nose. "You ready to die 'bout my bitch, fool? I suggest you two back the fuck up."

"You got that, yo," said Mr. Smooth, nudging his homie. "Let's clear it, dawg."

"You don' fucked up now, little nigga." The second brotha looked Dooley in his eyes, then turned away.

Dooley thought fast on that simple threat and knew he shouldn't take it lightly—especially with the way dude had looked at him with murder in his eyes. Then the man looked back over his shoulder and sneered at Dooley.

That's all it took.

Dooley rushed him from behind and bashed him in the back of the head with his pistol. It was definitely goin' down when dude hit the floor. Dooley pounced on him like a lion on a poodle.

Maya jumped down and looked from the scene to the direction she last saw Big Lee—or any of her other four bouncers.

"Aw, shit!"

Mr. Smooth made a move like he was fixin' to jump in and help his boy, but T.K. was all over him at once. From that instant on, shit went wild. When T.K. drew her gun, people moved immediately and ducked for cover. Before she was about to use it, Big Lee grabbed her wrist and reassured her that he had it under control now.

As for Dooley—who was now beatin' his victim nearly senseless with the butt of his pistol—he was lost in his rage. It took T.K.'s gentle touch and her sweet voice to pull him out of his beast mode.

"It's over, baby. Come on, let's go."

Dooley looked up into those hazel eyes of hers and saw nothin' but love in them.

"Fuck these punks, baby," she added. "They ain't even worth it."

"I think y'all need to leave—for now," Big Lee said, snatchin' Mr. Smooth up to his wobbly legs.

"I got 'em," Maya said. "Just get these fools out my club—and make sure they don't return."

Big Lee nodded, and Big Hurt and Road Block shoved and dragged both men toward the exit.

"We good, man. I'm takin' T.K. home," Dooley said, takin' hold of a tipsy T.K. and leadin' her in the same direction where their foes had just been taken.

Luckily, they got away without further incident, leavin' T.K.'s car to be picked up later. All Dooley wanted now was to get his girl safely home.

If it wasn't one thing, it was another.

Chapter 29

After another few weeks of straight hustlin' and tryin' to survive the street life, Dooley and his crew were still whole. Though the heat was still on in response to the double murders of Bean and his homie, Detective Stuart Collins had played his part as promised with the video of the shooting. Nadja was a little paranoid about being closely watched by the police regarding the restaurant murder. Although she'd taken the rap and convinced them it was a self-defense act, she still remained cautious. So she decided to distance herself from T.K. and Dooley during the daytime, just to be safe.

As for Dooley and Jon-Jon, the two friends were still just as close as two blood brothers. However, Jon-Jon's habit still remained, but definitely not around Dooley and Cash. He and Lyric had gotten closer by the day, and it was official that they were an item. Wizdom couldn't help but respect her wishes, because they never were a couple. Moving in with Lyric was something he didn't expect Jon-Jon to do.

To each his own, Dooley thought.

There was nothing that would separate the two friends—nothing at all. Now that they'd built a name for themselves in the drug game, and on some real killer shit with some major players in their circle, they were highly respected. If Jon-Jon and Dooley's name wasn't ringin' no bells to anyone, then they weren't deep enough in the streets. Pushing major weight was their thing, and they supplied many surrounding areas with some of the best cocaine in the city of Miami. Thanks to Sin and Fedo, they couldn't be stopped. There was no way they would grow hungry anymore—now that they were eatin' from the same table.

The haters still hated, the money kept coming, and the bitches came in flocks, only to get shut down in the process. With T.K. being pregnant with his child, Dooley saw other women as *nothing but shit* in his eyes. Everything he did or said was either pertaining to his girl or his unborn child. There was nothing more he cared about in the world . . .

Until he received his next phone call.

"Hello?" Dooley answered groggily.

"How is my boy?" came Mama Lizzy's soft, loving voice.

Dooley sat upright in the middle of the bed.

"Hey, Ma. What's up, baby?"

"Missin' my child. And T.K.?"

"She . . ." Dooley paused and looked around the room. "She pregnant and doin' good—"

"Pregnant? Dooley, how far along is she?"

"A little over a month."

"Thank you, Jesus! You've given me anotha grandbaby. Where is T.K. now? Tell her to get her behind right to this phone, right this minute."

"T.K.!" yelled Dooley. "T.K.!"

"Boy, hush all that fuss in my ear!" snapped Mama Lizzy.

"My bad."

When T.K. didn't answer, Dooley climbed out of the bed and padded toward the door.

"Anyway, I called to see when y'all comin' to see me. I really wanna see my babies. I wanna see Jon-Jon too," she said in her serious tone.

"I wanna see you too, Ma."

"Then do somethin' about it, baby."

Dooley searched the apartment for T.K. to no avail. Then he went for the front door.

"Ma, can I ask you a question?" said Dooley.

"Anything, baby."

"If I send for you, would you come? I mean, I know you don't like long trips—"

"No. No. No! I am not leavin' my house. That question is dead, baby. I'm sorry. I can't leave. I love all of y'all wit' my heart and soul. But Elizabeth is not fixin' to leave her domain."

"I figured that," he grumbled.

Down below in the street, T.K. was talkin' to some nigga whom Dooley had never even seen before. To him, their conversation was a very serious one, by how T.K. was lookin' as she spoke. The man was dressed quite elegantly.

"I'm comin', Ma. I'll be there soon. I just got to tie up some loose ends here."

She interjected, "Liah misses you so much. She wants to see you before she leave for college next semester. She's goin' to FSU."

"Whaaat! When did she . . . Damn, I been gone *that* long?"

"You have too. And it's time for you to—"

"I gotchu, Ma. As soon as I can, I gotchu," he promised.

"Then I shouldn't have to ask you again. Be careful, baby, and take care of that girl and my grandchild. My great-great-grandchild."

"I love ya, Ma. I gotchu."

"I know," Mama sighed. "I know."

A moment later, Dooley retreated back into the crib and strapped on his Nikes after tossin' on some shorts and a tank top. Then he was back outside and descending the stairs down to the ground.

What appeared to be now a heated conversation between T.K. and the stranger made Dooley speed up his approach. One look at Dooley, and T.K. gasped in sudden surprise.

"What's up, T.K.?" Dooley demanded to know.

"T.K.," said the stranger, confused.

"Dooley . . ." T.K. stepped over and took his hand nervously.

Dooley felt her hand shakin' in his.

"This is Frank."

"Frank?" Now it was Dooley's time to look confused.

"My stepfather, Frank, baby," she said.

Dooley then was speechless.

Chapter 30

"Where the fuck you come from?" Dooley glared at the man.

"He followed me from—"

"I'm down here on a business meeting with some very respectable investors," said Frank, sweating badly in his business suit. "I'd never known I'd find you here."

T.K. turned to Dooley. "I was just coming back from seeing "F" on them thangs . . . then next thang, I see him," she nodded in Frank's direction. "Flaggin' me down. But I kept right on going until now."

"Fuck all that!" Now it was Dooley's turn to look at the man whom T.K. had so highly despised. "What do you want, man?"

"For my daughter to come—"

"I'm not yo' muthafuckin' daughter, nigga!" T.K. shot back as she fumed. "We ain't never been shit."

Frank looked thunderstruck, shocked by her profanity usage of language. He never heard her talk in such a language. Even when they were back home in Atlanta and at times so frustrated she wanted to explode, she had never cuss at him.

"What about your Mama, Takira?" pleaded Frank.

"The same bitch's mind you poisoned too?"

"Listen here, young lady!" Frank was tired of playing around now, jabbing his finger in front of her face. "How dare you humiliate us the way you do by running away. After all we've done for you—after everything I'd sacrificed for you to see that you live a comfortable life. And this how you repay me—us! Your parents?"

"You ain't shit but a child molester, nigga. Tell that! T.K. bellowed. "Tell how you took my pussy when I was ten— how you made me suck yo' little ass dick when mama wouldn't be up for it. Tell that. Tell that!"

People began focusing their attention on the scene in the parking lot. Even the children had been caught up in the sudden act of brewing violence and hidden truth. Dooley stood mouth agape at what T.K. had just said. She'd never said the man had raped her, and the look on Frank's face was all the evidence he needed to see to know that it was true.

"I...Takira..." Frank avoided her piercing glare. "Your accusations will not work—"

"Accusations!" Then, T.K. drew back and punched the man squarely in the mouth.

She went wild on the man—the only real monster she knew. The same one who'd haunted her dreams at night. Together, both Dooley and T.K. beat his ass with anything and everything they could get they hands on. It was several minutes later of nearly beating the now bloody Frank into a coma that the unexpected happened.

Pulling up before the apartment building was a rental car. It stopped just yards away from Dooley and T.K.'s attack on Frank. Then the car that Frank had been driving was now backing up to a stop in reverse. The rental car had blocked its way of escape as all four occupants exited the rental at once.

Missy came running down the stairs after waking up to find her two friends in the act of violence. The surrounding area was in a state of shock and confusion as those who had grown to love and respect Dooley and T.K. watched in unmistakable surprise. By the time, T.K. had drawn her blade and sliced her mama's husband across the face with it. Then again and again, and again. Frank screamed in pure fear and agony.

"Dooley!"

"T.K.!"

"Oh shit!" Missy said.

At the sound of the familiar voices, both Dooley and T.K. stopped instantly and turned around. Then next thing later, Dooley's eyes widened as he watched Shantel rush to him and take him in her arms. The same as NeNe and Passion did with T.K.; both girls crying as they embraced one another. Tanisha just stood there with Bryon in her arms and waited her turn.

"Oh my god, T.K." Shantel said after taking T.K. in her arms next.

"I miss y'all so much."

Quietly, Passion and NeNe stood before Dooley as if they were not sure what to do next. Neither did Dooley, but when he opened his arms to them, they rushed into them without hesitation. At the same time, Frank lay panting and bleeding all over the place on the pavement.

Then the next thing later, a loud crash sounded off, and everybody turned in its direction. To their surprise, the car that Frank had driven there in was crashing back into Tanisha's rental, and the woman that was behind the wheel was desperately trying to get away the only way she could. In between two parked cars—and the one behind it—was difficult, but after seeing it was a woman, T.K. took off in a run while retrieving her tucked pistol at the same time.

"Oh Lord!" said Shantel.

"Oh shit!" repeated Missy.

Dooley then took after her.

"Bitch, get out the car 'fore I kill yo' stupid ass right now!"

Boom! T.K. shot out the car's front tire. Bryon shrieked in horror while the other children ran, for this was a side of T.K. they'd never seen. The car ceased its attempts to crash its way through to escape, but when T.K. and the female locked eyes, she gasped and stepped back a few steps. Then she stepped forward again, with the pistol at aim.

"Oh hell naw! Oh-hell-fuck-naw! Get . . . Get the fuck outta the car, bitch!" T.K. shouted.

"Chill, baby." Dooley stepped up and literally snatched the woman through the open driver's side window.

Now everybody's confusion heightened; they stood by and watched the two lovers operate in such a vicious way. The woman screamed, struggled, and cried the whole entire way out.

"Now strip that bitch! Take all that bitch's clothes off, Dooley," T.K. ordered.

Dooley looked up at her with a silent, crazily odd expression.

"Do it!" T.K. stomped her foot stubbornly.

With a bit of difficulty, Dooley snatched away the woman's blouse and skirt.

"Oh-my-God!" Shantel's mouth dropped.

"Pussy muthafucka!" whispered Dooley, stepping quickly away after his task was done.

The woman had actually been a man—as in, his penis was now exposed for all to see. There was a woman's set of breasts upon him as well—a transsexual. Now, the reality of it was more shocking to many of them than the actual violence. The element of surprise.

"Sonavabitch!" Dooley whispered. "Hell naw!"

"The police!" someone shouted.

Then came the sound of screeching tires and the roar of a car's engine turning the next corner—Jon-Jon and Cash. Then the blaring of sirens nearby.

"Let's go, T.K., Dooley!" Tanisha finally spoke up and stepped behind him to grab ahold of his hand.

Shantel grabbed T.K. and led her away as well.

"What's up, bruh? What's goin' on?" Jon-Jon demanded as soon as he exited his car.

Dooley looked at his crony. "Take care of that nigga for me, dawg." He nodded at Frank. "That's T.K.'s stepdaddy."

That was all Jon-Jon needed to hear before he and Cash grabbed a hold of Frank and tossed him in the trunk. Next thing later, they were speeding toward the nearest exit—the same time the police was making their entrance—and that was the last they heard of Frank.

***

Four hours later, after the initial shock was over, everybody was surprisingly relaxed and comfortable. They all were gathered up in Dooley's apartment—now the one he only shared with T.K.—laughing and hangin' out like a big family. There was nothing like having loved ones around. Tanisha had really surprised them by bringing Shantel and her girls when Dooley and T.K. least expected it.

Though he had planned on doing just that later on after all was situated, today served their presence with just as much joy. While Bryon played with T.K., Dooley was catching up on Passion, NeNe, and Shantel's life.

"So you finally leavin' home, huh?" asked Dooley.

"Both of us will be attending Florida State University," NeNe replied.

"That's the second time today I done heard about goin' to FSU."

"I don't know why they wanna be so far away," Shantel said. "But I know they mannish asses gon' be up to no good now that I won't be around."

Both Passion and NeNe burst out laughing. Then Bryon did the same for the apparent reason that laughter was in the midst. The boy was silly like that.

"But I'm happy for my girls," Shantel added.

"T.K. thinkin' 'bout going to night school—"

"I'm taking the course over the internet for now," T.K. cut Dooley off. "It'll be a good accomplishment before the baby comes."

"The baby?" Shantel blurted out.

"What baby?" NeNe asked.

"A baby...?" Passion fell in last.

Missy said, "Yeah, a baby. Dooley is 'bout to be a daddy."

Dooley attempted to get up and sneak out of the living room at the curious glances.

"Unh-uh, Dooley! Sit yo' butt down, boy," Shantel said. "You mean to tell me—"

"I gotta go pee," he lied.

Then there was a knock at the door, which gave him another excuse to escape their boiling, endless stares—especially Passion's, who was grinning over at him. Bryon bolted from T.K.'s lap and followed Dooley to the door.

After seeing it was Lil Scrappy, one of Dooley's young street hustlers, he opened the door and stepped outside with Bryon in tow. Lil Scrappy was a sixteen-year-old hustler from Homestead, the son of one of Miami's most infamous crackheads. He, Drake, and Konflict were cronies, and Dooley's foot soldiers. The trio never ceased to come up whole or show any flaws in their characters.

They had been waiting for someone to put them on, but many declined due to their reputation of terrorizing the streets, fighting, and vandalizing everything. It took Dooley to give them the benefit of a doubt, and the three proved themselves more than worthy.

"What'z up, fool?"

"Just chillin', man. I heard you been havin' some pro'lems, so I had to leave the post," Scrappy replied, referring to his spot on the University of Miami campus. The young nigga was makin' a killin' there.

"Everything is settled." Dooley took Bryon's hand and led the adventurous boy down the stairs. "What'z up with Drake and Kon?"

"Oh, them fools doin' they thang. They know what's up—I told 'em I was comin' to see what's up."

"Park? Park, Doolee?" Bryon pointed.

"Who this lil' fool is?"

"My nephew," Dooley headed for the park. "Bryon."

Scrappy nodded, relighting the blunt he had behind his ear. Then he was silent as they walked, and Dooley picked up on the odd quietness between them.

"What's really up, Scrap? What's on yo' mind, man?" Dooley questioned, surveying their surroundings.

Without hesitation, Scrappy said, "It's Kon's brotha, Sergio. Fool is on some other shit now that Kon is gettin' money wit' you."

"What he doin'? What he said?"

Bryon snatched away from Dooley and charged over to play with the other kids once they made it to the park. This was usually Drake's spot—and that one over in Little Haiti where he's originally from. That must be where he's at now that Jon-Jon had dropped more work in his hands earlier that morning.

"Twice I'd had to come outta my pockets—Kon too—to go up against Serg, no matter how much heart he got," said Scrappy. "He just let the nigga take his shit like he's some bitch or somethin'. I don't like that shit, fool."

"And don't Serg got his own work?"

"Yeah, he fuck wit' them clowns over there in Brown Sub. Them outta town niggas from Tampa who moved down our way and put down."

Dooley nodded.

"But the thang is—whatever Serg take from the nigga and he can't clean it up, he'll go knock off the next muthafucka so that he can keep his money up. That's why you never expected shit yet." Scrappy passed Dooley the blunt. "But I know that shit won't last long."

"What shit?"

"You," Scrappy said. "If I ain't stepped to you about this shit, and yo' shit come up short or anything—I know you'll take that shit out on all us since we tight. I just want to... I want Kon to put his foot down."

"And that's exactly what we gon' make 'em do. Or he is out—definitely."

"That's what I'm sayin', fool."

"After my people leave, it's goin' down. Just try to keep shit from poppin' off 'til then."

With that, Scrappy gave him some dap.

"You know I got you, fool. Real niggaz do real thangz."

Dooley nodded. "And it's 'bout to get realer."

Then a piercing scream rang out over the complex as a little girl slid down the long sliding board.

Dooley sighed in relief.

Chapter 31

The next morning had come in a flash. The night before had been spent eating at the finest diner, going to the movies, clubbing, and back to the crib where they all hung out some more. Dooley was feelin' himself, totally, that Passion, NeNe, Shantel, and Tanisha had come to stay the weekend with him. But it was Bryon who had been the light of the moment—so much like Walt he was. Dooley couldn't get enough of seein' his big brother through his nephew.

It was like Walt was still livin' within his child. Dooley had even dreamed about Walt the night before—something he cherished despite its aching effect.

"Where everybody at?" Dooley said.

"At the beach." Shantel looked up at him from the sofa.

"Why you didn't go?" He yawned loudly.

Shantel shrugged. "It's too early in the morning to be at the beach. I'll prolly go later on."

"Oh." Dooley padded over into the kitchen and prepared himself a bowl of Trix cereal.

Shantel stood up from her TV show and followed him into the kitchen.

"You ate already?" he asked.

Shantel shook her head. "My breakfast is a cup of coffee."

"Well, you fixin' to have some cereal with me then," he replied and took down another bowl.

All she could do was shake her head. She knew how stubborn he could be at times.

"Why you lookin' at me like that, man?"

"Just wonderin', that's all."

His eyebrows raised. "Wonderin'... About what?"

"Everything. But most of all—fatherhood. I wonder would your unborn child end up like Bryon."

"What?"

"You heard me, Dooley."

Dooley detected the seriousness in her eyes and sighed, sliding the bowl of cereal in front of her.

"That's why you didn't go out with them—'cause you wanted to be alone wit' me. You wanted to talk . . ."

She interjected. "And you're absolutely right. That's exactly what I want, and you better goddamn listen too."

"Yes, mama," he attempted a little humor, but Shantel didn't go for it.

Yeah, Dooley thought. *She is graveyard serious.* Then he sat down before her. "I'm listening."

"Dooley, I know about Kirk. I know you killed my brotha," she said softly, and held up a patient hand to silence his attempt to speak. "Let me talk."

"Hell nah! You on some real bullshit if you think I had somethin'—"

"I don't 'think', Dooley, I 'know', nigga!" Shantel banged her fist against the table. Tears spilled from her eyes now. Pain etched in her face.

"After doin' my own investigation, I was told by several different people that Kirk left the club that night with you and Gangsta. He was last seen with y'all. Then somebody else witnessed you and Gangsta dumpin' my brotha's dead body behind that RadioShack building. The so-called witness had been anotha street nigga who got knocked off by the police on a big case. So now he's turnin' state against y'all. But he don't know you, only Gangsta," she said, wipin' her tear-streaked face. "Gangsta is locked up right now on the murder of my brotha. They want him to tell who—"

"How in the fuck!" Dooley blurted out.

"Gangsta was dumb enough to think he'd wiped his car down good enough. The police found traces of Kirk's blood still in Gangsta's car. That mistake—of not destroyin' that car—cost him greatly. He won't tell who you is. Gangsta ain't no snitch. Anyway, I went to visit him last week, and his eyes told me everything I needed to know. I saw the truth in his eyes. Now, I'm askin' you, Dooley . . ." Shantel ceased her fallin' hot tears. "Tell me. Why did you kill my brotha?"

Dooley rose from the table and slowly turned away from her sad eyes. He opened one of the counter drawers and retrieved a Peach White Owl blunt. Then he went to his weed stash and took out a few buds. He needed to smoke bad now.

"I love you, Dooley. You made me love you. But all I ask for is the truth. Why?" she spoke again.

Dooley sat back down quietly and busted the blunt down.

"Remember that gun you left the night your brotha died? Well, your prints are all over it, but you not in the system. All it takes is for them to connect that gun to Kirk's murder—if that's the same one you used. Bein' that your brotha got killed that same time, it wouldn't be hard for the police to—"

"Whatchu tryna say, Shan? You gon' snitch on me?" Dooley looked up at her.

"I could've already did that and been over with it if I wanted to," she said. "But Mama ain't raised no 'snitch.'"

"Hmph." Dooley returned back to his task. A minute later, he was fillin' the kitchen with weed smoke.

"Don't make me beg you for somethin' I deserve to know, Dooley. You lied to me. You crushed me and hurt so many people. Do you even care about my feelings? Better yet—Passion's?"

"You know I care—"

"Then tell me, dammit! I promise on my own life I will not tell anotha soul if you tell me the truth. Straight up."

Despite the situation, Dooley believed her, and then, owing her that much, he gave her the truth. He admitted killing Kirk due to Kirk takin' his brother's drugs. It was a sensitive truth, but Dooley knew Shantel deserved it. He was goin' against his own laws; however, he wasn't tellin' her anything she didn't already know. Just the details of what really happened.

"I had no choice, Shan. It was already a life or death situation with me havin' them bricks."

"I understand," she sighed.

Dooley said, "It ain't like I planned it or somethin'. It was somethin' I had to do in order to—"

"You don't have to keep explainin', Dooley. Believe me, I know. I understand the game," she said. "Now, I hate to see you end up like Walt and leave a child behind without a father. I think it's time for you to leave the streets, Dooley."

He nodded, not sure if it was somethin' he wanted to do right now. He was in too deep to just give up so easily. Regardless of the fact that he was about to become a father—and that so many people counted on him—he couldn't leave the streets.

"I feel ya, Shan," he said. "But I'ma play it smooth until the baby comes."

"You're gonna leave it now, Dooley. No exceptions."

"I can't," he said. "You said you know the game, then you should know—in my position, in order to leave the game, you must clean yo' slate."

"You right," she said. "And that's what I thought I had done ten years ago when I was in the game. I didn't clean my slate, Dooley. Therefore, that's somethin' I must do."

That statement caused Dooley to frown, confused. "Whatchu talkin' 'bout, Shan?"

That's when she brought her right hand into view from underneath the table. Dooley froze rigid at the sight of the small black pistol. Then he looked up into her eyes and was shocked at what he saw. The murderous glare he met in her gaze brought a cold chill up his spine.

"It's my turn now, Dooley," she sneered, and aimed the pistol directly between his eyes.

Dooley swallowed hard.

"Now get down on the floor," she demanded.

"So you gon' kill me now?"

"I'ma ask you one more time, nigga. Get down on the floor."

Slowly but surely, Dooley did as he was told. He lay down on the floor and blinked back the tears that threatened to come. He didn't plead for his life or nothin'—because he knew it would be a worthless act. It was a life for a life. He thought about his unborn baby developin' in T.K.'s stomach. He thought about all he had accomplished ever since enterin' the game. His Grandma Lizzy, Jon-Jon, Cash, T.K.—The sound of Bryon's laughter exploded in his conscience. His whole life flashed before his eyes.

Then he felt the pillow cushion from the kitchen chair placed at the back of his head. The pistol was then pressed into the pillow next.

"Your mission is over, Dooley," she said.

"Nah, not yet," Dooley told her. "It ain't over—"

Then she squeezed the trigger, ending his life the same way he had done Kirk.

***

Ten minutes later, Shantel reached for the phone and dialed Tanisha's number. She had trashed the apartment as much as she could to make it look like a robbery. Shantel puffed on the blunt Dooley had been smokin' earlier as she waited on someone to pick up.

"Hello?" It was T.K.'s voice instead.

That's when Shantel burst out cryin', playin' her role.

"T.K., Dooley is dead. Somebody killed Dooley!" she sobbed uncontrollably.

"What!" T.K. shrieked into the phone.

"I was . . . in t-the s-sh . . . Please come and get me from here! Come get me . . . Come get me!"

Shantel smiled to herself. *It's a wrap.*

232

Soon the whole crew would be there, and hearts would be broken. Worlds would be crushed. But in all, life would continue to move on. The hustle never stops.

But to Shantel—revenge was a tasteful effect.

Epilogue

(Two Years Later)

T.K sat on the porch of her three-bedroom townhouse, watching as her son, Damarcus "Noony" Robinson, played with his pitbull puppy in the front yard. It had been a painful journey without Dooley, but she made it through the storms. There had been some terrible storms. Now back in Raleigh, North Carolina, several houses down from Momma Lizzy, T.K. was content with her current life. For burying Dooley was the hardest thing she ever had to experience in life, but bringing some part of him back to life into this world through Noony—that was the most special. Through him, and within her heart and mind, Dooley would forever live. His young legacy would always be remembered.

"Mommy, look!" Noony pointed.

T.K. smiled at the sight of Noony's puppy, Boo, standing up on his hind legs as if posing for a brief photo. Then he dropped down just as Cash's Mercedes-Benz pulled up in front of the house. Both Noony and Boo ran to meet Cash as he exited the silver car.

"What's up, lil Noony?" Cash scooped the boy up and gave him some dap. "Uncle Cash fenna take you and lil Boo out to the football game. You wanna go?"

Noony nodded eagerly. "Yea," he said.

Carrying Noony toward the porch where T.K still sat, Cash dropped down next to her on the wooden bench. Boo decided to find something else to do underneath the porch, while Noony looked around for him to no avail.

"What's happen', lil sis?"

"You late, that's what. But I got that package for you. It's in the freezer inside the Ego box."

"A'ight."

"You heard from Jon-Jon?"

Jon-Jon was still back down in Miami living with Lyric. They also had a daughter on the way, which T.K. was asked to be the godmother of.

"This morning," said Cash, draping his platinum chain over Noony's neck on top of his own little chain Passion bought him for his birthday. "Lyric will have the baby next week. But bruh should be here by Tuesday to bring them twenty bricks you ordered."

T.K. nodded.

"Yep." Cash sighed. "That's what it is, boss lady."

That was the essence of it. From Walt to Dooley, and from Dooley to T.K., and she maintained her position just as discreetly thorough as anyone of them had. For Fedo and Sin never switched lanes on her after Dooley's death. The torch was handed down to her, just as she demanded. To sustain Dooley's legacy was her promise to him, and by any means necessary, she was determined to do just that—even if she died trying.

"A'ight then, let's get this paper," she said.

"And don't let the paper get you, sis," Cash added.

The mission was yet underway.

A mission of survival.

Lock Down Publications and Ca$h Presents
Assisted Publishing Packages

Due to an increase in the price of services we have increased our prices. The prices below reflect the price increase as of 11/1/24.

BASIC PACKAGE	UPGRADED PACKAGE
$699	**$1000**
Editing	Typing
Cover Design	Editing
Formatting	Cover Design
	Formatting
	Upload eBooks to Amazon
	Upload Paperback to Amazon
ADVANCE PACKAGE	**LDP SUPREME PACKAGE**
$1,400	**$1,700**
Typing	Typing
Editing (line editing/content)	Editing (line editing/content)
Cover Design	Cover Design
Formatting	Formatting
Copyright Registration	Copyright Registration
Proofreading	Proofreading
Upload eBooks to Amazon	Set up Amazon Account
Upload Paperback to Amazon	Upload eBooks to Amazon
	Upload Paperback to Amazon
	Advertise on LDP's Amazon and Facebook Page

***

Other services available upon request.
Additional charges may apply

Lock Down Publications
P.O. Box 944
Stockbridge, GA 30281-9998
Phone: 470 303-9761
Email: lockdownpublications@gmail.com

Submission Guideline

Submit the first three chapters of your completed manuscript to ldpsubmissions@gmail.com. In the subject line add **Your Book's Title**. The manuscript must be in a Word Doc file and sent as an attachment. Document should be in Times New Roman, double spaced, and in size 12 font. Also, provide your synopsis and full contact information. If sending multiple submissions, they must each be in a separate email.

Have a story but no way to send it electronically? You can still submit to LDP/Ca$h Presents. Send in the first three chapters, written or typed, of your completed manuscript to:

LDP: Submissions Dept
P.O. Box 944
Stockbridge, GA 30281-9998

DO NOT send original manuscript. Must be a duplicate.
Provide your synopsis and a cover letter containing your full contact information.

Thanks for considering LDP and Ca$h Presents.

NEW RELEASES

BLOODLINE OF A SAVAGE 1-3
THESE VICIOUS STREETS 1-3
RELENTLESS GOON 1-3
BY PRINCE A. TAUHID

THE BUTTERFLY MAFIA 1-3
BY FUMIYA PAYNE

A THUG'S STREET PRINCESS 1&2
BY MEESHA

CITY OF SMOKE 3
BY MOLOTTI

GET IT IN SLUGS 1 &2
BY B. STALL

STANDING ON HER BUSINESS 1&2
BY DG SANTANA

STEPPERS 1,2&3
THE REAL BADDIES OF CHI-RAQ
BY KING RIO

THE LANE 1&2
BY KEN-KEN SPENCE

THUG OF SPADES 1&2
LOVE IN THE TRENCHES 2
CORNER BOYS
BY COREY ROBINSON

TIL DEATH 3
BY ARYANNA

AMBITIONZ OF A SLIDER | IRA B.

THE BIRTH OF A GANGSTER 4
BY DELMONT PLAYER

PRODUCT OF THE STREETS 1-3
BY DEMOND "MONEY" ANDERSON

NO TIME FOR ERROR
BY KEESE

MONEY HUNGRY DEMONS 1-2
BY TRANAY ADAMS

HUB CITY MENACE 1-3
BY J. WHITE

A THUGGISH PASSION 1&2
LAND OF DA HOOLIGANZ 1-4
KILLAZ ON STANDBY 1&2
BY IRA B.

FO'EVA ROLLIN 1&2
BY ASSA RAYMOND BAKER

THE LEVEL UP 1&3
BY LUXURY KING

Coming Soon from Lock Down Publications/Ca$h Presents

IF YOU CROSS ME ONCE 6
ANGEL V
By Anthony Fields

A THUGS STREET PRINCESS 3
By Meesha

CORNER BOYS 2
By Corey Robinson

THA TAKEOVER
By Keith Chandler

BETRAYAL OF A G 2
By Ray Vinci

SAVAGE FAMILY EMPIRE 1&2
SOULLESS GOON 1,2&3
THE DIRTY SIDE OF MONEY 1,2&3
By Prince

FOR MY ENEMY'S SAKE
AMBITIONS OF A SLIDER
FRESH OFF DA PORCH
By IRA B.

THE TRUCKLOAD 1-4
TIPPIN' THE SCALES 1-3
BAD BITCHES WIT GUNZ 3
PROBLEM SOLVED 2
By Christopher "Diesel" Hornezes

Available Now

RESTRAINING ORDER 1 & 2
By **CA$H & Coffee**

LOVE KNOWS NO BOUNDARIES 1-3
By **Coffee**

RAISED AS A GOON I, II, III & IV
BRED BY THE SLUMS I, II, III
BLAST FOR ME I & II
ROTTEN TO THE CORE I II III
A BRONX TALE I, II, III
DUFFLE BAG CARTEL I II III IV V VI
HEARTLESS GOON I II III IV V
A SAVAGE DOPEBOY I II
DRUG LORDS I II III
CUTTHROAT MAFIA I II
KING OF THE TRENCHES
By **Ghost**

LAY IT DOWN I & II
LAST OF A DYING BREED I II
BLOOD STAINS OF A SHOTTA I & II III
By **Jamaica**

LOYAL TO THE GAME I II III
LIFE OF SIN I, II III
By **TJ & Jelissa**

IF LOVING HIM IS WRONG…I & II
LOVE ME EVEN WHEN IT HURTS I II III
By **Jelissa**

PUSH IT TO THE LIMIT
By **Bre' Hayes**

AMBITIONZ OF A SLIDER | IRA B.

BLOODY COMMAS I & II
SKI MASK CARTEL I, II & III
KING OF NEW YORK I II, III IV V
RISE TO POWER I II III
COKE KINGS I II III IV V
BORN HEARTLESS I II III IV
KING OF THE TRAP I II
By **T.J. Edwards**

WHEN THE STREETS CLAP BACK I & II III
THE HEART OF A SAVAGE I II III IV
MONEY MAFIA I II
LOYAL TO THE SOIL I II III
By **Jibril Williams**

A DISTINGUISHED THUG STOLE MY HEART I II & III
LOVE SHOULDN'T HURT I II III IV
RENEGADE BOYS 1-4
PAID IN KARMA 1-3
SAVAGE STORMS 1-3
AN UNFORESEEN LOVE 1-3
BABY, I'M WINTERTIME COLD 1-3
A THUG'S STREET PRINCESS 1&2
By **Meesha**

A GANGSTER'S CODE 1-3
A GANGSTER'S SYN 1-3
THE SAVAGE LIFE 1-3
CHAINED TO THE STREETS 1-3
BLOOD ON THE MONEY 1-3
A GANGSTA'S PAIN 1-3
BEAUTIFUL LIES AND UGLY TRUTHS
CHURCH IN THESE STREETS
By **J-Blunt**

CUM FOR ME 1-8
An LDP Erotica Collaboration

AMBITIONZ OF A SLIDER | IRA B.

BLOOD OF A BOSS 1-5
SHADOWS OF THE GAME
TRAP BASTARD
By **Askari**

THE STREETS BLEED MURDER 1-3
THE HEART OF A GANGSTA 1-3
By **Jerry Jackson**

WHEN A GOOD GIRL GOES BAD
By **Adrienne**

THE COST OF LOYALTY 1-3
By **Kweli**

BRIDE OF A HUSTLA 1-3
THE FETTI GIRLS 1-3
CORRUPTED BY A GANGSTA 1-4
BLINDED BY HIS LOVE
THE PRICE YOU PAY FOR LOVE 1-3
DOPE GIRL MAGIC 1-3
By **Destiny Skai**

A KINGPIN'S AMBITION
A KINGPIN'S AMBITION II
I MURDER FOR THE DOUGH
By **Ambitious**

TRUE SAVAGE 1-7
DOPE BOY MAGIC 1-3
MIDNIGHT CARTEL 1-3
CITY OF KINGZ 1&2
NIGHTMARE ON SILENT AVE
THE PLUG OF LIL MEXICO 1&2
CLASSIC CITY
By **Chris Green**

AMBITIONZ OF A SLIDER | IRA B.

A GANGSTER'S REVENGE 1-4
THE BOSS MAN'S DAUGHTERS 1-5
A SAVAGE LOVE 1&2
BAE BELONGS TO ME 1&2
A HUSTLER'S DECEIT 1-3
WHAT BAD BITCHES DO 1-3
SOUL OF A MONSTER 1-3
KILL ZONE
A DOPE BOY'S QUEEN 1-3
TIL DEATH 1-3
IMMA DIE BOUT MINE 1-6
DYING FOR LIKES
By **Aryanna**

A DOPEBOY'S PRAYER
By **Eddie "Wolf" Lee**

THE KING CARTEL 1-3
By **Frank Gresham**

THESE NIGGAS AIN'T LOYAL 1-3
By **Nikki Tee**

GANGSTA SHYT 1-3
By **CATO**

THE ULTIMATE BETRAYAL
By **Phoenix**

BOSS'N UP 1-3
By **Royal Nicole**

I LOVE YOU TO DEATH
By **Destiny J**

I RIDE FOR MY HITTA
I STILL RIDE FOR MY HITTA
By **Misty Holt**

LOVE & CHASIN' PAPER
By **Qay Crockett**

TO DIE IN VAIN
SINS OF A HUSTLA
By **ASAD**

BROOKLYN HUSTLAZ
By **Boogsy Morina**

BROOKLYN ON LOCK 1 & 2
By **Sonovia**

GANGSTA CITY
By **Teddy Duke**

A DRUG KING AND HIS DIAMOND 1-3
A DOPEMAN'S RICHES
HER MAN, MINE'S TOO 1&2
CASH MONEY HO'S
THE WIFEY I USED TO BE 1&2
PRETTY GIRLS DO NASTY THINGS
By **Nicole Goosby**

LIPSTICK KILLAH 1-3
CRIME OF PASSION 1-3
FRIEND OR FOE 1-3
By **Mimi**

TRAPHOUSE KING 1-3
KINGPIN KILLAZ 1-3
STREET KINGS 1&2
PAID IN BLOOD 1&2
CARTEL KILLAZ 1-3
DOPE GODS 1&2
By **Hood Rich**

THE STREETS ARE CALLING
By **Duquie Wilson**

AMBITIONZ OF A SLIDER | IRA B.

STEADY MOBBN' 1-3
THE STREETS STAINED MY SOUL 1-3
By **Marcellus Allen**

WHO SHOT YA 1-3
SON OF A DOPE FIEND 1-4
HEAVEN GOT A GHETTO 1&2
SKI MASK MONEY 1&2
By **Renta**

GORILLAZ IN THE BAY 1-4
TEARS OF A GANGSTA 1/&2
3X KRAZY 1&2
STRAIGHT BEAST MODE 1&2
By **DE'KARI**

TRIGGADALE 1-3
MURDA WAS THE CASE 1-3
By **Elijah R. Freeman**

SLAUGHTER GANG 1-3
RUTHLESS HEART 1-3
By **Willie Slaughter**

GOD BLESS THE TRAPPERS 1-3
THESE SCANDALOUS STREETS 1-3
FEAR MY GANGSTA 1-5
THESE STREETS DON'T LOVE NOBODY 1-2
BURY ME A G 1-5
A GANGSTA'S EMPIRE 1-4
THE DOPEMAN'S BODYGAURD 1&2
THE REALEST KILLAZ 1-3
THE LAST OF THE OGS 1-3
By **Tranay Adams**

MARRIED TO A BOSS 1-3
By **Destiny Skai & Chris Green**

KINGZ OF THE GAME 1-7
CRIME BOSS 1-4
By **Playa Ray**

FUK SHYT
By **Blakk Diamond**

DON'T F#CK WITH MY HEART 1&2
By **Linnea**

ADDICTED TO THE DRAMA 1-3
IN THE ARM OF HIS BOSS
By **Jamila**

LOYALTY AIN'T PROMISED 1&2
By **Keith Williams**

YAYO 1-4
A SHOOTER'S AMBITION 1&2
BRED IN THE GAME
By **S. Allen**

TRAP GOD 1-3
RICH $AVAGE 1-3
MONEY IN THE GRAVE 1-3
CARTEL MONEY 1&2
By **Martell Troublesome Bolden**

FOREVER GANGSTA 1&2
GLOCKS ON SATIN SHEETS 1&2
By **Adrian Dulan**

TOE TAGZ 1-4
LEVELS TO THIS SHYT 1&2
IT'S JUST ME AND YOU
By **Ah'Million**

AMBITIONZ OF A SLIDER | IRA B.

KINGPIN DREAMS 1-3
RAN OFF ON DA PLUG
By **Paper Boi Rari**

THE STREETS MADE ME 1-3
By **Larry D. Wright**

CONFESSIONS OF A GANGSTA 1-4
CONFESSIONS OF A JACKBOY 1-3
CONFESSIONS OF A HITMAN
CONFESSIONS OF A DOPE BOY
By **Nicholas Lock**

I'M NOTHING WITHOUT HIS LOVE
SINS OF A THUG
TO THE THUG I LOVED BEFORE
A GANGSTA SAVED XMAS
IN A HUSTLER I TRUST
By **Monet Dragun**

QUIET MONEY 1-3
THUG LIFE 1-3
EXTENDED CLIP 1&2
A GANGSTA'S PARADISE
By **Trai'Quan**

CAUGHT UP IN THE LIFE 1-3
THE STREETS NEVER LET GO 1-3
By **Robert Baptiste**

NEW TO THE GAME 1-3
MONEY, MURDER & MEMORIES 1-3
By **Malik D. Rice**

CREAM 2-3
THE STREETS WILL TALK
By **Yolanda Moore**

THE STREETS WILL NEVER CLOSE 1-3
By **K'ajji**

LIFE OF A SAVAGE 1-4
A GANGSTA'S QUR'AN 1-4
MURDA SEASON 1-3
GANGLAND CARTEL 1-3
CHI'RAQ GANGSTAS 1-4
KILLERS ON ELM STREET 1-3
JACK BOYZ N DA BRONX 1-3
A DOPEBOY'S DREAM 1-3
JACK BOYS VS DOPE BOYS 1-3
COKE GIRLZ
COKE BOYS
SOSA GANG 1&2
BRONX SAVAGES
BODYMORE KINGPINS
BLOOD OF A GOON
By **Romell Tukes**

CONCRETE KILLA 1-3
VICIOUS LOYALTY 1-3
BLOODY MONEY BAGS
By **Kingpen**

THE ULTIMATE SACRIFICE 1-6
KHADIFI
IF YOU CROSS ME ONCE 1-3
ANGEL 1-4
IN THE BLINK OF AN EYE
By **Anthony Fields**

THE LIFE OF A HOOD STAR
By **Ca$h & Rashia Wilson**

NIGHTMARES OF A HUSTLA 1-3
BLOOD AND GAMES 1&2
By **King Dream**

GHOST MOB
By **Stilloan Robinson**

HARD AND RUTHLESS 1&2
MOB TOWN 251
THE BILLIONAIRE BENTLEYS 1-3
REAL G'S MOVE IN SILENCE
By **Von Diesel**

MOB TIES 1-7
SOUL OF A HUSTLER, HEART OF A KILLER 1-3
GORILLAZ IN THE TRENCHES
OOPS CRY TOO 1&2
THE DAUGHTER OF A CARTEL BOSS
By **SayNoMore**

BODYMORE MURDERLAND 1-3
THE BIRTH OF A GANGSTER 1-4
By **Delmont Player**

FOR THE LOVE OF A BOSS 1&2
By **C. D. Blue**

KILLA KOUNTY 1-5
TENDER
By **Khufu**

MOBBED UP 1-4
THE BRICK MAN 1-5
THE COCAINE PRINCESS 1-10
STEPPERS 1-3
SUPER GREMLIN 1-4
A GANGSTA'S SON
By **King Rio**

MONEY GAME 1&2
By **Smoove Dolla**

AMBITIONZ OF A SLIDER | IRA B.

A GANGSTA'S KARMA 1-5
By **FLAME**

KING OF THE TRENCHES 1-3
By **GHOST & TRANAY ADAMS**

BAD BITCHES WIT GUNZ 1&2
PROBLEM SOLVED
By "Christopher Diesel" Hornezes

QUEEN OF THE ZOO 1&2
By **Black Migo**

GRIMEY WAYS 1-3
BETRAYAL OF A G
By **Ray Vinci**

XMAS WITH AN ATL SHOOTER
By **Ca$h & Destiny Skai**

KING KILLA 1&2
By **Vincent "Vitto" Holloway**

BETRAYAL OF A THUG 1&2
By **Fre$h**

COUNTDOWN OF A KILLA 1&2
SEX, MURDER AND GOD 1&2
GUNS DOWN, BOTTOMS UP 1&2
By Lo-Life

THE MURDER QUEENS 1-7
By **Michael Gallon**

FOR THE LOVE OF BLOOD 1-4
By **Jamel Mitchell**

AMBITIONZ OF A SLIDER | IRA B.

HOOD CONSIGLIERE 1&2
NO TIME FOR ERROR
By **Keese**

PROTÉGÉ OF A LEGEND 1,2&3
LOVE IN THE TRENCHES 1&2
By **Corey Robinson**

THE PLUG'S RUTHLESS DAUGHTER 1&2
By **Tony Daniels**

BORN IN THE GRAVE 1-3
CRIME PAYS
By **Self Made Tay**

MOAN IN MY MOUTH
By **XTASY**

TORN BETWEEN A GANGSTER AND A GENTLEMAN
By **J-BLUNT & Miss Kim**

LOYALTY IS EVERYTHING 1-3
CITY OF SMOKE 1-3
By **Molotti**

HERE TODAY GONE TOMORROW 1&2
By **Fly Rock**

WOMEN LIE MEN LIE 1-4
FIFTY SHADES OF SNOW 1-3
STACK BEFORE YOU SPLURGE
GIRLS FALL LIKE DOMINOES
NAÏVE TO THE STREETS
By **ROY MILLIGAN**

PILLOW PRINCESS
By **S. Hawkins**

AMBITIONZ OF A SLIDER | IRA B.

THE BUTTERFLY MAFIA 1-3
SALUTE MY SAVAGERY 1&2
By **Fumiya Payne**

THE LANE 1&2
By Ken-Ken Spence

THE PUSSY TRAP 1-5
By **Nene Capri**

DIRTY DNA
By **Blaque**

SANCTIFIED AND HORNY
by **XTASY**

BOOKS BY LDP'S CEO, CA$H

TRUST IN NO MAN
TRUST IN NO MAN 2
TRUST IN NO MAN 3
BONDED BY BLOOD
SHORTY GOT A THUG
THUGS CRY
THUGS CRY 2
THUGS CRY 3
TRUST NO BITCH
TRUST NO BITCH 2
TRUST NO BITCH 3
TIL MY CASKET DROPS
RESTRAINING ORDER
RESTRAINING ORDER 2
IN LOVE WITH A CONVICT
LIFE OF A HOOD STAR
XMAS WITH AN ATL SHOOTER